Tentatively he

It was redolent of decaying plants, fresh bark, a hint of blood—and sweat, coming from the corner to his right.

Bolan took his hand away from his face to find it clenched into a fist, just like the one at his side. What the hell is happening to me? he thought. Every sense was preternaturally aware. Every inch of his body overflowed with energy, as if he could run a dozen marathons back-to-back.

But above all, his mind was filled with the overwhelming basic instinct of fight-or-flight. But it was difficult to consider flight as a viable option anymore. Instead, there was only the burning need for combat, to dominate his opponent—any opponent— and leave the person bleeding and defeated in the dirt.

Almost unaware that his lips had peeled back from his teeth in a feral grin, Bolan stepped farther into the room, his eyes wide and searching.

Hunting for his prey.

DON PENDLETON'S MACK BOLAN®

Nightmare Army

A GOLD EAGLE BOOK FROM

WORLDWIDE®

TORONTO • NEW YORK • LONDON
AMSTERDAM • PARIS • SYDNEY • HAMBURG
STOCKHOLM • ATHENS • TOKYO • MILAN
MADRID • WARSAW • BUDAPEST • AUCKLAND

Recycling programs
for this product may
not exist in your area.

commentary
First edition December 2014

ISBN-13: 978-0-373-61573-5

Special thanks and acknowledgment to
Travis Morgan for his contribution to this work.

Nightmare Army

Printed in U.S.A.

It is a man's own mind, not his enemy or foe,
that lures him to evil ways.

—Buddha

The evil ways of evil men will eventually bring
them down. And if it takes too long, I'll step
forward to hurry things up.

—Mack Bolan

PROLOGUE

Labored breath loud in his ears, bare feet shuffling down the dark path, Motumbo staggered through the dark jungle. His side, red and sticky with blood, pulsed with pain at each step, but he didn't stop. Instead he kept scanning around, nose flared to scent possible prey, red-rimmed, watery eyes staring wide into the darkness.

Time held no meaning for him anymore—he couldn't say whether it had been twenty minutes or two hours since he had broken free of his captors. Now all that was left in his mind was the relentless desire to move, to hunt.

Normally the Congolese jungle held no fear for him, even at night. Although there were creatures in the dense forest that should be avoided, such as the stealthy leopards, the territorial gorillas and the wide variety of poisonous snakes, spiders and insects inhabiting the lush underbrush, Motumbo knew them all and how to avoid them. Growing up in the isolated northern region, the twenty-year-old had been fortunate to avoid the violence that had swept much of his country for the past decade. But he hadn't been so lucky avoiding the silver ghosts haunting the deep tropical forest.

They had appeared about six months ago, mysterious, gleaming beings appearing seemingly out of nowhere to snatch whomever they could find: men, women and children. Appeals to local law enforcement had been ineffective; the men who had tried to find the elusive beings had either come back empty-handed—or disappeared, as well. The populations of the scattered villages in the area, still on edge from the violence of the simmering civil war that had been slowly cooling for the past few years, didn't enter the jungle unless they absolutely had to. But they had to eat.

That was how Motumbo had been captured one day, hunting in the jungle against his father's wishes. The ghosts had appeared like magic around him, one of them tossing a small canister at his feet that had spewed a noxious yellow gas. One whiff had made him pass out in seconds.

When he'd awakened, he had been in a place unlike anywhere he had ever seen before. Bare, bright rooms with hard, white walls. Strange currents of cool air came from square holes in the ceiling. And he'd been surrounded by quiet, pale men and women, all dressed in long, white coats with paper masks over their faces, their dark brown or bright blue eyes measuring and cold.

And the screaming. From the moment he woke to the night he was able to escape, Motumbo always heard someone screaming. Sometimes it was a man, the voice hoarse and low, sometimes a woman, the shrill shrieks lancing through his head. But it was constant, unrelenting, endless.

The men and women poked and prodded him, weighed him, made him do physical tests that he didn't understand. Failure to comply was met with shocking force, administered by large men with devices that shot strange darts with wires attached to their handles that made Motumbo's entire body feel as if it was on fire. He'd only needed to experience that once and afterward he had complied with their demands as quickly as possible.

In some respects, it wasn't so bad. He was dressed and well-fed. He was even allowed to watch television for an hour each day, but sometimes the programs gave him headaches. The tests weren't hard—at least, not in the beginning. Then one day he had been given an injection of a thick, black liquid and brought into a room with another person, a woman. Motumbo had just stared at her for a moment, as she had looked back at him. Then he had felt a strange sort of pressure in his head, as though his skull was about to split open if he didn't do something *right now,* and a funny kind of warmness in his arms and legs, and the only thought in his mind was to—

No! He banished the rising memory before that terrible nightmare replayed behind his eyes again. Instead he concentrated on how he had escaped, catching a scientist by surprise when he had come in to check on the teen's progress after the latest round of injections of the black stuff that made his limbs pulse with a warm, drowsy fire. The man hadn't even had time to shout before Motumbo had leaped on him, bearing him to the ground and smashing his skull until it leaked blood. He had taken the man's lab coat, identification and mask, and headed out a maintenance door he'd noticed was often left unguarded. Outside, he'd thought he was free, but had encountered another guard, who'd seen through his flimsy disguise. Motumbo hadn't hesitated then, either. He had grabbed the man and battered his face until he had slumped to the ground. It was only afterward that he realized the guard had stabbed him in the side. He'd left the strange place, running at first, trying to put as much distance between himself and it.

The wound in his side throbbed now, but Motumbo's pace never slowed. One hand pressed to his right side, the other held out to block low branches or to fend off a predator, he kept moving forward. Occasionally he glanced around the unfamiliar terrain, having no idea where he was or which direction his village might be. But always, always there was the insistence demand to hunt, to find…

A rustle in the trees to his right made the teenager freeze, cocking his head to pinpoint the source of the noise. He turned in time to see a blur of fur and fangs leap straight at his face The mouth of the leopard was opened wide to sink into his cheeks while the jungle cat's front claws reached out to pierce his arms or shoulders and the rear claws raked across his abdomen to disembowel him. All of that would normally happen in the next half second as the jungle predator efficiently killed him.

But the moment Motumbo's vision locked on to the leaping predator, time seemed to slow. The pupils of his eyes dilated even farther, taking in every detail of the large cat, from the snarl on its face to the scrap of rotting meat wedged near its upper left canine to its left paw extended a few inches ahead of the right one to hook into him first. The soaring cat turned sluggish, floating through the air instead of flying at him in the blink of an eye.

Along with the time slowdown, Motumbo was immediately filled with an insensate, killing, red rage.

Reaching out with his right hand, he gripped the

left paw, heedless of the extended claws, and grabbed the right paw with his left hand. As soon as his fingers closed on both limbs, he wrenched them sideways, as far apart as he could with all of his strength, which now seemed limitless.

The crack and tear of snapping bones and ripping flesh sounded in the night. The leopard's ferocious expression turned to agony as its forelegs were almost ripped off its body. Using the momentum of the cat's leap, Motumbo whirled and threw the sixty-kilogram animal ten meters away. The crippled animal landed against a moss-covered tree with a sickening thud. Unable to rise, it let out a shocked yowl, as if unable to comprehend how it had gone from supreme hunter to mortally wounded in two heartbeats.

As soon as the overwhelming urge to kill had come over him, it abated, and Motumbo regained control of himself as though coming out of a daydream. He hadn't suffered a scratch from the beast's attempted attack, but his head felt thick and sluggish, and his muscles burned from the effort to protect himself.

A low mewling came from the base of the tree where the leopard had landed, and Motumbo walked over to it, seeing the animal writhing in pain, its front legs twisted and useless, its back legs limp and unmoving. Broke its back when it hit the tree, he thought. Careful to avoid the sharp teeth, he grabbed it behind the scruff and, with an amazing burst of strength, snapped its neck.

As he did so, bright lights popped on all around the small clearing. Motumbo looked up to see the three of the silver ghosts appear at the far end. The red rage fell over his vision again and he sprang at them, fingers outstretched to tear them apart, if he could only get his hands on one...

A loud hiss of compressed air sounded from his left and Motumbo felt the bite of the darts again, followed by searing agony that locked his limbs and sent him crashing to the ground, his face twisted in pain, a choked cry forcing its way from between his gritted teeth.

The silver ghosts looked at him from behind the strange masks they wore, and one of them held a small vial of something under his nose that made him dizzy and sleepy.

His last conscious thought before the blackness took him was what one of the ghosts said to the others. "Killed a full-grown, healthy leopard while unarmed. The company will be very pleased with our results so far, don't you think?"

CHAPTER ONE

Fingers clenching the grip of his silenced SIG-Sauer P-229 pistol, Mack Bolan listened to the two men as they walked closer to his hiding spot. Talking in rapid-fire Armenian, they were close enough now that he could smell the harsh smoke from their Turkish cigarettes as it mixed with the tang of the gun oil on the hunting rifles slung over their shoulders.

Normally he wouldn't hesitate to take them out if they got too close. The two men weren't taking any security precautions. He could easily hear them, even over the constant wind at this altitude. Their steps were slow on the goat trail, their conversation casual, unhurried. At the moment they had no idea where he was.

When they reached the ideal position, he would stand from cover and put both men down with double taps to the chest in under two seconds. The .40-caliber bullets would smash through their woolen sweaters, crack their sternums and plow into their hearts, mangling them before exiting their backs in a spray of blood. Two quick steps forward, along with a third shot into each man's forehead, and all he would be left with would be to make sure these men were never found.

But this situation was anything but ordinary.

Bolan had spent the past four days surveilling the mountaintop headquarters of Aleksandr Sevan, the leader of the Jadur clan, currently at the top of the Armenian mafia hierarchy. Tightly knit and bound by a strict code of honor and ethics, as well as family ties, the Armenians had resisted all attempts at agents infiltrating their ranks, with even local agents with impeccable jackets either found dead or simply vanishing, never to be seen again.

Meanwhile, over the past few decades, the Armenians had extended their tentacles from their small landlocked country to encircle both Europe and America in a stranglehold of crime and fear. With a well-deserved reputation for savage brutality and the use of violence in response to even minor threats against them, they had made inroads into every type of crime on both continents, from street crimes such as kidnapping, bank robbery, drug smuggling and sex slavery to white collar offenses such as wire fraud, bank fraud, racketeering and embezzlement. Along the way, the Armenians were willing to work with local, established mafias, such as the Russians or Mexicans, to get what they wanted, but also had no qualms about going toe-to-toe with larger mobs to get in on the action, wherever it might happen.

All that was why Bolan was here. When INTERPOL intelligence had managed to get a line on Sevan's movements, they'd expected him to end up back at the walled town of Artakar, twenty miles east of Tumyanan, where the Jadur clan ruled it and the surrounding mountainous countryside with a heavy hand. Every village and farm in ten kilometers had been co-opted by the syndicate, with large rewards for reporting any suspicious behavior, and illegal shipments of contraband ranging from heroin to guns to women often stored in farms before being moved on to their final destination.

The mission had been straightforward: Bolan would go in, alone, infiltrate the headquarters, kidnap Sevan and extract him to an airfield near Tumyanan, where Jack Grimaldi waited to fly them both to Washington, D.C. No one in European law enforcement would know he was in-country—the Armenians were as free with their bribes with law enforcement as with anyone else, and rumors ran rampant of corrupted police officers and administrators in a half-dozen countries. In and out, no muss, no fuss, the whole operation had been scheduled to take no more than thirty-six hours.

That deadline had passed two days ago. When Sevan hadn't showed up, Stony Man Farm had put out cautious feelers about what was behind the deviation. A change in plans, or was the entire mission some kind of smokescreen or diversion? Careful intel-gathering and analysis by Aaron "the Bear" Kurtzman and Akira Tokaido, members of Stony Man's cyber team, revealed that the criminal ringleader had been held up by a supposedly minor matter involving a meeting with Salvatore Gambini, one of the heads of the Italian Mafia with whom the Armenians were very close. The meeting had run long, with the two crime family heads celebrating their partnership. When he'd heard about the change in plans, Bolan had cursed not being able to try to get to that one. There were few things he liked better than capturing two scumbag mobsters for the price of one. Gambini would simply have to wait until another day.

Instead he had sat and watched and waited, preferring to take the chance of staying to capture the mob leader rather than leaving and attempting to pick up his trail another day. The longer he stayed in place, however—even with moving his base camp once already to obscure traces of his being here—the odds were greater that he would be detected sooner or later.

Although the Jadur patrols didn't come out this far, Bolan couldn't take a chance on a shepherd or farmer stumbling across his base of operations. His low-slung, camouflaged tent was covered by the native grasses so artfully so that an intruder would have had to step on it to discover it. When the flap was closed, it was just another grass-covered hillock among a cluster of them scattered on the mountainside. Bolan had been living on cold MREs—meals ready to eat—and doing anything outside the tent under the cover of darkness, using night-vision goggles to see if the moon was obscured. He hadn't lit a fire, awakening on the brisk autumn morning to heavy frost and a chilly tent, nor showered in the past two days, as well.

Despite the uncertainly and rough conditions, Bolan lived for situations like this, pitting himself against both the elements and his enemy. Unlike just about anyone else who found themselves in this situation, he thrived on the challenges of remaining undetected while completing his mission, no matter what obstacles might be thrown in his path.

All of which brought him back to the moment at hand, and the two men walking just a few paces away from his hidden lair. The odds were good that they might be part of Aleksandr Sevan's mob. On the other hand, they might be two farmers, perhaps a father and his eldest son from a nearby farm, out hunting game birds. Either way, if they found Bolan, the odds were very good that they were both going to die. While he tried to avoid civilian casualties—that was the kindest term he could use to refer to any of the population of the area—these tough, hardy mountain people had compromised themselves by accepting deals with the devil that lived in the walled city.

Sevan's control of the region was ironclad, and Bolan couldn't take the chance of anyone seeing him and telling the mobsters. His mission was too important to risk because of a chance encounter. Therefore, he waited; every sense locked on what he could hear and smell of the two men, and stood ready to execute both of them, even while hoping they would simply keep walking.

"Doesn't look like they've spotted you, Striker," a voice said in his ear. Bolan didn't reply. The voice came from Akira Tokaido, about six thousand miles away in the Stony Man Farm Computer Room, watching the two men through the 1.8 gigapixel eye of an ARGUS camera mounted on the underbelly of a Predator Hawk drone flying overhead at 15,000 feet. "Hunting rifles are confirmed. I think they're old Mosin-Nagants. Anyway, they've passed your site, and are moving south-southeast, still walking and talking. Looks like they're headed down the mountain. We'll keep tabs on them in case they come back your way."

Even with the all-clear sounded, Bolan waited until the men's conversation faded from hearing before he uncurled his fingers from his pistol and replied. "Copy that."

"That was way too close for my comfort," Kurtzman grumbled. Bolan imagined him watching several monitors at once from his wheelchair while drinking from a cup of his abominable coffee that was always brewed 24/7 at the Farm. "Far be it from me to second-guess you, Striker. We've backed you on a lot of high-risk missions before, but even before the delay, this one seems a bit, well—"

"Suicidal?" Akira offered.

"I was going to say high-risk, but if the combat boot fits…" Kurtzman's voice trailed off

Slowly, cautiously, Bolan unzipped his observation port and stuck out his camouflaged high-powered binoculars. First he spotted the two hunters, watching them for a few seconds as they trudged away from him. It wasn't that he didn't trust Tokaido or the incredible technology watching over him; it was just that, when out in the field, Bolan preferred to always verify what information came his way with his own eyes whenever possible.

"Duly noted, Bear." After the hunters had disappeared from view, Bolan turned his attention to the walled city below him.

There was a pause from Stony Man and Bolan imagined the two men, Kurtzman grizzled and older, Tokaido younger, with his ever-present earbuds pressed into his ears, exchanging puzzled glances. "You've seen the plans," Tokaido said. "It's a fortress, and I'm not talking about one from the Middle Ages, either."

As he studied the high stone walls, with lookout towers cleverly built in so they seemed to be a part of the medieval defenses, not to mention the small army of alert guards and attack dogs backing up a twenty-first-century web of high-tech surveillance equipment, Bolan had to admit that Tokaido was correct. Even so, his mouth curved into a sardonic grin.

"Yeah, but if it wasn't, it wouldn't be any fun sneaking in, now would it?" he replied. "Look, I appreciate the concern, but we've been over all this before." Bolan didn't drop his field glasses while talking, just continued scanning the city on the plateau beneath him. "It's a complete stealth op. Infiltrate, acquire the target, exfiltrate, all without anyone being the wiser."

"Yes, and that all sounds great," Kurtzman replied. "The part that concerns me is our intelligence showing that more than sixty percent of the town's inhabitants are members of the Jadur clan mafia. It's one thing if you were sneaking into a village of civilians, but about two-thirds of the people in this place are some kind of criminal, and we know the Armenians don't mess around. It'd be one thing if we had Phoenix Force on hand to back you up—"

"But they're busy in Australia right now, so, I'll just have to do it real quiet..." Bolan trailed off as he spotted a caravan of black SUVs coming up the lone dirt road to the main gates of the village. Sleek and squat, they boasted tinted windows and were undoubtedly armored.

"Akira, you see what I see?"

"The small fleet of sport-utes at the gate? Roger that." Bolan heard the faint click of keys as the whiz kid accessed information. He kept his eyes glued to the four-vehicle procession, which was swept underneath with mirrors for bombs, as well as what looked like electronic sniffers.

After a minute Tokaido came back on. "They originated from Erebuni Airport, south of the capital city of Yerevan. Left there at 10:30 a.m. and traveled straight through until they reached their destination."

"Aleksandr Sevan is in one of those SUVs." Bolan watched as the caravan was allowed inside the walled village, then lowered his binoculars. "And tonight, I'm going in and bringing him back out with me."

CHAPTER TWO

Seventy-two hours earlier

Dennis Kuhn struggled out of unconsciousness to find his head pounding, his dry mouth tasting like sandpaper, and his arms and legs feeling like he was moving them through thick syrup.

Raising his head from the cot he was laying on, he looked around in confusion. The white walls of the bare, windowless room were completely unfamiliar. Kuhn pushed himself up onto his elbows and paused, fighting a sudden wave of nausea. *Don't throw up, don't throw up...*

After a minute his queasiness subsided enough for him to carefully sit up and look around. Other than a white table on the other side of the room and a sturdy-looking white door to his right, the room was empty. Blinking in confusion, Kuhn looked down to find himself wearing the same clothes—an indigo Hugo Boss button-down and gray slacks, both wrinkled from being slept in—that he had worn to the office...yesterday? Patting his pockets, he found that his smartphone and wallet were both missing.

Where the hell am I? Mind whirling, Kuhn pushed himself to his stockinged feet, swayed unsteadily, and glanced over to find his wingtip shoes set neatly at the foot of the bed. He walked to the table, which was stocked with bottles of spring water in an ice bucket and a variety of energy bars. Removing the bottles, he opened one, swished a huge gulp of ice-cold water around in his mouth, then spit it out in the bucket. After draining the rest of the bottle, he found himself ravenously hungry and tore one of the bars open and devoured it. Selecting a second, he was peeling it open when he was interrupted by a click near the door and a familiar voice emanating from a concealed speaker somewhere over there.

"Greetings, Mr. Kuhn. I am glad to see that you are awake and recovered from your recent journey."

Kuhn looked up from his protein bar in surprise. "Mr. Stengrave?" The water he'd just drank seemed to coalesce into a ball of ice in his stomach. *He doesn't know—he* can't *know—* "What's going on here? Where am I?"

"You are a guest at my winter home, Stengrave Castle, on the north end of the Gulf of Bothnia."

Kuhn knew the place his boss was talking about: a modern update of a medieval castle, built to Kristian Stengrave's exacting specifications. He'd even visited the place once before, three years ago, a reward for certain top-level executives for surpassing their lofty sales goals, even during the recession that had been sweeping Europe at the time. But last night, he had been in Stuttgart—more than 1,500 miles away. Not only had he been kidnapped by the very company he worked for, but someone had brought him to this forlorn place near the top of the world—all without anyone being the wiser.

"Where is my family?"

"They are safe and sound at your home. They have

been told that you were called away to a top-level emergency conference, so suddenly that you didn't have time to contact them."

"Okay... Why am I here?"

"You have been brought here to discuss a very serious matter—your attempted theft of proprietary research and materials for one of our rivals."

Kuhn's stomach lurched so hard he thought he was going to throw up, but he maintained his poker face while opening another bottle of water. "Sir, I have no idea what you're talking about."

But of course he did; in fact, Kuhn was as guilty as hell. He worked as a computer programmer and analyst at one of Stengrave Industries' facilities in Germany, producing top-of-the-line medical equipment for sale throughout the rest of the world. Hired straight from graduation at the top of his class at Heidelberg University, with a double major in computer science and business, he'd spent the past decade with the company, rising steadily through the ranks.

And yet it had never seemed to be enough. Although he was paid well, his wife had expensive tastes combined with a desire to keep up with their well-to-do neighbors, and when their children had arrived, the pressure to maintain their lifestyle had only increased.

So when a rival bio-manufacturing firm had offered him ten years' salary to deliver test data on one of Stengrave's most propriety lines of gene research, he had agreed, seeing a way out of his increasingly pressure-filled life. What he hadn't counted on was how much more pressure he was under now; not only from his wife, but also from both masters, keeping appearances normal at his regular job while satisfying the increasingly strident demands of his new boss.

"Do not bother protesting your innocence, Mr. Kuhn, it will not help you. All of the evidence has been collected and presented to me, and I have already made my decision."

Even though the room was perfectly comfortable, sweat appeared on Kuhn's brow and the back of his neck. He gulped more water even as his gaze flicked to the door, which he knew was locked. "Okay, then why have you brought me here?"

"To offer you a chance to reclaim your lost honor."

Of all the things his boss might have said, that was the last thing he expected. "Wha—what are you talking about?"

"Finish eating and we will discuss what will happen next," Stengrave replied.

Kuhn tossed the bar on the table—there was no way he could stomach any more. "I'm ready now."

"Very good." The door clicked. Kuhn walked over to it and tried the handle. The door swung open easily under his touch, and he walked into the next room.

Lights came on as he did, revealing a long hallway lined on both sides with full suits of armor. As the door to the other room closed behind him, Kuhn blinked and stared at the at least two-dozen suits standing silently in the hall, ten on either side, each one on its own small dais; a warrior's uniform from another time.

In the middle of the room was a rack of swords, containing various blades from a typical medieval long sword to what looked like a Scottish claymore. Other than the armor and the swords, the room appeared to be empty. There was a door at the end of the room, but it had no knob or handle.

"Mr. Stengrave?" Kuhn asked. "What is all this?"

"As I said…" His boss's voice came from somewhere in the room. "It is a place for you to reclaim your honor."

"I—I don't understand."

"Choose your weapon."

Kuhn frowned. "What?"

"Choose your weapon. There are twenty suits of armor in this room. I am in one of them. If you select the correct one and strike me, you will be free to go. If you do not select the correct one, then we will fight to the death."

Kuhn's blood pounded in his ears as he heard the terms of his "exit interview." He shook his head. "This is insane! You can't just kidnap me and hold me hostage and set up this ridiculous contest like some James Bond villain!"

"Yet you are here, and I am here. So it would seem that is exactly what is happening," Stengrave replied in the same calm, measured voice.

"I refuse— I refuse to participate in this madness," Kuhn said. "Have me arrested, tried, thrown in jail, whatever, I'll deal with it. But this…this is madness."

"Perhaps you should have thought of that before you chose to steal from my company—and me."

Kuhn squinted as Stengrave spoke, trying to figure out where his voice was coming from. He studied the metal suits of armor closest to him, thinking it would be easy to figure out which one his boss was wearing, but each one looked as if it held a mannequin filling out the clothes underneath the polished steel plates. Even as he did this, a part of his mind screamed that all this had to be in some kind of nightmare, and that if he could just wake up, he'd find himself back at home, in bed next to his sleeping wife, and all of this would simply be a bad dream...

Except he felt his sweaty palms and his increased heartbeat, and the blood pounding in his ears, and knew—absolutely *knew*—that this was real, that it was happening to him right now.

"Surely you are not such a craven man that you would prefer the ignominy of a public trial," Stengrave continued. "With your name dragged through the mud as you are found guilty—and you will be—and sentenced to a very lengthy prison term. Your wife and children will be forced to fend for themselves, and they will probably have to sell their home and move out of that wonderful neighborhood you've been living in for the past three years."

"Why are you telling me all this?" Kuhn asked while edging closer to the rack of swords. He had fenced in college, even done some reenactment fighting of the German sword techniques, but all that had been more than a decade ago. Plus, he wasn't in the best shape after ten years of sitting at a computer behind a desk. His wife, Helene, had been hounding him to take better care of himself, but he had always said there'd be time for that later. Now he found himself desperately wishing he had listened to her.

"I am telling you this because if you face me and win, all record of your transgression will be erased. You will, of course, have to leave our employ, but no doubt a stellar recommendation from your immediate superiors will allow you to find employment elsewhere with ease…perhaps even with the company you've been moonlighting for."

"You'll have to excuse me for finding it hard to believe that you would simply let me go after all this."

"Make no mistake, if you defeat me, you will have earned your freedom."

"Okay…" Kuhn nodded. "And if I lose?"

"If you lose, you will be dead. Your family, however, will not suffer in your absence. As I said, they are not complicit in your crime, and I bear them no ill will. As a matter of fact, they would be eligible to receive the life insurance payout on your untimely death."

"Sure—while you go to prison for murder." Kuhn regarded the nearest few suits of armor, noticing that none had a weapon sheathed at its side. *If he is truly in here somewhere, he's* unarmed *right now…*

"Mr. Kuhn, do you really think that I have not planned this down to the last detail?" his boss asked. "Officially, you will have died in an unfortunate car accident. And yes, there will be a scenario created that will explain the injuries on your body. Stengrave Industries will mourn the loss of one of its own, and due to the life insurance policy, including double indemnity for your tragic but accidental death, your widow and children will be able to live lives of comfort, rather than being forced to fend for themselves— She does have a degree, I recall, but has not worked since your children were born, yes?"

Kuhn's head spun at the casual yet definitive way Stengrave has defined the two paths he faced, as if there were no other options at this point. He listened as Stengrave continued. "You have sullied the honor of your family name with your deception and insulted me, as well. All I am offering to you is a chance to make it right, for you to reclaim your honor and perhaps die with your integrity restored. And who knows, you may even win."

"And what if I sit on the floor and refuse to participate in your crazy game?"

"Then eventually I will grow tired of waiting and come to kill you. But surely that is not how you wish to die, is it, Mr. Kuhn? Sitting passively on the floor, meekly accepting your fate? Your family forced to continue their lives knowing their father was a criminal—for I will definitely have to let them know of your misdeeds—"

Kuhn's brow furrowed. "So now you're trying to blackmail me into playing, fighting for my life?"

"I am offering something you will not find anywhere else—a chance to redeem yourself, to pass from this world to the next with your head held high."

Kuhn looked back at the door leading to the room in which he had awakened, then at the hall of armor in front of him. As he stood there, he realized with a strange frisson of combined horror and honesty that Stengrave was right—there was only one way out.

"All right." Striding to the rack of bladed weapons, he selected the long sword—the only one that even came close to the fencing blades he'd used in college, and tested its heft and reach. He couldn't explain it, but it somehow felt…right in his hand. "I'm ready."

"Good. You may begin at your leisure."

Gripping the hilt in both hands, Kuhn slowly began walking down the rest of the hallway, searching for that one suit of armor that had the telltale sign of a real person inside it.

That one? Or maybe that one? He stared at each one, trying to discern something, *anything* that would give him the edge.

There! Spotting what he thought was a flicker of movement out of the corner of his eye, Kuhn whirled and drove the tip of the blade as hard as he could into the lower abdomen of a spectacular suit of fluted armor that was engraved everywhere with delicate golden filigree.

The armor suit tipped backward and crashed to the ground. On impact, the helmet flew off, revealing a mannequin's featureless face.

Sword held high, Kuhn turned, looking for one of the suits to come at him. None of them moved. *Come on...come on!*

He lashed out at another suit nearest to him, this one a simpler, unadorned collection of steel armor. It, too, went over in a clatter of metal and mannequin limbs. Kuhn turned to the next one, only to find it had stepped off its dais and was coming right at him.

Stengrave rushed him like a striker charging for a loose ball—a striker sheathed in sixty pounds of metal.

Kuhn didn't even think about trying to get his sword up—he just leaped out of the way. Stengrave didn't change course or attempt to stop, however, he just kept going, only slowing once he'd reached the sword rack. Grabbing a heavy-bladed Walloon sword by its basket hilt, he whirled, slashing out with it in a move that would have sliced Kuhn's chest open if it had connected.

The younger man, however, wasn't there anymore. He'd gotten up and backed away, sword held out in front of him. Now armed, the six-foot-five Stengrave regarded him for a moment from inside a visored basinet that covered his entire head. Stengrave raised his sword in front of him in a brief but sincere salute, then began advancing on the smaller man.

Kuhn stepped back and then did so again. His foot brushed against a helmet that had fallen off one of the other suits, and he reached down, groping blindly for it, as he dared not take his eyes off his attacker. Stengrave kept coming, and just when Kuhn thought he'd have to abandon the piece, his fingers gripped an edge and he grabbed the helmet and whipped it up at Stengrave.

He'd thrown it in his opponent's general direction, so the programmer was surprised to see his improvised missile clang into Stengrave's helmet, throwing the man off course for a moment. Seizing the opportunity, Kuhn didn't follow up with an attack, but instead darted off deeper into the hallway, trying to find a place to hide and hopefully figure out some way to take the armored man by surprise.

Despite the odds against him, Kuhn hadn't felt this alive in years. Also, from what he had seen, he thought he might actually have a chance to take the other man. Stengrave's closed-face helmet protected him, but it also limited his vision to a tiny strip right in front of his eyes. Plus, as the helmet was attached to the rest of the armor, it didn't allow him to turn his head! Finally, there were many places where he wasn't nearly as heavily armored, like his neck, elbow and knee joints.

If I can just take him by surprise, I might be able to pull this off, Kuhn thought. And I think I know exactly how...

Hiding behind the last suit of armor near the far door, he tried to get his breathing under control as he peeked out just enough to locate Stengrave. The bigger man had returned to the middle of the hallway, standing a few steps away from the rack of swords. Although he was looking around, Kuhn's evaluation of his helmet was correct—Stengrave couldn't turn his head. He ran through his plan one more time in his mind. *Here goes...*

He shoved the armor he was hiding behind over as hard as he could, counting on the movement to attract his boss's attention. The moment he felt it tip, he ducked and ran, keeping low, down the row to the suit of armor closest to Stengrave.

The falling suit hit the floor with a clatter. Kuhn didn't wait for Stengrave's reaction, but shoved the suit he was standing behind over, as well, straight at the big man. His plan was to follow that up with an attack, hoping to injure the other man as he dodged the falling armor.

It wasn't a bad plan, and went off more or less as he had planned it. The only trouble was that Stengrave ended up facing Kuhn to fend off the falling armor, and as such, saw the smaller man coming at him. Already committed, Kuhn kept going, even as Stengrave sidestepped the second distraction. Kuhn angled over to the other man's left side, where his sword wasn't, already raising his sword to swing down at the armored man's left knee, hoping to chop into the joint and maim him.

Kuhn wasn't exactly sure what happened next. As he started bringing his sword down he caught a blur of movement from Stengrave out of the corner of his eye, then it felt as though he had run into a horizontal railing with such force it knocked the breath out of him. He kept moving forward, his sword forgotten in his hand, even as he felt a strange pressure on his chest, which was gone as soon as he'd sensed it. He stumbled a bit, falling to one knee. Sensing that something wasn't right here... Where did all this...blood come from? he wondered as he stared down at the pattering of droplets on the floor in front of him. With a gasp, he realized the front of his shirt wasn't indigo anymore, but black... black with wet, fresh blood.

Oh, my God... A long, horizontal tear had cut his shirt in two. Kuhn moved numbing fingers up to pull the top part away, revealing a long slash across his stomach, through the abdominal wall lining and into his abdomen. With mounting horror, he thought he saw the pinkish-gray of his own intestines as he fell backward to sit on the ground. Blood was everywhere, on his hand, in his pants, covering his shoes. Oddly, there was no pain, which surprised him, as he would have thought being sliced open this way would have hurt like a son of a bitch.

Kuhn's sword dropped from his other hand as a wave of weakness crashed over him. Dumbly, he looked up to see Stengrave looming over him. The owner of Stengrave Industries had raised his visor and now stared down at Kuhn with cold, slate-gray eyes. His face looked as if it might as well have been carved from granite. Again, he raised the sword, its edge now covered in blood, to salute him.

"You lasted longer than I expected. *Farväl.*"

Drawing the sword back, he swung it forward and down, the heavy blade slicing through Kuhn's neck and spinal cord, and cutting off his head. It rolled to the ground while the jet of blood that spurted from the stump was already subsiding as the body fell backward to the floor.

KRISTIAN STENGRAVE REGARDED the body of his former employee as dispassionately as he did most of his investments. The strongest feeling he would admit to at the moment was annoyance—annoyance that someone in his employ, whom he had spent considerable resources to retain and improve—would have turned on him for such a base reason as money. It was only through the most fortunate circumstance that the hapless programmer hadn't realized the true value of what he was stealing. If he had, then anyone he would have come in contact with, from his minders at the other company, to his family, would have had to have been killed, as well. Secrecy was simply that vital for his largest project, one that would irrevocably alter the world as humanity knew it.

Stengrave cleaned his sword and set it back on the rack before unstrapping his helmet and removing it, revealing sweaty, white-blond hair that fell to his shoulders. He tapped his wireless earpiece. "It's done."

The door at the far end of the hallway opened and a whip-thin man with a shaved head entered. Dressed in an impeccable three-piece dark gray suit, he walked to Stengrave, careful not to get any blood on his handmade shoes. "I sure hope that isn't the severance package you have planned for me." His voice held the smooth, supple tones of a top-class British education.

"Do not betray me, Mr. Firke, and you will never have to find out," Stengrave replied, not taking his eyes off the body. "Have this hallway restored, and set up the accident as we had discussed."

"Of course, sir." The second man eyed the head with pursed lips. "I suppose there wasn't any way you could have avoided beheading him, perhaps? That will make it more difficult to, uh, disguise his condition."

"He deserved an honorable death. Just make it happen."

"Of course, sir. Don't forget that you have the update call in an hour. The lab in the Congo says it has news."

That tore Stengrave's gaze from the body, and he began divesting himself of the rest of the armor. "Excellent. I look forward to hearing about their progress. I suggest that you keep a travel bag prepared. If all goes well, you may be overseeing a field test shortly."

"Of course, sir, I'll prepare that just as soon as I've had this—" Firke nodded at the mess "—cleaned up."

CHAPTER THREE

Sixty hours earlier

Dr. Gerhardt Richter sighed as he leaned back in his chair, trying to avoid the chill breeze blowing on the back of his neck. Shaking his head, he walked over to his single upright dresser, pulled out a black, silk scarf and draped it around his neck. Although the laboratory needed the air conditioning to maintain the temperature throughout the complex, it was difficult for him to get re-acclimated, particularly after two days in the field. Now, he always felt cold, no matter where in the complex he was, and that damnable breeze seemed to follow him around the room. Richter walked to the thermostat mounted next to the door and tapped it, not sure if the damn thing was regulating anything anymore.

This is not how groundbreaking science is achieved, he thought, activating the VOIP—voice over internet protocol—program on his machine. "The thermostat in my office is malfunctioning again, Sharene. Please get someone in maintenance to take a look at it as soon as possible."

"Yes, sir. Yours is the third complaint I've received, and maintenance is already looking into it. I'll pass on the status update as soon they get back to me. Also, I just received word from the lab that they're ready to begin the next round of tests."

"Good, I'll be there shortly." Richter closed his computer and tucked it under his arm. With a grimace, he glanced at the roof above him one last time, as if willing it to stay up long enough for him to get out of the room. Rising from his desk, he left his cramped office and walked into the even more cramped hallway.

His backers had built the complex to be sturdy—at least, that's what they had told him—but the German was forced to stoop as he walked, so that his balding head wouldn't hit the ceiling. He was slightly concerned that he would develop a permanent hunch from the past five months of work.

After this, I'm due a long vacation, he thought, maybe somewhere sunny and bright instead of humid and hot all the time.

The idea cheered him a bit and he nodded to the other white-lab-coated men and women he passed as he headed for the main laboratory.

He stopped only once before passing two security men half carrying one of the test subjects—a quivering young African male—between them, with another technician trailing them.

"Hold it." Richter thumbed back the sagging youth's eyelid, revealing an eye that had rolled back into his head. "Where'd he come from?"

"He's the security breach we recaptured at 2100 last night," the tech said. "Filmed him killing a full-grown leopard out in the jungle. Emailed you the video this morning."

"Right." Richter pressed fingers to the young man's neck. "Erratic heartbeat. I don't like that. Place him in the guarded ICU and monitor his condition for the next twenty-four hours."

"Yes, sir." The three men left with their prisoner, and Richter continued on his way.

Arriving at his destination, Richter entered the airlock, waiting for the doors to close. He walked to the center of the small corridor, where a powerful stream of antiseptic air washed over him, removing any small biological organisms that might contaminate the lab. When the tone sounded, indicating his cleansing cycle was completed, he stepped into the next room.

The laboratory was state-of-the-art, with a half dozen of the current shift's white-coated scientists working at computer stations and lab tables. One of them, a tall, Nordic-looking blond woman, noticed his entrance and walked over.

"Good afternoon, Doctor. Here to witness the next test?"

"Correct."

"Good, we're about to start. Follow me, please." She led him to the other side of the laboratory, where a large, thick pane of laminated glass separated them from the occupants in the other room.

Richter watched as the first creature in the room roamed around. It was a chimpanzee, about three years old, circling the perimeter of the bare, five-meter by five-meter room with apprehension in its eyes.

"This is a young male, captured two weeks ago, weighing ninety-three pounds and measuring forty-five inches tall. We've limited its calorie intake and have taken steps to ensure a suitable aggressive reaction to the second test subject."

A door slid open on the right side and a slender black man wearing a pair of white shorts and a T-shirt was prodded through the door, which slid closed behind him.

The chimp's head swiveled to stare at the newcomer, whose eyes also locked on the animal. The chimpanzee rose, standing on its back legs and supporting its front body on its knuckles. It bared its teeth at the man, who looked confused for a moment.

The blond woman spoke, not taking her eyes off the window. "The primate senses that something isn't right with the human subject."

"When does the reaction start, Dr. Estvaan?"

"Any moment n—"

She hadn't even completed her sentence when the two creatures in the room exploded into action. The man's face turned into a rictus of rage that suffused his features, his lips peeling back from his teeth in a savage snarl, his fingers outstretched into curled talons as he rushed at the chimpanzee. The animal stood on its hind legs and charged, screaming in rage, its fangs also bared.

"Normally the chimpanzee has the advantage, since it is five times as strong as the average human, despite being outweighed by fifty pounds." Dr. Estvaan sounded as though she might be discussing two Olympic wrestlers. "But watch."

The two combatants clashed in the middle of the room. The chimp established early dominance with its opposable hands on the lower legs clamping onto the man's torso while its upper set of hands grabbed the head of its soon-to-be victim as it zoomed in to bite at the vulnerable face.

Usually that would have been the end of it. However before the chimp could attack, the man's hand swiped down with inhuman speed, raking the animal across the eyes and causing it to screech in pain. The man continued his attack, curling his hand into a fist and battering it against the monkey's skull again and again, his hand blurring with the effort. The chimpanzee rocked back with each punch.

"Subjects have been observed to break their fingers and dislocate their wrists and elbows from repeated forceful blows against their targets," Dr. Estvaan stated, jotting notes on her tablet.

The chimpanzee's hands tore at the man, scoring a hit on his genitals and twisting hard, but the man didn't stop his frenzied assault. He lunged forward, sinking his teeth into the side of the chimpanzee's neck and savaging it with all his might.

The chimpanzee screamed in agony and redoubled its efforts, grabbing one of the man's ears and tearing it off his head. But its struggles grew weaker as bright red blood spurted from the terrible wound in its neck. It brought around its right fist, the fingers covered in blood, trying to smash the man's temple. Without stopping his attack on the chimp's throat, the man's left hand rose to block the attack, his open palm meeting the monkey's arm whistling through the air and stopping it cold.

The chimpanzee struggled to extricate its hand, the muscles shaking with strain as it tried to free itself, while the man's hand closed around the chimp's fist, squeezing it tighter and tighter. The chimp now shook all over, its ropy muscles spasming as it went into shock. It moaned once, then its head flopped back.

The man shoved the chimpanzee's body off him and stood in the center of the room, his chest heaving as he sucked air in through his gore-caked mouth, his own blood mingling with his victim's to spatter on the floor.

"First assault to critical wound in eight point nine

seconds." Dr. Estvaan noted that data on her tablet. "Impressive."

"Yes, yes, the lethality results of the compound have been noted a dozen times. It is the next phase that is critical. Are your men ready?"

Estvaan tapped her earpiece. "Send them in."

The door the man had come through slid open again and a man dressed in heavy padding and ballistic protection, with a riot helmet and visor on his head, appeared in the doorway. The test subject whirled, his dilated eyes locking on the new person. His nostrils flared as he scented the air, a low growl building in his throat, then he crouched and leaped to attack. The new man fired a pair of darts into his assailant's chest, then ducked back behind the door, which began to close. The subject hit the barrier and forced his arm through the shrinking hole to block it. Bracing himself against the wall, he began levering the door open.

"Do we have a problem?" Richter asked, setting down his laptop.

Estvaan pointed. "No, look—the energy is draining out of him even now. However, he does not pass out as the early subjects did. The drug is containing him, for lack of a better term."

Their test subject's efforts grew more labored and he sank to the floor, still trying to shove the door open, but failing as the tranquilizer coursed through his body. With one final growl that sounded more like an anguished groan toward the end, he slumped over, chest rising and falling rapidly as he sank into unconsciousness.

"Restrain and stabilize him. After-team, run the standard battery of tests and send me the results."

Richter ran his hands over his head, resisting the urge

to clench them into fists and hammer the wall. "I thought this variant had so much promise, but we are no closer to arresting the effects once the cycle begins. What good is true superhuman strength and reflexes without the control to stop using them when the immediate threat has been neutralized? And if the subject cannot remain active once the surge is done, that is another problem."

Dr. Estvaan nodded. "Perhaps. We are close. Another few modifications and we'll be able to turn this on and off in subjects at will, either by neuro feedback or by remote control."

"Yes, but I've got to tell Stengrave that we haven't gotten any closer to controlling the virus's effects."

Estvaan nodded again. "Keep in mind the potential this compound also has as a weapon by introducing it into unknowing or unwilling subjects."

Her last words sparked something in Richter's mind. "What about the transfer vectors you've been working on?"

"Well, you would have seen it if the chimpanzee had survived. Within six to eight hours, it would have been exhibiting the same pretest symptoms as the human subject. Currently the virus is best transmitted via blood or saliva."

"And the genetic safeguards we've tailored it with have been effective?"

"One hundred percent so far." Dr. Estvaan glanced at him. "As I have stated before, we cannot guarantee that a mutated form wouldn't be able to cross genetic types, but the self-destruct safeguard should prevent that, as well."

"Lastly, you have confirmed that the virus cannot survive independently outside of a host body?"

"Correct, Doctor. If exposed to open air, it begins

breaking down at the cellular level immediately. There is no chance of an active strain using an airborne or fluid-borne vector to contaminate others. Of course, the infectious strain can be introduced into food or water in its dormant state and, once ingested, begin affecting its victims within two hours."

"Good, I'm glad to see that parameter has been maintained. Prepare a dormant sample large enough to affect…oh, say thirty to fifty people. I'll need to update our superiors, but I see no reason to halt our tests on a limited public group. It's time to begin phase two." Dr. Richter smiled. "After all, if this cannot be used as a controllable weapon yet, perhaps its application lies in using it as a less-controlled one."

Just then his smartphone beeped. Richter glanced at it and saw the reminder he'd been waiting for. "Prepare your after-test reports and forward them to me once they are finished. I'll be in my office, but am not to be disturbed for the next hour."

AS HE STRODE through the halls toward his office, Richter dictated his notes.

"Although the virus appears to have potential practical applications on the battlefield, there will need to be more tests done to refine a more controllable variant. This is not to say that the research here has been in vain, on the contrary, we have done more here in six months that has been possible in the past three years. With additional time and experimentation with the various strains we have cultivated, I am sure that we can create a version that will give us the abilities we're looking for, along with the necessary control."

His laptop chimed and Richter frowned at the interruption to his train of thought. He reached over and paused the computer recorder, then hit the answer button. *"Ja?"*

The voice on the other end of the satellite connection was smooth and cordial but hard underneath—like silk over a steel glove. "Dr. Richter, I hope I'm not interrupting you."

Richter recognized the voice instantly. "Of course not, Mr. Stengrave. I am ready to present our status to the board, as directed."

"What can you tell me about your recent progress?"

"We are making progress, but it has slowed considerably." Verifying their channel was secure, he summarized the recent tests. "We cannot seem to strike the balance between the advantages the drug gives the recipients and the negative effects afterward."

"I see. How do you intend to mitigate this situation?"

"One of our potential uses for the virus in its current form would be as an inflammatory agent, which could be tailored to fit a specified population. Spiking the water would introduce it into their systems, and chaos would follow. I had wanted to discuss a possible test of this scenario—"

"I already have something in mind for that—a geographically-isolated test on genetically-limited population. I'm sending Mr. Firke down with the necessary genetic sample. He will stay until the batch is ready, and will escort it to our on-site team within thirty-six hours." He chuckled. "Sometimes it's easier to make a point with a little bloodshed. Spun properly, I think this could be just as effective as our first projected use of the virus."

"I'll have the samples ready for splicing the moment

he arrives. If you do not mind my asking, how will you handle the meeting today?"

"I'll put them off for now, saying you are in the middle of a delicate series of tests and cannot be disturbed. Make it happen, Doctor. If the results are good enough, I may have you conference in to a later meeting to field questions. I'll let you know once we know how the field test has gone." Stengrave broke the connection with a click.

Richter stabbed his intercom button. "Sharene, please ready the guest quarters. We're going to have company soon."

CHAPTER FOUR

Fifty hours earlier

Dr. Richter stood at the main doors of the lab, watching as a man dressed in jungle fatigues rappelled from a helicopter to the small clearing in front of their concealed facility. The moment his feet hit the ground, he unclipped himself from the rope, which was swiftly drawn back up as the helicopter was already flying away from the area. It had hovered over the site for maybe a minute at the most.

"Dr. Richter," the man said as he walked up to him. "I'm Reginald Firke. Interesting place you have here."

Well, at least he didn't try any sort of "I presume" crap, Richter thought with a disdainful glance at the man's crisp new fatigues and polished combat boots. "Come inside."

The two men headed across the small vehicle bay to the outer airlock, past the half-dozen mud-splattered Range Rovers, and stood in front of an industrial glass-and-stainless steel door as the large outer doors closed behind them, throwing the large room into semi-shadow. "I assume your cargo is intact?"

Firke shrugged off a small backpack and held it out. "In here are all the samples you will need. I'm sure our mutual boss has informed you that time is of the essence."

"Of course he has." Richter didn't move to take the pack, nor did he spare the shorter man a glance as the outer airlock door opened. "The emphasis was unnecessary, however. You'll have the tailored viruses and be on your way soon enough."

If the slender man was insulted by Richter's annoyed tone, he didn't visibly react as they headed into the airlock. "No need to insult the messenger, Doctor. I'm simply passing on the message, that's all."

"Humph." Richter stared straight ahead as compressed air jets containing a powerful disinfectant covered their clothes and exposed skin. He didn't think much of Stengrave's hired goon. He'd had the man researched and learned he was ex-SAS, the British special forces arm of the military. That information did not faze him in the least. In Richter's opinion, a gun was only used to accomplish a goal when those involved neglected to use their brains to find a more elegant and much less obvious solution. "I assume that Mr. Stengrave has also let you know of my requirements for this experiment?"

The safe tone sounded and the inner airlock door opened, revealing the cool tile and sterile-white hallway. Richter stalked forward through the corridors, brushing past men and women who knew to get out of his way when they saw the tall man walking with such purpose.

"Yes, that is not a problem. You'll have all the eyes on-site you requested."

"Good." Richter turned a corner and lengthened his stride, making the shorter man hasten to catch up. It was a faint jab at the other man, but the doctor took his pleasure where he could find it.

"You realize, of course, that observing is all you will be doing."

Now Richter did turn to the other man and let a small, mirthless smile appear on his face. "Of course, Mr. Firke. Just as you would never presume to tell me how to do my job, I would not feign to know the slightest bit of knowledge about how to carry out yours."

The ex-military man's only physical response was a raised eyebrow. "So glad we understand each other."

Richter didn't reply until they reached the culture room. White biohazard-suited figures, their faces obscured by full hoods, worked on various trays and at various lab machines and microscopes. The doctor stopped by a drawer set into the wall and hit the switch on an intercom.

"Dr. Estvaan to the transfer drawer, please." A lithe figure on the far side of the room approached. Richter pulled the drawer out of the wall, then turned to the other man and held out his hand. Firke unzipped the backpack, pulled out a small metal case that was cold to the touch and handed it to the scientist.

After placing the metal case in the drawer, Richter closed it, sending it into the room as he activated the intercom again. "This is the package you were briefed on. You have the entire lab at your disposal to create as many strains using the DNA in here as possible over the next sixteen hours. This assignment takes priority over all others."

With a curt nod, Estvaan took the case and pulled the rest of the suited workers to her as she began assigning tasks.

"Why Armenia?" Richter asked as he watched the group begin its work.

"Stengrave told you about the final destination, then," Firke replied.

"Of course." Richter glanced sidelong at the ex-soldier. "That is the one thing I don't understand about this experiment. There are plenty of isolated places with a limited population around here. I could find several villages that would suit his needs within a half-day's travel." He turned to the other man. "So, why Armenia?"

"You know, I asked him the very same question." Firke's mouth curved into a grim smile. "Apparently, about fifteen years ago, a shipment of medical equipment was hijacked and its contents sold on the black market. Don't ask me who bought it. I didn't even know there was a black market for plasmapheresis machines, but apparently there is. Anyway, the thieves stole from our boss, at a time when his company had invested everything in this new technology. That shipment was not only worth several millions dollars, it was supposed to open up an entire new world of sales opportunities for Stengrave Industries. When the shipment was lost, insurance didn't cover nearly enough to make up for the loss. The company almost went under."

Richter blinked. "And you're telling me that Mr. Stengrave is now about to exact his revenge on the Armenian thugs who did this to him?"

"Well, over the past fifteen years, that small family of Armenians that took that shipment has grown into one of the largest crime families in the country. The file that my predecessor was required to keep on them is almost 20 gigabytes of data and pictures. Their leader has a vacation place in the mountains, inside a walled city."

Richter held up a hand. "Just to be clear... Mr. Stengrave has been holding on to these DNA samples for all this time?"

"Well, you know the old saying 'keep your friends

close, and your enemies closer'? Mr. Stengrave has quite a collection of both."

"But to collect all of these various samples… It seems, I don't know…"

"Obsessive?" Firke shrugged. "Perhaps. Let's just say you're not the only one who's spent time in a lab coat over the years." He cleared his throat. "Regarding what you and your people are about to do, one could say that Mr. Stengrave just wants to run a test in a controlled area, where there is the least likely possibility of your little tailored friends in there getting loose. The fact that he's selected that particular place to do so—also delivering a particularly gruesome revenge on an old enemy who by now has most likely forgotten the reason why this biological death is about to rain down on him—could be a staggering coincidence…or you could chalk all of this up to simple Stengrave efficiency, and take out two birds with one carefully aimed stone."

Firke turned to the other man. "Fortunately, down here in the Congo, you do not have to worry about such things. Just keep working on what Mr. Stengrave wishes you to work on, and all will be well." He looked up and down the corridor. "Since I'm basically stuck here for the next several hours, I'll be in my quarters. Notify me an hour before the batch is ready."

He walked down the hall, leaving a silent Richter staring after him and trying to repress the shudder that quivered its way down his spine.

Thirty-three hours earlier

AT 0200 LOCAL TIME, Reginald Firke's eyes popped open without the aid of an alarm.

Swinging his legs over the side of the cot he'd been sleeping on, he sat up and reached for his tablet. Logging in to the local network, he accessed the security cameras and saw that just about everyone was down for the night, except for Dr. Estvaan and her busy crew, still working hard in their lab. He brought up the camera in the main security room and recorded about three minutes of the lone sentry there, then got up and left his room.

Firke walked through the corridors until he came to a room marked Security. The door had no handle on this side, just a keypad and a card slot on the wall next to it. Firke pulled a black key card out of his pocket and swiped it through the reader. The door opened with a soft click.

"What are you doing back?" the guard at the monitors asked as he began turning in his swivel chair, a finger reaching for a large red button. "You're not due for another thirty minutes…"

Firke held up the black key card. "Good reflexes. You know who I am, correct?"

The guard nodded dumbly, removing his finger from the alarm button.

"And you know who I work for?"

Another nod.

"Very good. I am conducting a surprise inspection of this facility's security. I am pleased to see that you are at your post and alert. However, I must now ask you to step outside for a few minutes."

Still nodding, the guard slowly got up from his chair and walked toward the door. He didn't take his eyes off Firke, who watched him leave, not turning back to the main security console until the door was completely closed. Once it did, he casually glanced at the panel, which controlled every camera both inside and outside the complex, as well as doors that sealed off particular areas and even overrode controls for power, temperature and air intake. Firke didn't bother with any of these; he just pushed the guard chair aside and sat on the floor.

Taking a screwdriver with an unusual, star-shaped tip from his pocket, he unscrewed six screws in a small panel under the console. Removing that panel revealed a small, unmarked console with another keypad next to five switches, each one underneath a small light and all in the down position.

Firke carefully punched in a long, memorized series of numbers. Then, taking a deep breath, he flipped each switch one by one from right to left. In each case, a green light came on. When they were all activated, he let out the breath he had been holding. If he had input the code wrong, activating the last switch would have been the end of him and the base—literally. Carefully, he replaced the panel and screwed it back into place.

Getting up, he checked the display on his tablet, which showed the camera's view of the security room in what was supposed to be real time. Instead of him, however, the screen showed the footage of the guard Firke had recorded earlier. With a satisfied nod, he replaced the chair behind the console, then walked to the door and opened it to let the guard back inside.

"Is everything all right?" the man asked as he walked to his station.

Firke nodded. "Everything is exactly as it should be. You are doing a fine job. Keep up the good work and we may have a promotion for you once you've completed your duty here. And the best way you can do that is by never mentioning that you ever saw me here, all right?"

"Yes, sir."

Firke nodded. "Excellent. As you were."

The young man almost raised a hand to salute, but turned it into scratching an itch on his cheek. Smiling thinly, Firke stepped outside the security room and let the door close.

Retracing his steps, Firke was back in his room without a soul seeing him. Sitting on his cot again, he activated a control panel that showed a full blueprint of the base with small red Xs revealed in every room and ringing the outside perimeter of the complex. Below all of that was a simple sentence: BASE SELF-DESTRUCT SYSTEM PRIMED.

Satisfied, Firke cleared his tablet and set it aside, then lay down and was asleep within sixty seconds.

"YOU HAVE everything you need. Introduce it into the water supply, or even food will work. It can survive being boiled or cooked, so whatever way you find will get it into the target populace will be best. Of course, you and your men would be best advised to not eat or drink anything in the area once the contamination has been implemented."

"Of course not." Firke raised his voice over the sound of the approaching helicopter. "It has been a most interesting visit, Doctor. Thank you for your hospitality." He reached behind him to check on the backpack strapped to his back.

Richter only nodded curtly as the helicopter stopped over the clearing and a line was dropped. Firke hooked his harness onto it and was drawn upward. The moment he was clear of the tree line, the helicopter rose higher into the air, carrying him, still on the line, with it.

Richter watched it shrink until it vanished into the sky, then turned and headed back into the lab complex.

CHAPTER FIVE

Seventeen hours earlier

"To Armenia!"

Josh Tyrell clinked his raised his bottle of beer against his friends' glasses. He took a healthy swallow, his dark brown eyes roaming over the mix of tourists and locals mingled in the bar of the Pergomesh Hotel in Arkatar. His eyes settled on an olive-skinned, raven-haired beauty who gave him a friendly glance and smile as she walked by in a miniskirt and sleeveless blouse. *"Bari yereko."* Stumbling over the unfamiliar Armenian, he grinned as she smiled wider but still kept going.

"Would you keep your voice down? Jesus, could you sound more like a tourist?" With a frown, William Scott raised his glass of pilsner and sipped it, then waved his other hand in front of his face to try to move some of the haze of cigarette smoke that hung in a cloud over the entire room. "Probably going to get us all mugged and killed before the trip is over."

"Jeez, Billy, would you relax?" Tyrell replied. "This isn't Slovakia, and we're not in *Hostel*. These are my people, remember? They're gonna get my money one way or another, so I might as well enjoy myself while I'm here, right? Hell, we all might as well enjoy ourselves while we're here, if you get my drift." Waggling his thick eyebrows, he grinned conspiratorially at the other two men, earning an aggravated sigh from Scott and a nervous smile from the third member of their group.

Gary Alcaster sipped his own beer and watched the two friends bicker. He wasn't sure what made him more uncomfortable: Tyrell's outspoken swagger and brashness, Scott's peevishness and worry over seemingly every minute of this weekend getaway, or the fact that he was ostensibly here to get his cherry popped.

I should get my brain scanned for agreeing to all this, he thought. Of course, it had all been Tyrell's idea. The three had met while preparing to attend their second year at King's College School of Medicine in London. Tyrell was a broad-shouldered former linebacker from Dublin, Texas, with a knee injury that had effectively ended his football career and left him with a slight limp when he walked. Blond-haired Alcaster was born and raised in the slightly larger city of Glace Bay, Nova Scotia, and this was his first time out of his hometown, not to mention Canada. Scott, rail-thin and bespectacled, hailed from the small town of Haltwhistle, in the northern part of England. Despite their differences, the three had quickly bonded over their status as outsiders in the sprawling, cosmopolitan city.

Over beers and a Texas Hold'em game with a couple other students one night, Alcaster had lost a side bet and, red-faced, admitted that he hadn't yet slept with a girl. Ever since, Tyrell had talked about nothing else, not even their upcoming exams, but helping his friend lose his virginity.

That was how they had ended up here, during a bank holiday weekend when they probably should have been studying instead. After four days of persuasion, with Tyrell saying the three of them would have a story unlike anything else in their lives, he'd convinced Scott first and then the two of them had persuaded Alcaster to take the plunge, so to speak. The Canadian's biggest concern had been to go somewhere where he wouldn't be seen by anyone who might recognize him. Tyrell said he had the prefect place for them to go.

The three had taken the Chunnel to Paris, then a day on the train traveling to Bucharest. From there they had rented a car and driven north-northeast, with Tyrell saying his ancestors came from around the area. A few hours later they had checked into the hotel and had spent the afternoon seeing the small town's sights, of which there were few.

Other than Scott's increasingly worried demeanor, they'd only encountered one spot of potential trouble so far. While walking through the old, cobblestoned streets, they'd seen a large, modern house, surrounded by a high stone wall with unfriendly-looking iron bars, looming over the rest of the village. Oblivious to the two thickset men at the gate and his friends' warnings, Tyrell had wanted to get a closer look and had crossed the street to look through the gate. He had been intercepted halfway across by one of the men, who'd had a quick, firm conversation with him, while opening his light jacket to reveal something inside.

While Scott and Alcaster watched with their hearts in their throats, trying to figure out whether they should grab Tyrell and run, or just take off themselves, the Texan pointed the other two students out, and the two men laughed about something. Then the gate guard pointed back the way they had come, said something with an emphatic nod, and sent the med student on his way with a smile that never came close to his pale blue eyes.

When he returned, Tyrell was ecstatic. "Dudes, that guy was in the *mob!* He showed me his pistol and everything!"

Scott had nearly lost it right there. "I swear to God, Josh, you're going to get us killed!"

The taller American flipped black hair out of his eyes. "Would you relax? He knew exactly why we're here. Tourists come from all over to sample the nightlife, so to speak. He said to stick around the bar in our hotel, especially after eight. That's when the best girls start coming in for drinks."

Although Alcaster had his misgivings about any truth in the information they had been given, that was how they all found themselves sitting in the hotel tavern, which could have been just about any older drinking establishment in Europe, with a long, dark wooden bar along one side of the room, surrounded by several round tables and a row of booths along the far wall.

They'd had a surprisingly good dinner, washed down with a variety of regional beers, ranging from pale golden pilsners to a weak, dark dunkel that all three had agreed was the worst of the lot. Now, with dinner behind them, Tyrell tapped his fingers restlessly on the tabletop, obviously anxious for the evening's entertainment to begin. Scott looked uneasy, while Alcaster was engaged in his internal struggle—which he'd been waging with himself since the trip began— as to whether he was really going to go through with this. His mind churned with equal parts anticipation, nervousness and flat-out fear. He swallowed through a suddenly dry throat and his palms were sweating so much he nearly dropped his beer glass when he went for a drink. He could back out right now, say he wasn't feeling well from dinner or something—

Having made up his mind to do just that, Alcaster was rehearsing what he was going to say before excusing himself and going back to their room when the cuckoo clock on the wall over the bar began chiming the hour. As if drawn on cue, the main doors of the small lobby next to the bar opened and a parade of young women in tight dresses, high-heeled shoes and a range of makeup entered the bar. Although most of them had game smiles on, it was relatively clear that none was here of her own free will. However, that really didn't seem to matter to the men waiting in the bar.

All of the men there—many of whom had been furtively counting the minutes, much like Tyrell, Scott and Alcaster had—perked up, smiling and waving as they looked over the night's offerings. The three students huddled together, eyeing the women as they made the rounds, with Tyrell urging the other two to make their selections quickly.

"We need to cull the ones we want out of the herd, or they're gonna go elsewhere," he insisted.

"For God's sake, Josh, these are people, not cattle!" Scott hissed.

Tyrell rolled his eyes. "Yeah, yeah, would you pull that stick out of your ass for just one night? Look, we all know why we're here, and so do they. If we don't take advantage of the situation, someone else will. Now—" Tyrell craned his head up as three women, a blonde, a brunette and a dark-haired woman somewhere in their twenties, all dressed in different varieties of brightly colored, skintight dresses, approached their table. The trio of younger women had headed off a pair of more mature-looking prostitutes who had glared at the interlopers but still retreated. "Uh…can we help you ladies?" Tyrell asked.

"You are Americans, yes?" the brunette asked in decent English. "We *love* Americans."

"Well, I am, and my friends are from Canada and England, but don't worry, they're all right." Tyrell's weak joke made all three ladies laugh, however, and he nodded at the other two to push a table over to make more room as he waved them in. "Won't you join us?"

"Thank you." The brunette introduced herself as Anoush, the blonde as Lusine and the raven-haired young woman as Siranush. Once Scott and Alcaster had gotten another table and chairs, the three women sat among the suddenly tongue-tied young men.

"You are all here on vacation?" Lusine asked.

"Er, yes," Scott said. "We're medical students on holiday, that's right."

The three women exchanged glances. "You are going to be doctors, yes?" Siranush said, placing her hand on Alcaster's thigh. "We *love* doctors."

"Well, we're not—" he began.

"Great!" Tyrell interrupted a bit too quickly. "We were just about to order a bottle. Is there anything you would recommend?" he asked, ignoring the sudden warning glance from Scott.

Again, the three girls glanced at each other. "You all seem like nice boys," Aroush said, her voice low. "You should know to be careful about asking that sort of thing here. A lot of bars in the cities have arrangements with the girls, who get a kickback for steering tourists to higher-priced drinks."

"Oh, they do?" Tyrell asked. "Well, thanks for the tip. I think you all deserve a drink just for telling us that."

Siranush swept her long, dark hair back over her shoulder, exposing generous cleavage as she nodded at the beer bottles on the table. "You are all drinking beer. Perhaps you would care for something a bit stronger?"

The three students exchanged hesitant glances. "Perhaps…?" Tyrell said.

The blonde flagged down a server and rattled off an order in Armenian, then leaned back in and snuggled up to Scott. "He will bring us a bottle of Ararat cognac. It is very good, and not nearly as costly as other bottles."

"All right…" Scott leaned over to Alcaster. "What about 'beer before liquor, never sicker'? I don't want to be ill for…you know, what comes later."

Alcaster considered the adage for a moment. "Well, we've already eaten, so it shouldn't be a problem—"

Tyrell cleared his throat. "Guys? Would you mind keeping your heads in the game here, please?"

Their server had returned with a squat bottle and six small glasses. With a flourish and a small bow, he presented the cognac to the group, then set it and the glasses on the table.

"Now, if I remember correctly—" Tyrell said as he distributed glasses to each person and began filling them with the dark amber liquid "—there's supposed to be a toast with each round, right?"

"Very good, Josh," Anoush said as she raised her glass. "What would you like to drink to?"

With a broad grin, Tyrell stood and raised his glass. "To a night we'll never forget!"

CHAPTER SIX

Ten hours earlier

"We're ready for you, Doctor."

Richter took the offered headset with its attached microphone and slipped it on, adjusting it on his oblong head. "Testing, testing, one, two. Mr. Firke, can you hear me?"

"Yes, and that had better be all I hear from you until we're finished, understand?"

"Unless I feel the situation warrants it, I will leave the execution of this mission entirely in your hands. On the ground, you are in charge."

Richter was pleased he'd gotten Stengrave to go along with wiring the infiltration team for video and sound. He'd pushed hard for it, saying he wanted a record of the entire experiment, and that the data they collected on the Armenian village before the test began would be vital for their results. He figured Firke wouldn't be pleased about it, but as Richter had suspected, he had gone along when he realized there was no getting around his boss's orders.

Now he watched as the squad of six armed men drove down the deserted mountain road, their vehicle's headlights barely illuminating a few yards through the foggy night. Cresting a hill, they spotted the lights of the target village a mile away. Firke killed the lights and the engine, and the men got out and checked their gear one last time. Slipping a pair of night-vision goggles on his forehead, he made sure his team was ready to go and led them into the night.

Although the distance wasn't that great as the crow flies, the steep mountainside varied from passable to almost vertical, and the men had their work cut out for them on some of the rougher sections. Halfway there, two of the men, each carrying a long, hard-shell case slung across his back, split off and began climbing an escarpment overlooking the village. Covering the rest of the mile while making sure they weren't detected on the way took just over an hour, about as long as Richter had estimated.

He made sure the digital recorders, a primary and two backups, were all running perfectly, then turned his attention back to the over-the-shoulder view he had of the men as they cut their trail, as though he was walking right behind them. After a few minutes of quick, silent movement to get as close to the wall as they dared, Firke held up a fisted hand. All of the men stopped immediately.

Richter checked on the pair that had split off. They had reached the top of their hill and had a great view of the darkened valley, lit only by the lights of the walled village below. Both men unslung their cases and began removing equipment. One uncased a long sniper rifle, uncapped his scope and turned it on, then lay down. After adjusting his position one last time, the second man covered him with camouflage netting, then lay down behind a spotting scope and covered himself.

When both men were ready, they radioed in to the rest of the team.

Meanwhile, Firke had reached what looked like a four-foot-high water outflow pipe buried between two hills. An ankle-deep rivulet of water splashed out and trickled down the hillside. The opening of the pipe was covered by a latticework of what looked like rebar. Checking to make sure he couldn't be seen by anyone on the walls, Firke took a small cutting torch from a pocket, turned it on and began cutting through the bars. Within five minutes he had burned through enough of the latticework to bend back a large portion of it.

He signaled the rest of his men forward to the entrance. Turning on their night-vision goggles, they entered the sewer pipe, the tunnel lit only by the eerie, bright green of the NVGs. Occasionally, Richter saw the fleeting shape and heard a squeak of a rat in the pipe, but Firke and his men didn't seem bothered in the least.

They progressed deeper into the pipe, until Richter estimated they had gone at least one hundred yards. At an intersection Firke pushed his goggles back onto his forehead and peeked around a corner to see a dim shaft of light and a trickle of water coming down into the sewer from above. He waved his men forward again. When they reached the light and water, Firke took a hand-held screen attached to a small cable and fed the cable up through the sewer grate. A picture flickered into life on the screen and he studied it for a few minutes before stepping past the grate and waving two of his men forward.

They pushed the grate up and turned it sideways to fit it down the hole with them. Carrying it back, the other three hunkered down a few meters away and watched as Firke carefully stuck his head above the hole and looked around.

His camera took in cobblestoned streets and a neighborhood that could have come right out of anywhere in nineteenth-century Europe. Sturdy, wattle-and-daub buildings that had probably been built sometime in the last century lined the street, their tiled roofs two stories above the street. At this hour, the entire place was deserted. The camera caught the glow of the wall lights above, but none was turned to look inside the perimeter.

"What are they doing, Doctor?" The scientist monitoring the recordings, a callow youth of twenty-five—a near genius when it came to breeding virus stock, but relatively untutored in much of the outside world, including this sort of operation—blinked in confusion.

"They're taking stock of the situation, making sure there will be no surprises when they make their move on the water supply."

"But there's no one there now. They could be in and out in just a few minutes."

"I am sure Mr. Firke knows exactly what he is doing. I suggest that you concentrate on your duties and leave him to concentrate on his."

"Yes, sir." The scientist bent over his monitors again, while Richter and the rest of the watching scientists also waited. Five minutes passed, then ten. The other lab-coated men and women fidgeted or grew distracted as the time stretched out. Only Richter did not move a muscle, waiting for the operation to truly commence.

Finally, Firke rose out of the pipe and signaled his men to take their positions. Two men fanned out, one going left, one going right to flank. Kepler and the fourth man waited until the first pair were both ready to cover, then they quietly replaced the drain grate. Pulling their silenced pistols, the two men moved into the village square, staying low.

Like most Armenian villages fortunate enough to have one, the water tank was mounted on top of a tall building that looked to be some kind of hotel. This would be the trickiest part of the op, getting to the tower without being detected. Richter had stressed the importance of planting the compound in the tank itself, not in any kind of well. He didn't know what if any effects it might have on the groundwater table, and they weren't ready for any sort of test on that scale—at least, not yet.

With the two flanking men covering the intersection, Firke and his partner headed down a narrow alley that would give them access to the roof where the water tower was located. At the end was an industrial garbage bin, with bags of garbage piled next to it. Taking a folding grappling hook from his harness, he set the rubber-coated tines, then twirled the rope and let it fly up onto the roof. It didn't connect the first time and came tumbling back down, smacking the team member's hand when he tried to catch it. The second time was the charm, and soon both men had climbed the rope and were on the roof.

They reached the water tower without incident. Kepler stood guard at the base while the other man climbed a strut hand-over-hand until he reached the top. This was the crucial point—the man would have to drill a small hole into the pipe to insert the compound. Kepler alternated his glances up with a slow scan around the perimeter walls, watching for any potential trouble.

It came in the form of a door creaking open down the street. Two people slipped out of a building at the far end of the village. A young man and woman, both giggling, snuck through the silent streets, holding hands as they flitted from shadow to shadow.

The four-man squad froze. Richter listened to the conversation between them.

"Leader, I have visual on both approaching targets. Permission to fire?"

"Negative, keep them covered, but let them approach. We'll take them out only if necessary. Tank, hold your position." Firke melted into the shadows on the roof, holding his pistol in front of him with both hands as he disappeared.

The couple came closer, and Richter saw that they were tourists, maybe two students hooking up on a trip across Europe. They both took shelter in a darkened doorway, the man tilting the woman's head up for a long kiss, his hand stealing down to cup her breast. She moaned and pressed her body against him, her mouth opening to his. Ordinarily, Firke wouldn't have cared about them, but they were now blocking the escape route, and their noises might eventually attract the wall guards, which could not happen.

"Three, take them."

Lost in each other, they didn't notice the urban-camouflaged man emerge from the shadows and slowly creep toward them. When he was a few steps away, he aimed his silenced pistol and fired two carefully placed shots, one into the head of each. The couple, still locked in each other's arms, collapsed to the ground. The man strode over and put one more bullet into each unmoving form. "They're down."

"You and Four remove the bodies. Put them in the large garbage bin at the back of the alley. Longshot, keep your eyes open for others, and sing out the moment you see anyone. Tank, resume your mission."

Richter watched as the woman's body was picked up and slung over the man's shoulder as he began walking down the alleyway. Over Firke's microphone, the faint whine of a small cordless drill could be heard in the background. At the garbage bin, he dumped the limp form inside and waited for his partner to dump the other body. The two men covered both of them with bags of garbage before returning to their original positions.

Waiting for the cry of alarm that could come at any moment, Richter scarcely remembered to breathe while Tank finished his job, dumping the viscous, black liquid into the water tank, then sealing the hole with a bit of fast-drying putty. He affixed a small, wireless camera to the top of the tank, aiming it down so that the entire street could be seen, then descended just in time to rejoin Firke. The two men tied off their rope and climbed down, then retrieved the rope at the bottom by untying the slipknot and coiling it up. They picked up their flankers and were on the way back to the sewer grate at the spot where they had first come out of the jungle.

"Mr. Firke." Richter's words froze the Englishman in his steps. "I want you and your other men to place at least two more cameras in other areas, so that we can get different views of the experiment. There is no need to acknowledge my orders, just do it."

Firke didn't say a word, but Richter sensed the fury coiled in the man, ready to be unleashed on any available target. Without a sound, he gave the commands to his other two men by hand, sending them off to place the cameras in the best vantage points they could find. Each man completed his task in less than three minutes, giving Richter three lines of sight on the main roads of the small village. It was better than he could have hoped for.

The two men retraced their steps back to their leader, who led them all to the grate and down into the pipe. They left the area without incident, re-bent the grate into place and snuck away from the village. At a rendezvous point, they waited for the sniper team to rejoin them. The six-man team jogged back to their vehicle and drove down the road a few kilometers until they came to a telephone pole that led to the village. One of the men put on climbing spikes and a tree strap, ascended the pole and cut the wires. Once that was done, the vehicle disappeared into the night.

"Mission accomplished, Doctor." Firke had to have switched off the camera on his shoulder, for that monitor went dark right afterward.

"Don't forget to launch the drone over the property, Mr. Firke." Richter straightened, easing his kinked back muscles while around him the men and women drifted away, having either lost interest in what was happening or moving on to other tasks.

The doctor pulled up a chair and checked his watch: 1140. In several hours the townspeople would be up and about. He pulled his notebook closer to him and rechecked that the camera on the water tower was transmitting properly.

Now it was simply a matter of waiting for the experiment to begin.

CHAPTER SEVEN

At 0545, Mack Bolan was almost finished preparing for his insertion into Alexsandr Sevan's walled fortress city.

The breeze was blowing even harder in the early morning hours, making him smile as he unfolded what looked like an oblong, matte-black parachute that was rounded off at both ends. Four lines led from his loose harness to the odd-shaped canopy, splitting up three times along the way to attach at equidistant points along its edge to give the pilot maximum control. The stiff wind gusted even harder, making one side of the sail flap in the night.

Of all the things they'd planned about this operation at Stony Man, the insertion had been the most discussed, argued about and refined. They had simulated just about every possible method of entry, from a HALO—high altitude low opening—drop, insertion by the sewer system, posing as a tourist and entering through the front gate, and scaling the wall. In the end, they had gone with Bolan's suggestion, initially thrown out as an off-the-cuff remark, but which gained more converts as the planning progressed. It wasn't the surest insertion method, but because he would already be on the ground, and given the pros and cons of the other methods, it was the best way for him to reach Sevan's house with the least chance of detection. The final deciding factor was that the majority of the security measures at the village were directed at the ground around the perimeter, with no radar or any obvious air-detection capability. Of course, it has also necessitated him taking a crash course in paragliding forty-eight hours before he left the U.S., but after ten practice runs, Bolan thought he'd gotten the hang of it, so to speak.

"How's the weather?" Tokaido, monitoring his insertion, asked.

"Overcast and breezy," Bolan replied. "At least I'll have no problem getting there."

"So, you're still green?" The hint of doubt in the hacker's voice was clear.

"When I'm back, you'll have to come up with me—you'll love it."

"Uh, yeah, we'll see about that."

Bolan grinned again. Tokaido often talked a good game, but the few times he'd called the younger man on it, he had preferred to stick with what he knew best—hacking and computer infiltration. And he was among the very best, no doubt, but it was obvious that his skill set lay in a completely different direction.

Now, as he prepared for a reverse launch, facing the canopy to make sure his lines were clear, Bolan felt a mix of adrenaline and anticipation, mixed with a healthy respect for what he was about to do. The wind up here was stronger than what he'd trained in, and he was already recalculating his speed toward his target, and most importantly, controlling his descent and sticking the landing once he got there. He'd be dead if he fractured an ankle or got hung up on power lines.

Bolan snugged his night-vision goggles over his eyes and checked his pistol, spare magazines and equipment in their various holsters and pouches. He took one more look at everything, weighing the pros and cons of the current conditions. His insertion window—the time just before daybreak, when guards would be tired and their perception and reaction times would be slower—was still open. But he had to go right now, before the first rays of sunlight lit the still-black horizon.

"Beginning insertion," Bolan said. "Affirmative."

Tokaido's tone was all business, as well. "Good luck, Striker. Stony Man standing by."

Taking up the slack lines, Bolan twitched them to make the sail lift into the air. The second the edge caught the steady breeze, the whole canopy inflated and shot up with a snap, making him brace himself to not get pulled off his feet. He glanced at the dim lights of the city below, the auto gating adjusting to prevent him from being blinded. When the next gust came along, he walked with it down the hill, letting the wing begin carrying him along until, with one more stop, he floated off the ground and into the night sky.

The wind off the mountains swiftly carried him high into the air. Bolan concentrated on getting enough altitude to ensure he was far enough above the sentries to avoid being spotted. Below his dangling feet, the valley was swathed in darkness, broken only by the eerie green circles of light coming from the wall. Toward the rear of the enclosure, the large villa they'd identified as Sevan's loomed above every other building, almost topping the wall. Its large, tiled roof was Bolan's target, and he steered toward it while keeping an eye on his variometer, which would tell him if he was leaving a strong wind current.

Maintaining his elevation wasn't turning out to be a

problem, but Bolan was a bit concerned about his forward speed. Even allowing for the stiff wind, he was approaching the village faster than he preferred and was concerned about bleeding enough off to land safely. They'd discussed aborting if the conditions weren't right, but having gone this far, he was even more loath to come so close, only have to leave with nothing to show for his efforts.

About a kilometer out, Bolan pulled on both outer A-lines, bending the ends of the sail down in a formation called "big-ears." This made the paraglider begin to slowly lose altitude while still heading toward the roof of the villa, exactly as he had planned.

The large, black canopy, with Bolan dangling underneath, passed silently over the rear of the village and the bored pair of thugs on that wall, close enough that he heard a brief snatch of their conversation. His auto-translator picked up the words and told him that one was complaining about not feeling well. The two men were both in the roofed guardhouse—as they had been every evening at this time—instead of patrolling. The hole in the security and the pattern of the prevailing winds across the valley were two reasons Bolan had used this approach.

Alternating his attention between the approaching roof and his variometer, he kept his approach steady, trying to bring himself down as gently as possible. Less than ten meters from the roof, the wind gusted hard, making the paraglider suddenly rise again. He tugged on his B-lines to bleed more air from his canopy, dipping down twice as fast as when he had used the "big ears" method.

Unfortunately he was also gliding right past the villa. Even though he shifted his weight hard right to bring himself around, Bolan skimmed past the edge of the rooftop, missing it by less than a meter.

"Striker?" Tokaido said. "GPS shows you've missed the primary landing zone. Is there a problem?"

"Let you know in a second—" Bolan whispered as he fought for control. He had lost too much altitude now and was in danger of either getting entangled in power lines or gliding into the side of a building. Releasing the B-lines, he pushed hard on his speed bar with his foot, decreasing the angle of attack on the wing's leading edge in a desperate attempt to gain height.

It worked—sort of. Entering the airspace of what looked like a wide, main road that ran through the village, Bolan felt the wind channeled here shove him up—straight toward the wall of a house. Easing up on the speed bar, he lifted his legs as high as he could, narrowly avoiding smacking the top of the roof. He missed, but now out of the air channel, he began losing altitude again.

"Striker? You're still moving. What's your sitrep?" Tokaido asked.

A pancake, if I don't find a place to set down soon, Bolan thought but didn't say. Instead he was looking for any place he could set down without injuring himself in the next few seconds. The village sloped down from here, and Bolan saw what looked like a small, three-story hotel coming up. A large water tank took up a third of the flat roof, but it was his best chance— hell, his only chance—to land, and he took it, aiming for the flat expanse and pulling on his B-lines again to begin coming down.

The induced stall averaged a drop rate of about 5 meters per second, but as he got closer, it seemed the roof was rushing up even faster at Bolan. At the same time, he was sailing over the building and there was a very real danger he was going to overshoot his landing zone again.

Gritting his teeth, Bolan pulled even harder on the B-lines, spilling that extra bit of air and causing him to come down with a thump on the rooftop. The moment he landed, Bolan hit the ground in a forward shoulder roll, heedless of entangling himself in the lines. The canopy snapped and fluttered around him, but the moment he stopped moving, he quickly gathered in the paraglider before a guard happened to catch sight of the mass of flapping black cloth.

"Striker, are you all right?" Kurtzman was on the line now. "What is your sitrep, over?"

Entangled in a shroud of canopy and lines, Bolan was still listening for shouts or any sign that his entry had been detected. Only when he didn't hear any sort of alarm or doors opening did he whisper, "Striker is down. Overshot primary landing zone, had to go for secondary. No injuries." He began to stuff the paraglider into his backpack.

"You're a good half klick from your target and you have to improvise a way past his house guards. *And* the sun's about to come up."

Bolan glanced east and confirmed Kurtzman's biggest concern—the sky on the horizon was already shaded with pink and orange from the oncoming daybreak. "Then I better move out."

"Striker, you don't think we should abort?"

"Absolutely not, Bear. Look, I'm here now. Even if we called it off, I'd have to get out somehow anyway, so I might as well get what I came for before I do."

Bolan shrugged out of his harness and added it to the backpack, which he hid beneath one of the water tower's steel legs.

"Well, watch your ass," Kurtzman said. "The way this op started, it wouldn't surprise me if you tripped, fell off the roof and broke your neck."

Despite the circumstances, Bolan couldn't help grinning at the very real concern he heard under Kurtzman's grumbling. "Have I ever told you how much I love your optimistic attitude, Bear?"

"No, 'cause you know better."

"Exactly. Striker out." Trotting to the side of the building, Bolan tested the seemingly sturdy ceramic drainpipe that went all the way to the ground. When it didn't move under his weight, he swung a leg over, braced his feet on the wall and gripped the pipe with both hands as he descended to the ground. Halfway down, the pipe shifted enough to make him stop and wait in case it was coming loose. It didn't move again, and Bolan reached the alleyway without further incident.

At this hour the town was still quiet, although Bolan saw lights coming on in various windows as the populace began to wake up. There were still plenty of shadows to hide in, and Bolan made the best of it, flitting from darkness to darkness, all the while keeping an eye on the walls overhead.

He covered the distance to Sevan's villa in less than ten minutes and took a position in a narrow alley between what appeared to be a bakery—the smell of bread baking filled his nostrils—and what looked to be either an abandoned or holiday house for someone, with tightly shuttered windows and a securely locked door.

Bolan's attention, however, was on the front gate made from thick, black iron bars that guarded the entrance to Sevan's estate. The rest of the perimeter was enclosed by an eight-foot-high stone fence that had matching vertical iron bars at the top, which were themselves topped by welded spikes sticking out at a forty-five-degree angle. Two guards paced back and forth in front of the gate. Unlike the slackers on the wall, both these guys looked alert and ready. He studied the pair for a few minutes, noticing that although they were definitely on guard, they also seemed oddly distracted. One shook his head every few seconds, as if trying to clear it. The other kept wiping his forehead and cheeks with his sleeve. Viewing them in the monochromatic night vision, Bolan couldn't tell if either man was flushed or showed any other signs of incapacitation.

"Striker to Stony Man, I'm going to need that security window and camera break, after all," he muttered as he melted back into the shadows. "West wall, corner."

"Roger that, Striker," Tokaido replied. "What is your position?"

By the time the hacker finished replying, Bolan was at the rear corner of the empty house. As he knew from the overhead view, the road cornered at the fence and followed the perimeter. "Ten meters away."

"All right…bringing security camera online…"

Bolan divided his attention between the two guards who had paused by the gate and the steadily lightening eastern sky. "Let's go, Akira, the sun isn't going to stop rising."

"Just making sure the inside is clear. Won't help much if you drop down into the arms of a couple goons, now, would it? Okay, go on my mark… Three, two, one, mark."

Still mindful of the two guards, Bolan stepped out from cover and walked casually across the street to the corner of the fence, slightly stooped over, even muffling a yawn. Just another early riser heading to work. Out of the corner of his eye, he thought he saw one of the guards look in his direction, but he didn't turn or quicken his pace in any way as he reached the stone wall.

The second he was around the corner and out of view, Bolan leaped for the top of the fence, grabbing the rough stone with his gloved hands. Pulling himself up, he threw a leg over, grabbed the row of iron spikes and held there for a few seconds while scoping the inside. True to Tokaido's word, the immaculate lawn was deserted, with the villa increasingly lit from behind as the sun kept rising. Bolan gave it another five count, then climbed over the spikes and jumped to the ground, staying in the shadows formed by the inside wall corner. The area here was calm, with no breeze.

"I'm on the grounds," Bolan reported. "Keep that camera looped for another minute. I'll contact once I'm inside the building."

"Roger that."

Drawing an odd weapon that looked like a small paint gun, Bolan removed a plastic vial from a waist pouch and screwed it on to the receiver just ahead of the trigger. Taking his SIG-Sauer in his right hand, he checked right and left one last time, then started down the wall on his left, wanting to be sure he was out of sight of the gate guards before entering the main building.

He had only taken a few steps when two black-brown shapes trotted around the corner. Upon seeing him, the two Doberman-Rottweiler mixes didn't snarl or bark, just accelerated into a silent run, muscular legs churning the grass as they sped toward their target.

Waiting until they were only a few steps away, Bolan squeezed the trigger of the strange pistol in his left hand twice. The gun spit a fine mist into the dogs' path as they leaped at him. The second they jumped, Bolan dropped to the ground and rolled out of their path. After two turns, he rolled onto his back, brought the real pistol up and aimed at the dogs behind him.

Deprived of their target, the dogs landed on the ground and turned to come at him again. However they weren't moving as quickly as before; in fact, both dogs stumbled as they tried to charge at him and ended up sinking back to the ground, whining in confusion as they struggled to get back on their feet. Within a few seconds, both dogs were out cold.

Bolan got up, careful to stay several feet away from the dissipating cloud of a fast-acting, powerful tranquilizer. With a silenced pistol not all that silent, and dart guns, blowguns or crossbows only able to shoot one projectile at a time, John "Cowboy" Kissinger, Stony Man Farm's chief armorer, had come up with the best way to silently eliminate multiple guard animals with minimal risk of injury to the defender. The spray pistol had been extensively tested, and other than wind dispersal, performed excellently in the field.

Holstering both pistols, Bolan headed for the wall of the house. It was a tastefully built place, all heavy timbers and stone walls. The stone had to have been local; it was rough cut and arranged in a natural style to blend in with the rest of the grounds. The irregular rocks sticking out of the wall afforded perfect hand- and footholds for him to climb to the roof.

Once there, he had to negotiate the overhang of the longer-than-usual eave. Reaching out as far as he could allowed Bolan to just grab the edge with his fingers. Pulling back, he braced his hands against the underside of the eave while positioning his feet on the topmost line of stones on the wall. His next move would require split-second timing, not to mention a lot of upper-body strength. Fortunately, Bolan had both.

Pushing off from the wall, he grabbed the edge of the roof with both hands and used his momentum to hoist his upper body above the roof. Once there, he threw a leg over and rolled onto the roof.

Made it...and only twenty minutes behind schedule, he thought as he rose to his feet and headed up the slight incline to the second-floor windows of the master suite. The room took up the entire second floor, and the row of curtained windows facing him was dark. Bolan stopped at the window farthest from where he knew the bed was located.

"Open sesame," he whispered. After a few seconds there was a soft click and the electronically operated window popped open. Bolan watched it extend outward. When it was open far enough, he pulled a double-bladed dagger from its sheath on his leg, slit the screen open and slipped inside.

Bolan's brow knit at the clean, modern furniture in the huge bedroom. Most Eastern European criminals he'd encountered loved to show off their ill-gotten riches, overdecorating their rooms in ostentatious leather and silk. Sevan kept things minimal, his only indulgence being the four-poster canopy bed he and another blanketed form were lying in.

Keeping his knife out, Bolan crept to the right side

of the bed, where he figured Sevan would be sleeping. He was right. The head of the Armenian mob boss was turned away from him, breathing steadily. An open bottle of water sat on the nightstand, next to a small tablet computer.

Slowly, Bolan extended his free hand until it was just above Sevan's mouth. In one quick movement he clamped his gloved fingers down on the man's lips and put the keen edge of the blade to his throat.

Sevan's eyes flew open as Bolan whispered, "Don't move or you're—"

Before he could finish, a blur of movement from beside Sevan caught Bolan's attention. He raised his head just in time to see a vase flying at his face.

CHAPTER EIGHT

Gary Alcaster sat on the side of his bed, still breathing heavily from what had happened in the past few hours. "Goddamn, that was better than any hand job I ever had!"

After Josh Tyrell's toast, the cognac and other liquors had flowed for the next two hours. Although William Scott still worried that the women were planning to get them all drunk and rob them while they were passed out, after the third round he was just as into his chosen woman, the blond Lusine, who had moved to his lap and was toying with his glasses, saying he reminded her of Harry Potter. That had made everyone, even Scott, laugh, then blush when Lusine commented that she found the character very sexy. The curly haired brunette, Anoush, had paired up with Tyrell, and the two were making each other laugh over the silliest of things, such as the shape of the cognac bottle.

That left Alcaster with the quieter and perhaps just a bit sadder-looking Siranush. He had tried to break the ice by complimenting her name, which he really did like. He asked if it meant anything.

She smiled. "It means 'lovely' in Armenian."

"Well, it suits you." Alcaster snagged the bottle from a giggling Anoush. "Would you like another drink?"

"Yes, thank you for asking." After that she had

slowly warmed up to him. Alcaster felt as though their conversation was always on thin ice and was terrified of saying the wrong thing or insulting her. Although he didn't remember most of what he had said, she had never frowned or stormed off, and even smiled a few times while supplying very brief answers to any of his questions.

A couple hours later most of the other patrons had paired off with women, and the unluckier ones had taken to the streets in the vain hope of scrounging up some kind of business so they wouldn't return to their brothels empty-handed.

The young men had escorted the prostitutes to their shared room on the second floor, where Tyrell held up two more keys. "I spoke to the hotel manager and got a deal on two other rooms and the girls for the entire night." With a wink, he tossed one to each of the other guys. "Enjoy, and don't do anything I wouldn't do."

"Wait—what does that leave?" Alcaster asked in exasperation. He turned back to William to see the lanky Englishman roll his eyes.

"For God's sake, Gary, even *I* knew he was kidding." He nodded toward their room. "Now get in there and dip your wick." He waggled his own pale eyebrows as he slipped an arm around Lusine, who smiled and leaned into him. "I certainly intend to."

The couple staggered off to their chosen bedroom, leaving Alcaster and Siranush alone in the threadbare hallway. With a nervous glance at the woman, he unlocked the creaking, wooden door and opened it, inviting her inside with a wave. "After you."

She had walked inside and Alcaster had fiddled with the door after closing it, making sure it was securely locked. When he turned, Siranush was standing right in front of him, watching him with heavy-lidded eyes. She smelled of cheap floral perfume and stale cigarette smoke, which somehow combined to create an alluring scent. He thought she was breathtaking.

"You…seem nervous," she said, the hint of a smile playing on her lips.

Alcaster tried to speak, but couldn't around the sudden lump in his throat, so he just nodded instead. His heart was thumping madly in his chest and his palms felt like a river was flowing from them. He wiped his hands on his jeans.

"Is okay. I have had many… What is best word? 'First-timers.' Do not be afraid."

Alcaster frowned. "Well, I'm not."

"Good." The back of her hand brushed the front of his jeans and he was suddenly at full attention. Siranush's smile widened. "*Very* good. Come with me."

She took his hand, not seeming to care about the sweatiness, and led him to the sagging bed. "I will help, yes? Just listen to me, and do as I say, and it will be fine."

And it was. Actually, it was more than fine.

Now, sitting on his bed, with the woman who had taken his virginity sleeping on the other side, Alcaster was at a loss to describe how he felt other than…good.

Damn good.

Swallowing, he realized he was quite thirsty. The hotel was old enough to not have en-suite bathrooms. He'd have to go down the hall and get a drink from the old bathroom at the end of the hall.

Rising slowly to as not to wake Siranush, Alcaster pulled on his underwear and jeans, then crept quietly to the door and let himself out. Walking past the other two rooms, he heard the squeak of a mattress from one of them and smiled. A door opened down the hall and Alcaster didn't turn to see who it was, wishing to respect their privacy. Only when he heard footsteps approaching, along with what sounded like a growl, did he turn to behold a strange sight.

Another prostitute, one he didn't recognize, ran straight at him. The woman's face, smudged with makeup, was twisted into a snarl of pure hatred. A vivid purple-and-black bruise covered the right side of her head and she only wore a cream-colored slip, her breasts flying with every quickening step. Her arms reached out for him, fingers curled into hooked, bloody claws as her bare feet slapped against the dusty floor, sending little puffs up with each step. A high, keening noise burst from her throat, growing louder as she approached.

Alcaster had just enough time to take this in, hearing some kind of commotion coming from one of the nearby bedrooms, before the crazy woman was upon him. Instinctively he stepped aside, grabbing the woman's right wrist with his right hand and redirecting her force up and back. At the same time he stepped forward with his right leg and planted it behind the woman's furiously churning feet. Using the prostitute's own inertia, he swept her off balance and sent her crashing to the floor, the impact shaking the hallway.

Holy crap, it worked! Alcaster looked up—partly to keep his face away from her, partly because she stank of sweat and urine—as he held the woman down. "William! Josh! I need help—" was all he got out before the woman grabbed his hand and bent it back with unbelievable strength, the tendons in her neck standing out like taut cords with the effort.

What the hell? Alcaster watched, almost in shock, as his arm was levered into the air while the woman tried to claw at his eyes with her free hand. She had to be at least forty kilograms lighter than him, and didn't look very strong. He should have been able to restrain her, but that certainly wasn't the case at the moment.

Trying to wrench his arm free only caused more pain. He grabbed below the wrist of the hand that was about to break his fingers, and squeezed the ulna and radius bones as hard as he could. For a moment he thought he was too late, but then the pressure on her trapped hand lessened and the woman's unearthly shrieks became tinged with pain. Pushing his attacker away, Alcaster jumped to his feet and faced his opponent, arms out, hands up and ready. "Josh! William! Help!"

A door opened and Scott, straw-blond hair tousled with sleep, craned his head out. "What's all the noise about, man—?"

The woman, her head jerking around erratically, fixed on him. She whirled and tensed to leap at the student.

"Whoa!" Scott ducked back inside and tried to push the door closed, but she slammed into it and forced it partway open, then started pushing her way inside. "What's her problem?"

"Shit!" Alcaster rushed at the woman and tackled her, bearing her to the ground and pinning her arms. Despite outweighing his captive, he had to use everything he had to keep her subdued, practically sitting on her to keep her on the ground.

"Get—a belt or something—to tie her up—now!"

Alcaster ordered. Scott, mouth hanging open in shock, was jolted out of his stunned trance and ran back into his room, returning shortly with his belt. The woman snapped and hissed at them, unintelligible noises streaming from her mouth.

Alcaster fixed the British student with a steely gaze. "All right, first we're going to turn her over. Then I'll hold her arms together and you bind her hands."

"I—I am?"

"Yes, damn it, you are. Get over here. Ready—now!" With a lot more effort than should have been necessary, he and Scott flipped the woman onto her stomach and forced her arms behind her back. Meanwhile, her legs beat a rapid tattoo on the floor, then she began arching them back to try to hit either of the two young men. Scott ended up sitting on her legs to stop her from lashing out at them while Alcaster double-looped the belt around her wrists and cinched it tight.

From where he sat, the Canadian med student eyed the restraint with a critical eye. "Don't be stingy—we don't want her getting free any time soon."

The moment Scott finished pinioning her, the woman strained at her bonds with one final great heave, then collapsed on the floor, unmoving, only the rapid rise and fall of her chest indicating she still lived.

The two young men cautiously got off their bound captive. "What the hell was that all about?" Scott asked as he hurriedly dressed. Alcaster massaged his sore hand while staring at the panting, sweating woman. "You all right?" he asked.

"More or less. Except for seeing a woman I don't know from Adam try to claw my face off just now, I'm peachy, thanks."

"Yeah, that was certainly something you don't see every day." Scott's tone was so matter of fact—as though he was discussing a trip to the store—that Alcaster looked at him carefully to make sure he wasn't going into shock. But he seemed perfectly calm and collected as his gaze alternated between his friend and the woman.

"No, I suppose not." Taking a deep breath, Alcaster squatted next to their bound captive and carefully thumbed an eyelid back, ready to jerk his hand away if she tried to snack on it. "Any idea what's happened to her?"

Scott frowned. "Beats the hell out of me. We wouldn't know without a full medical workup, which we obviously can't do around here. Right now, the best thing to do is to keep her restrained until we can find some help. One that's done, they can try to figure out what's causing this."

After double-checking that she wasn't going anywhere, Alcaster straightened again. "Are you sure that's a good idea? After all, we don't want to panic the rest of the village."

Scott stared down at her. "I don't think we have any other choice. We can't risk moving her, and she'll kill anyone she comes across if she gets loose. Let's get her into my room."

"Grab her feet," Alcaster said as he bent to pick her up by the shoulders. Scott grabbed her ankles, holding tight as she tried to wriggle out of his grasp. Together the two young men carried her into Scott's room, where Lusine sat up in bed, clutching the sheets to her chest. Her smudged eyes widened when she saw the young men enter.

"What happened?"

"She tried to attack me," Alcaster said. "Can you move, please?"

Lusine scrambled off the bed, taking the sheet with her. "But that is Katar. She would not hurt a fly—never!"

"Well, that wasn't the impression I got when she charged at me in the hallway," Alcaster said as Scott and he set her on the bed. "Grab those sashes from the window," he said.

Scott scrambled to do so, tossing them to his friend.

"Okay, you're going to have to hold her down while I tie her to the bedframe—"

"You…you cannot do this," Lusine said just as Katar came alive again, throwing her bound arms around Scott's neck as he leaned over her. He barely got his hands up to block her as she snapped at his throat. He tried to rear back, bringing her with him. At the same time she scissored her legs at Alcaster. One foot kicked him in the stomach, driving him a step backward.

"Shit!" Scott tried to lever her arms off him, but couldn't without risking getting bitten. He fell on her chest, pinning her to the bed. "Lusine, grab her legs!"

The prostitute shook her head and backed into a corner. Alcaster had recovered by then and grabbed her hands. Together, the two men forced her arms above her head as she strained to bury her teeth in his throat. "Got her?" Scott asked.

"Yeah—hold her head."

Scott settled heavily on her chest, making her wheeze under his weight. Her struggles weakened, he immobilized her head while Alcaster unstrapped her hands and then bound each one to the sturdy iron railing at the head of the bed. Then he grabbed the belt, went to the smaller railing and tied her feet to it. "Okay—she's not going anywhere."

Only then did Scott feel secure enough to get off. Katar strained against her bonds, arching her back as she tried to pull free, but they held. She sank back on the bed, panting heavily as she glared at the two men with furious eyes.

"Lusine, do you know what's—" Scott looked over at where she had been, only to find the corner empty. "Figures. I suppose I wouldn't hang around, either, with all this going on. Do you think the other girls were affected?"

Alcaster shook his head. "Well, mine wasn't, as far as I know." He glanced up at Scott as the same thought occurred to both of them. "Josh…come on!"

The two closed and locked the door to Scott's room, then crept over to the one Tyrell had disappeared into several hours ago.

"Shit, shouldn't we get some weapons?" Scott asked

Alcaster frowned. "No time. Besides, where you gonna find one, one of those fake swords on the wall in the bar?"

"I was just saying—"

"Just back me up." Alcaster reached out and knocked on the door. "Josh…you in there, buddy?" He put his ear to the door. "I can't hear anything.

Scott followed suit as his friend knocked again. "Josh? Answer the door, man!"

"I think I heard someone move," Scott whispered.

"We gotta go inside," Alcaster whispered back, trying the doorknob, which turned under his hand. "Come on."

Slowly opening the door, the two stepped inside, trying to let their eyes adjust to the dim light coming in through the eastern window while being ready for someone to leap out at them from the shadows. Clothes were strewed around the small room, and the night table had been overturned. Spotting a huddled form moving back and forth on the bed, Scott nudged his friend, and they took a step closer.

Alcaster peered through the dimness. "Josh…you awake?" Just then, Scott went back and turned on the lights.

Blinking at the sudden glare, Scott was close enough now to see a head of brunette hair at the top of the bed. He smiled as he stepped to the side of it. "Look, I understand you want one more go, but we've got a serious—"

He trailed off as he saw the large, dark stain on the mattress and pillow. As he did, the prostitute he knew as Anoush turned to face him. Her mouth and jaw were covered in fresh, red blood.

And lying underneath her was Josh Tyrell's body, with its throat ripped out.

CHAPTER NINE

Voski Mardikian was not having a very good night.

For starters, the moment Sevan and his people had returned home, he'd been placed on gate duty for the next month. On their last night in Italy, he'd accidentally drank too much *grappa* and made a drunken fool of himself in front of their partners in crime to the southwest. Mardikian was fortunate he'd already been with Sevan for several years; newer additions to the crime family often only got one or two chances before punishment of a more permanent nature, such as arms or legs broken or fingers getting cut off, was inflicted. Plus, it really was his first major screw-up since he'd joined the Sevan mob after leaving what would be the equivalent of the eighth grade in Armenia.

Still, the thought that he had screwed up and made the boss look bad weighed on him. Dragging heavily on his cigarette, the guard cast a wistful glance back up at the house. There were three levels of security in the village: a newcomer started on the wall, staring out at the endless valley hills. Once the newcomer had proved himself by using brains, guts or both, he could get promoted to gate guard, making sure Sevan's personal residence was secure at all times. That was a big step up from wall duty, but the novelty wore off quickly there, as well, and then the newcomer became part of the crew walking back and forth in front of the big iron gate, waiting for who knew what, since nobody in the village would be crazy enough to try to take out the man who had modernized the whole place when he'd established his base of operations here a decade ago, installing such luxuries as regular electricity, a working water supply and satellite television.

The best of Sevan's guards ended up working in the house itself. Responsible for security of the villa and the grounds, they were expected to be on duty pretty much 24/7, but in many other respects they were almost like Sevan's guests, free to indulge in whatever the house had to offer when they were off duty.

Until his demotion Mardikian had planned on sampling some of the most recent shipment of exotic beauties that had come back with them from the Urals, Chechnya and places farther east. Sevan and his men broke in the girls before sending them off to earn their keep in one of a hundred brothels scattered across Europe. He still could have gotten his rocks off at the one established in town for the guards, if not for the second thing bothering him—he was coming down with something.

"Goddamn Italians…" he muttered, wiping his sweat-soaked, balding forehead for the tenth time that evening. Mardikian didn't know what he'd come down with in Italy, but it was driving him nuts. He'd been fine yesterday, but now felt sick. The fever, the sweats, the head and muscle aches, and most of all, he was just so damn irritable. Whatever it was, the last place he wanted to be was sweating his nuts off while tromping back and forth all night in front of his boss's house.

His guard partner, Kevork Ardzruni, was making that damnably irritating high-pitched whistle again…

"For the last goddamn time, would you stop that whistling?" Mardikian wiped his forehead again and rubbed his ears. "You're driving me crazy!"

"And for the last time, you ass, I'm not whistling!" Ardzruni shook his head again as he stomped over to his partner, who was already bristling at being called an ass, and got right in his face.

"Clean out your ears or get them checked, but get off my back!"

Mardikian was already pulling back his fist to punch the idiot's sweating face, but before he could unload, he was distracted by someone coming down the street. "Who is that?"

The figure wobbling toward them on high heels turned out to be Siran, one of the more recent arrivals from the last shipment. Mardikian never bothered to learn their last names, as they were usually gone too quickly for him to care. Tossing his cigarette on the ground, he nodded at the gate. "Stay here. I'll see what is up with her."

Without waiting for a reply, he turned and headed down the street to intercept her. The girls weren't supposed to be out of the brothel unless they had been requested by Sevan, in which case they were escorted to the house under guard. Even in his weakened state, Mardikian found himself looking forward to punishing her. Siran was lean and lithe, with high full breasts that nicely filled out the fabric of her cheap sleeveless blouse. Her pleather skirt barely covered her hips, revealing long legs and tiny feet. As she stumbled toward him, the Armenian caught the odor of cheap liquor the girls often used to pass out after a night servicing the guards and occasional tourists.

"What are you doing out? You know the rules! No one leaves the house alone!"

"I came…to get help…everybody at house is sick…" She pressed a palm to her forehead. "Everyone is hot…and bitchy…"

Mardikian sighed. "I suppose I should look into it, but first…" Taking her by the arm, he led her toward a nearby alley. "You're going to have to pay for walking the streets alone."

"No, please…I was only trying to…get help…" She clutched her forehead with both hands. "My head hurts…so much…"

"I do not make the rules, little one, but I must enforce them." He pulled her roughly down the narrow, garbage-strewed corridor until he found a reasonably clean spot and then unzipped his pants. "Get down there and don't stop until I'm done." Siran didn't protest or answer. Ignoring his order, she stumbled forward and nibbled his neck—then she bit down hard. Grabbing her hair, he pushed her away. "You bitch, how dare you bite me!" With his free hand, he backhanded her across the face.

Glowering, her eyes sullen, the prostitute attacked, biting his face. The pain was so intense he could barely think. Grabbing her hair again, Mardikian tried to pull her off, but that hurt even more. Blood leaked from her mouth along with low, guttural noises as she gnawed on him.

Screaming in agony, he punched her in the face over and over, blacking an eye, breaking her nose. But no matter how hard he hurt her, she would not release him.

"What is— Goddamn! What is she doing to you?" Ardzruni's startled voice pierced Mardikian's near-blinding haze of pain, and he turned to see the other man lumbering toward them.

"What do you…think! Get her off me!" As he said that, Siran arched back, tearing off a good chunk of his cheek.

"Oh my God!" Clutching his ruined face, Mardikian slumped over, vainly trying to stem the gushing blood with his hands. "Kill her!"

As Ardzruni drew his pistol, Siran spit out the piece of flesh and rose to face him. "Do not come any closer, whore!"

Bloody teeth bared, she leaped at him. Still shaken by the freaky scene, the guard fired, but missed his target. Before he could correct, she was on him, grabbing his arm and sinking her teeth into his gun hand.

"Goddamn it! Get off me!" Forced to drop the gun, Ardzruni cocked his free fist and swung. Still off balance, he only grazed her head. The smaller woman savaged his hand, then spit it out and went for his face with her fingers curved into claws.

Mardikian watched his partner try to fend her off, but she seemed to have the strength and endurance of five men, shrugging off his blows, while scratching and biting at his face. She got hold of his nose with her teeth and shook him the way a dog would a rat. All the while the larger man rained punches down on her, but they had no effect.

Suddenly light-headed, Mardikian tried drawing his own pistol, intending to shoot the woman before he died, but the grip slipped out of his blood-soaked hand and fell to the ground. Ardzruni had pushed her away, losing the end of his nose in the process, which now poured blood down his chin and shirt. He tried charging Siran, who met his charge and buried her face in his neck. His scream turned into a gurgle as he collapsed to the ground, arms outstretched, legs twitching. The woman sat astride his chest, worrying his throat like a wild dog.

Mardikian slipped to the ground, his arms and legs feeling as if they weighed a ton. Seeing his pistol through blurry eyes, he reached for it, intending to at least fire a warning shot for Sevan. Someone had to warn them about what was happening. He would. He just had to rest for a moment...

Fingers only inches from his gun, Mardikian succumbed to his blood loss and passed out.

HER FACE BLOODY and bruised, one eye nearly pulped from the abuse from the two men, Siran punished Ardzruni's face and neck until he was nothing but unrecognizable pulp. By then he'd stopped twitching, and she left the body to go in search of something else. All thought of trying to help the other girls at the brothel had left her mind, replaced by a singular, subconscious urge to find another person and pass on what now lived inside her.

Rising to her feet, she stalked out of the alley, where she saw a few other people emerging from their homes in the early morning light. Siran started after the nearest one, but when she got closer, she realized that he was just like her; a friend, not an enemy to be destroyed.

Hearing a noise from the other side of the black iron gate nearby, she turned toward it along with everyone else. Perhaps there they would find someone who could stop this incessant, shrill noise in her head...perhaps then she would be able to get some peace and quiet....

CHAPTER TEN

Even Bolan's combat-honed reflexes weren't fast enough to dodge the flying vase. He was saved by his night-vision gear, which absorbed the impact as the missile shattered against its casing in a spray of ceramic chunks.

Distracted and off balance, he tried to stay with Sevan, but the other man seized the distraction to grab his knife hand and lever it away from his throat. He was stronger than Bolan expected him to be. Sevan brought his other clenched hand around and clocked him in the jaw, then shoved him away, hard. Bolan stumbled back against the wall, where he regained his balance in time to see the entire blanket fly toward him.

"Run!" he heard a woman say in translated Armenian.

"To hell with that, I'll kill him myself!" a man replied. "Guards!"

Clawing the blanket off, Bolan drew his pistol, hoping he could salvage the situation without shooting Sevan. Rising to his feet, he saw the other man, large and fit and dressed in nothing but silk boxers, going for his pillow.

"Damn it, where are my guards?" Sevan bellowed as he reached under it.

"Freeze!" Bolan aimed his pistol's muzzle right between the big man's eyes. "Move that hand and you're dead!"

The other man froze on his hands and knees, one hand still under the pillow, his head swiveling to regard Bolan with appraising, slate-gray eyes. He had curly, shoulder-length black hair streaked with gray. "You're not here to kill me?" He wrinkled his nose. "My God, you stink."

Eyebrows rising in surprise, Bolan shook his head. "No. I'm here to take you and your organization down." As his translator program broadcast his words in Armenian, Bolan scanned the rest of the room, trying to locate the woman who'd thrown the vase.

"What? An American?" Sevan replied in lightly accented English. Even with the muzzle of Bolan's pistol a few inches away from his head, he didn't look too worried. "That will be more difficult that you think. Besides, I don't see how this sort of illegal kidnapping is going to stand up in any court."

"I've already gotten inside here, and I've got you," Bolan replied. "Don't worry, where you're going, a courtroom or lawyer is the last thing you'll be worrying about."

Sevan frowned. "I thought your CIA wasn't rendering anyone anywhere anymore."

"You'll find out soon enough. Take that hand from underneath the pillow—slowly. Twitch or try to shoot, and I will blow your head off."

The Armenian still didn't move, as if he was actually considering his choices. "Very well, you seem to hold the advantage—for now." He removed his empty hand from under the memory foam pillow.

"Please." Bolan waved him back with the pistol. "Kneel on the bed." He reached for the pillow and flipped it over, revealing a stainless-steel 9 mm Heckler & Koch P-9 pistol. "I'll hold on to this for now."

Tucking it into his belt, he walked to the end of the bed and leaned over to check the floor, but it was empty. He scanned the rest of the room for movement or anyone hiding, but saw nothing. "Where did your woman go?"

Sevan looked around. "If she is smart, she went to find out where the hell my guards are. They are going to tear you apart when they get here."

"Not with you as my hostage, they won't," Bolan replied, although he did wonder where exactly the Armenian's guards were. From what their surveillance had showed, his security wasn't *that* poor. "Hands above your head."

Sevan did as ordered. Holstering his pistol, Bolan removed a plastic zip tie from a side pouch and secured the man's hands behind his back.

"Oh, come now, surely you're going to allow me to get dressed?" Sevan said.

"Nope." Drawing his gun again, Bolan pulled the other man off the bed. "Base, this is Striker. Package is in hand, beginning extraction now."

"Affirmative, Striker," Tokaido replied in his ear. "Flight is awaiting your arrival and delivery of the package."

"I figured a big, tough man like you can handle a chilly morning," Bolan said. "Besides, we're not going far, just down to your SUV."

"And you think you'll just be able to drive out of here like nothing even happened?" Sevan snorted as he nodded toward the door. "Even now my men are taking up positions outside that door. You'll be lucky to leave this room alive."

"Many people have told me that before, yet here I

am." Grabbing the other man by the arm, Bolan prodded him in the back with his pistol. "Let's go."

They were halfway there when a heavy fist pounded on the door. At the same time, Bolan caught movement out of the corner of his eye. Before he could turn, a dark shape came out of nowhere to land on his back, clawing at the night-vision goggles and tearing them off.

Reacting instinctively, Bolan closed his eyes to protect them while bending at the waist. At the same time, he let Sevan go, reaching behind his head to grab his attacker. Finding a mass of long hair, he pulled hard, flipping his attacker over his head to land with a crash on her back.

Opening his eyes, Bolan stared into a woman's very attractive face. Her almond-shaped eyes glared back at him. It was accompanied by a foot flying at his head. He took the kick and straightened so she couldn't hit him there again, then returned the favor with a short kick behind her ear, which stunned her enough so that he could escape. Blinking to adjust his vision, Bolan saw the Armenian half facing him as he grabbed at the doorknob with his bound hands.

"Sevan, no!" Bolan raised his SIG-Sauer as a large shape barreled into the room, brushing the mob leader aside as he headed straight for Bolan. With the op blown, and not wanting the Armenian to escape, Bolan lined his sights up on the bodyguard and squeezed the trigger twice.

The big man jerked from the impact of the bullets, but didn't drop. He didn't even slow down. What the hell? Only crazed meth or PCP junkies were able to shrug off bullets like that. Aiming for his face, Bolan triggered his weapon once more and the guard crashed to the ground right in front of him. Sevan was nowhere to be seen.

"Striker, we have shots fired and a lot of activity in the house—" Tokaido began.

"Sevan is making a break for it!" Bolan replied as he stepped around the body and hit the door. "In pursuit now!" Outside the bedroom was a small landing with stairs leading down to the main level. Angry shouting could be heard below as Bolan hit the stairs.

"Goddamn it, what is wrong with all of you?" Sevan roared. "A killer's in my goddamn bedroom with Evie! Stop fucking around down here, cut me loose and go kill him!"

Reaching the bottom of the staircase, Bolan spotted Sevan in the middle of the large living room, filled with more sleek, modern furniture. Standing among three of his guards, the Mob boss nodded at the stairs, his eyes widening when he saw Bolan. "There he is!"

The three hardmen raised their pistols or submachine guns, but Bolan already had his weapon out and aimed. Three shots later, the trio was on the floor, dead or dying. But they had done their jobs, delaying Bolan enough for their boss to escape into another room.

The memorized floor plan in Bolan's mind told him Sevan was heading for the kitchen, where he'd no doubt find something with which to free himself. Swapping his half-empty magazine with a fresh one, the Executioner kept his pistol pointed at the three bodies, blood on their chests from his shots plainly visible as he began moving past them toward the kitchen.

That was when one of the strangest things Bolan had ever experienced happened.

One of them moved.

More specifically, a slick, sweaty hand reached out and grabbed his ankle, locking on it in a viselike grip.

When Bolan felt the hand grab his foot from behind, he whirled to see the man trying to pull his leg to his sweating face. But what was really weird was the bodyguard's mouth was wide open, saliva-flecked teeth white in the darkness, as though it was ready to take a bite out of him.

Bolan didn't bother wondering how this was possible—he'd seen plenty of crazies able to shrug off what should have been mortal wounds. Bringing his pistol around, he put a .40-caliber bullet into the man's open maw. The hollowpoint round blew out the back of his skull, dropping him for good this time. But even in death, the thug didn't let go, making Bolan pry his leg loose before resuming the pursuit of his quarry.

However, the grab stopped Bolan enough for the other two to attack him, one of whom tried to grab him around the chest while the other one sat up and wrapped both arms around his knees.

Bolan threw an elbow into the face of the one trying to hug him, snapping the man's head back and loosening his grip. He felt teeth try to sink into his leg, gnawing on his fatigues as he shoved his pistol behind his back and shot the man three times in the abdomen. His first attacker shuddered and slipped down his body.

Bolan looked down to see the last thug slobbering all over his knee as he tried to penetrate the poly/cotton weave. Grabbing one of the guy's arms, the soldier unwound him from around his legs, then put a bullet into his forehead before heading toward the kitchen door.

"Sitrep, Striker?" Tokaido asked. "What's going on there?"

"Apparently they grow them tougher here in Armenia," Bolan replied. "Shooters don't seem to know when they should lay down and die."

"Where's the package?" Kurtzman chimed in.

"I'm recollecting him right now." Standing to one side of the kitchen door, Bolan pulled it open, waiting to see if Sevan would be crazy enough to attack him. When he didn't, the soldier ducked inside, ending up next to a tall cabinet containing two industrial ovens, and swept the room with his pistol.

The kitchen was a vision of stone and hardwood, with a huge, granite-topped island in the middle of the room. Bolan couldn't see anyone from where he was, but that didn't mean the room was empty. He stepped over to the end of the island, expecting to hear shots fired, but nothing broke the silence.

The roar of a vehicle starting up outside turned his head and Bolan remembered that there was a door at the rear of the kitchen that led to a short hallway that connected the massive garage.

"Akira, disable the SUV in the garage!" Running through the kitchen, he reached the door and opened it while standing to one side. Several gunshots rang out and a fusillade of bullets drilled into the wall opposite the door. Sticking his pistol around the corner, Bolan emptied the magazine, firing in an X pattern in hopes of hitting at least one of the shooters. When the enemy returned fire this time, it was only one weapon firing now.

"Striker, I cannot access the vehicle's electrical systems. Whatever he's driving either doesn't seem to have much electronics in it or is shielded like crazy," Tokaido said. "If you want to stop him, you're going to have to move fast."

"What do you think I'm trying to do?" Bolan ejected his magazine and reloaded, then crouched and fired several shots at waist level across the hallway. There was silence for a moment, then the thump of something heavy hitting the ground. Peeking around the corner, Bolan saw two slumped forms in the hallway. He edged through the door and slowly approached the bodies. When he was only a few feet away, one twitched. He put a round into its head and then did the same with the second one.

The doorway to the garage was just beyond the limp forms, and Bolan kicked it open and came out with his pistol tracking for anything that moved. He was just in time to see a silver Range Rover surge from the garage into the early morning light. Bolan holstered his pistol and took off after it, but the SUV had too much of a head start—until it came to the gate. Slowing, it seemed as if Sevan was waiting for something, but the gate didn't budge.

"However, I can override the remote system to the outer security," Tokaido said, satisfaction evident in his tone.

Bolan was almost to the back of the vehicle when the engine revved and it shot toward the gate. "He's not gonna do what I think—" was all Tokaido got out before the Range Rover rammed the main gate, smashing it completely off its track and sending the bent metal flying into the road.

The impact slowed the SUV and Bolan was able to reach it as it began accelerating again. Grabbing the rear door handle, he pulled himself up onto the roof rack. The moment he got up there, he knew this wasn't an ordinary vehicle. He could barely feel the vibration as it roared down the road. Oddly enough, the light crowd of pedestrians didn't scatter out of the way, but seemed to be attracted to the loud, speeding vehicle.

"Akira, this thing's armored like a tank. I don't know how I'm going to get inside," Bolan said. The SUV slewed back and forth under him as Sevan tried to dislodge him.

"I may be able to help with that," Tokaido replied. "I couldn't access the engine, however I've got the security system up and... I've just unlocked all the doors."

"That's great." Bolan held on with all his might as the Range Rover took a left turn at such a high speed he felt the right tires leave the ground for a moment. "Now I just need to get in without killing myself!"

"Complain, complain, complain. Well, that's your only shot. The windows are made from bulletproof glass so thick they don't roll down."

"Great. All right, I'll try it." Wind whipping across his face, Bolan crawled to the passenger side of the vehicle and leaned down to try to hook the rear door latch with his hand. But as he did, the Rover jogged hard right. Although he was braced on the rack, it wasn't enough and Bolan flew off the SUV.

He slammed hard enough into the side of the vehicle to knock the wind out of him, but managed to hold on to the roof rack with his left hand. Gasping for breath, Bolan struggled to climb back up, but felt hands grabbing at him from the street. They almost pulled him off, but lost their grip and fell away. Bolan glanced back to see what looked like a villager rolling in the street behind them.

The SUV rocked on its wheels, swerving again, and Bolan saw another person—a woman in a simple peasant dress—try to jump onto the speeding vehicle, only to miss her grip and be flung back into the street. What the hell was going on here?

He didn't have any time to ponder that question, as the Range Rover started veering right again. Bolan looked ahead to see the side of a building that Sevan was aiming for, no doubt to scrape him off like a huge bug. They were about fifty meters away and closing fast.

With not enough time to pull himself up, Bolan kicked a leg onto the hood and climbed onto the front of the vehicle just as Sevan careened into the side of the building, shearing away the side mirror and scraping metal for a few seconds before he steered away.

He glared at Bolan from behind the wheel. The soldier glared back at him, then boosted himself onto the roof rack before Sevan got the bright idea of slamming on the brakes. He glanced around as they sped down the street, seeing more and more people out on the sidewalks and realized he had to stop this madman before he killed a lot of people.

"That was a waste!" he shouted. "Isn't there anything else you can do?"

"Well, there is the rear door—" Tokaido began.

"Pop it *now!*" Bolan shouted as he began crawling toward the rear of the vehicle. At he got there, the door opened and rose into the air. Grabbing the pneumatic cylinder that kept it held, Bolan swung down to pull himself inside.

As he did, he was hit from behind by another towns-person, this one snarling and grunting as he clawed at Bolan's chest and head. The added weight made Bolan's left hand slip loose, and for a moment he and his attacker were both dangling by the rod. Reaching behind him with his free hand, Bolan raked his attacker across the eyes, making him howl in pain. He did it again, and the second time the person fell off, landing on the cobblestoned street and rolling along until he skidded to a stop.

His arm trembling with the strain, Bolan hauled himself inside and reached for his pistol, only to find an empty holster—he'd lost it during the struggle with one of the villagers. Well, everything else about this had been hard, he thought as he started heading toward Sevan in the driver's seat.

"You are one tough American!" the Armenian said, pointing a pistol behind him and pulling the trigger. Bolan hit the deck as the bullet whined over him, then leaped forward, trying to get into the backseat before Sevan could shoot at him again. He was mostly successful; the second bullet plowing a furrow in his back as he fell over the leather seat. Bolan reached up and grabbed for the gun, struggling to wrestle it from Sevan's grasp.

The SUV pitched and yawed on the road as the two men fought. Bolan levered the gun toward the ceiling as Sevan pulled the trigger.

"No!"

His warning came too late. The bullet ricocheted off the armored ceiling and around the interior of the Range Rover. Getting his feet back under him, Bolan pushed hard on the pistol, smacking it into Sevan's head and bouncing it off the driver's window. The Armenian slumped over, hauling the steering wheel with him. Bolan grabbed for it, but he was too late again.

With a screech of tires and metal, the SUV tipped up on its side and ponderously rolled over. Tossed around inside, Bolan had a fleeting sensation of sky, then ground, then nothing.

CHAPTER ELEVEN

"Jesus Christ!"

William Scott, who had just stepped up next to Gary Alcaster, recoiled in shock. The Canadian med student also took an instinctive step backward as Anoush opened her mouth, still dripping with blood and scraps of flesh, and lunged at him.

He'd moved just in the nick of time. The crazed woman fell off the bed and crashed to the floor.

"Get out of there!" Scott shouted from the doorway. Spying the room key on the floor next to the nightstand, Alcaster grabbed it and ran for the door.

"Close it! Close it! Close it!" he shouted the second he was in the hallway. Scott pulled the door closed just as Anoush slammed into the other side. There was a pause, then the door was yanked inward hard enough to almost pull Scott off his feet.

"Help!"

Alcaster turned and put one hand over his friend's to hold the door closed while he attempted to lock it. Fumbling with the key in his sweaty hand, he nearly dropped it, but managed to insert it into the shaking keyhole. Twisting savagely, he felt the lock turn halfway, then stop. "It won't lock!"

"What the bloody hell!" Scott checked around the door and found the trouble—a blackening toe—

Anoush's—was crushed between the edge and the jamb. "When she pulls again, on three, we shove her away, then slam the door and lock it. Go when I say three, okay?"

"Okay." Alcaster unlocked the door again and tensed, straining to keep it closed while waiting for the signal.

"One...two...three!" Just as she strained at the door again, both men let go. As Scott had planned, Anoush was caught off guard and staggered across the room, falling on the bed, while the door smacked against the wall and rebounded toward them. Even so, by the time Scott was reaching for the knob to close it, she was already getting up and about to come for them again.

"Get it! Get it! Get it!" Alcaster shouted as Scott slammed the door firmly closed. The second he did, Alcaster turned the key, locking the door just as it trembled in its frame from the impact of Anoush's body on the other side. The door shook from more blows, but held firm.

"Holy shit..." Alcaster said as both men fell back from the door, watching it shake and tremble in its frame. "This is insane!"

"Yeah, we gotta get the hell out of here!" Scott replied.

"What? What about Josh?"

"What do you mean? He's fucking *dead!*" Scott said. "And if we don't get out of this...this brothel of psychotic cannibal hookers, we're gonna be next!" He looked around nervously and lowered his voice. "Which makes me wonder about where the rest of the people are." They looked down the corridor at the rows of closed doors on either side. "After what we saw with Josh..."

The Brit's face paled as the realization of what they had just seen hit him. Without another word, he ran for the bathroom at the end of the hall, and Alcaster was soon treated to the sound of him puking his guts out. He kept a watch on the hallway while Scott finished up, and soon he returned, ashen-faced but steadier. "All I know is I'm not knocking on any of those doors."

Alcaster couldn't argue with that logic. "Yeah, we need the police or the army, or whatever Armenia has, to get over here."

"Great idea! We need to call someone—anyone, for help!"

"Right. First, let's get out of the hallway. Come on, back to our room." Alcaster led his friend back into his room and locked the door. Siranush was still asleep in the bed, breathing heavily.

"You gotta be shittin' me!" Scott stared at her as he pulled out his cell phone. "She slept through all that?"

"Guess so," Alcaster replied. "Probably exhausted."

Scott swiped his screen a few times with a shaking hand, then shook his head. "Got no coverage out here. How about you?"

Alcaster rolled his eyes as he sat next to Siranush. "My phone barely works in London. No way will it function out here."

"Jesus, you're calm. How come you aren't, like, freaking out over all this?" Scott asked.

"Probably 'cause I grew up on a big farm in Nova Scotia," Gary replied. "I've seen dead things—even humans—before. Puked then, don't need to now."

He gently shook the woman's shoulder. "Siranush? Wake up. You have to get up now."

"What? Just a few more minutes…come back to bed…"

"Believe me, there is nothing I'd like more at the moment, but we have to get up and go—"

"Wha—what's this 'we' business?" Scott asked. "You're not taking her with us?"

"Of course we are, and when we get down the stairs, you should find Lusine, too. I'm sure as hell not going to leave someone who isn't affected by—whatever's going on here to get infected, too."

Siranush was starting to come awake under Alcaster's gentle but insistent shaking. "What? What is happening?"

"Yeah, you're right, sorry. I'm just not thinking right." Scott slumped into the rickety wingback chair in the corner and rubbed a hand over his face. "Just—everything that's happened, y'know?"

"Yeah, this is— It's all nuts."

Alcaster turned to face Siranush. "A lot of people seem to be sick here. You have to get dressed, and then we're going to go to our car and leave town right away, okay?"

"Sick…sick how?"

"Sick in, like, they want to tear our faces off, that kind of sick," Scott said.

"Will, ease up, okay?" Alcaster said without looking at him. "But he's right. They're very aggressive and dangerous. Do you hear that?" They all fell silent, hearing the continued banging against the bedroom door down the hall. "That's Anoush. She…she killed Josh—"

Siranush's blue eyes grew wide and her hands flew to her mouth. "No…"

Alcaster nodded. "We—we saw his body…and she

was covered in his blood. Will and I locked her in the room, and captured another woman who tried to attack me in the hallway."

"I don't understand…"

"That makes three of us," Scott said from the chair. "But the sooner we get clear of the area, the better off we'll be, not only in not getting attacked, but being able to get some help."

"Exactly, although we're going to see if we can use a phone downstairs and call someone first," Alcaster said. There were no phones in the individual rooms. If you wanted something, you went down to the bar or front desk and asked for it.

"Right. If she—" Scott waved at the still nearly nude woman "—would kindly do us the favor of getting dressed, we could get down there, find Lusine and call for help."

Having grasped how serious the situation was, Siranush had pulled on her dress and began putting on her shoes. Alcaster shook his head. "Go barefoot. If we have to run, you're done."

She looked at the ridiculous four-inch heels, then nodded. Picking one up, she regarding the spike on the back, hefting it for balance. "I think I will keep them, however."

Alcaster glanced at Scott, who shrugged. "Better than anything we've got. Speaking of…" Rising from his chair, he tipped it over. "Give me a hand."

Together the two tore the chair apart enough to get the legs off. Alcaster swung one through the air, getting the feel of it.

"A very serviceable club," Scott said as he swung

his own back and forth. "Much better than going down empty-handed, right?"

"Yeah." Licking his lips, Alcaster looked at the door, then at his friend. "You sure you're up for this?"

Scott stared back at him for a moment. "No. But there isn't any other choice. We have to get out of here, and the sooner the better." He held up the thick piece of walnut. "And I'm not letting anyone get in my way."

"All right, then." Alcaster walked to the door and quietly unlocked it. "Will, take the other side," he whispered. "Siranush, get behind him."

Scott took his position behind the door, improvised club held high to clobber anyone who might come at his friend. Taking a deep breath, Alcaster looked at his buddy, who nodded. Holding his own club high, and turning the knob as slowly as possible, he cracked the door open, braced for someone to charge at him.

Nothing happened. Other than the creak of the hinges, he didn't hear a sound from the hallway. Even the crazed Anoush had finally stopped beating against the door of her prison.

Alcaster opened the door just wide enough to stick his head out. The hallway was empty. Where is everyone else? he wondered. The answering thought—they're all dead—made him shudder.

"All right, let's go," he whispered. Opening the creaky door just wide enough to slip through, he stepped into the empty hallway, looking both ways. "Follow me."

The stairway was in the middle of the building, bisecting the upper hallway. Alcaster, with Scott and Siranush trailing him, crept over there, wincing every time one of them stepped on a creaky board. Every time they passed a room, Alcaster held his breath, sure that the door would fly open and he'd be attacked by a blood-thirsty psycho.

By the time they reached the staircase, he was sweating all over, and quickly wiped his hands on his pants so he could hold on to his club. "Watch the other hall. I'm going to take a look down the staircase."

He was about to step down when a hand grabbed his arm. He looked back to see Scott's worried face staring back at him. "Not too far, okay?"

Alcaster shook his head. "Don't worry, first sign of trouble and I'm hightailing it back up here."

His friend nodded. "Be careful."

Alcaster nodded back, then eased around the corner. The staircase had a landing about ten steps up, and he would have to get down there before he could see through the railing into the bar. Step by creaky step, he descended, his heart in his throat. At the landing, he leaned down and peered through the wooden balusters. The main desk and a small sitting area were on one side, with the bar on the other. At this hour of the morning, the whole place should have been empty.

However, it wasn't.

Scanning the main desk area, Alcaster turned to see Lusine standing at the bottom of the stairs, staring up at him. Even in the dim light, he could see the sheen of sweat on her face, and was pretty sure her eyes were red-rimmed. Still, she hadn't immediately leaped for him—yet.

"Uh, Lusine? Are you all right?" he asked quietly.

She didn't reply, just put her foot on the first step. Her cheek twitched and she raised a pale arm to absently wipe her glistening forehead. When she did, Alcaster noticed the new, raw bite mark on her arm, still oozing blood. "Stay where you are," he said a bit louder while raising his club. "I don't want to hurt you." Again she didn't answer, but took another step up.

"Gary? What's going on?" Scott whispered from above him. "Is that Lusine?"

"Yeah, and I think she's got what the others have," he said over his shoulder while not taking his gaze off her. She took another step up. "She's not listening to me."

"What do you want to do?"

"I want her to stay the hell down there!" Alcaster said as she took another step. His arms trembled from the strain. It was one thing to defend himself against someone who was clearly out to hurt him, but she hadn't done anything like that yet. She just kept coming closer and closer...

"Not another step, I mean it!" he said as he cocked his club back, trying to keep his voice from shaking.

Lusine took another step, moving faster now.

"Lusine, stop..." Siranush said from the top of the staircase. Her friend paused for a moment, cocking her head to regard the other woman, then kept coming toward him. As she took the final step, her face darkened, mouth dropping open to reveal dingy teeth, and her hands came up, fingers curved into grasping claws.

"I'm sorry—" When she was a step away, Alcaster swung his club toward her head. She didn't duck or dodge, and the end of the chair leg smashed into her temple. Lusine stood there a moment as blood trickled down from where the corner had split her skin open. Then she fell backward and slid down the stairs, coming to a graceless heap at the bottom.

Alcaster stood there for a long moment, the bloody

club nearly forgotten in his hand. Sensing a presence beside him, he turned to see Scott and Siranush standing there.

"You—you had to do it, man. She would have ripped into you otherwise," Scott said.

"I—I know. That doesn't make it any better." He took a deep breath. "I'll be all right. Come on, let's find that phone."

The three ran to the main desk, where Alcaster grabbed the receiver of the old, black phone on the counter. He put it to his ear as he jiggled the receiver. "It's dead."

"Fuck it, then!" Scott said as he whirled and headed toward the front door. "We've got a car. Let's get the hell out of here!"

"Will, wait!" Alcaster ran after him, but the towheaded Brit was already fumbling with the old-style bolt.

"Got it—let's go!" He began pushing the door open.

"Hold up," Alcaster said, reaching for him. But it was too late.

As he trotted outside, the dozen or so people already on the street all turned to look at him at once, their eyes practically glistening red in the light of the rising sun.

CHAPTER TWELVE

"Evie," as Alexsandr Sevan knew her, came back to consciousness on the floor of the master bedroom. Her head pounded as though a hammer was beating it, and a dull ache throbbed at the base of her skull.

What...happened? Pushing herself up on her elbows made the pain shoot to the front of her head and bounce around her brain for a minute. Squeezing her eyes closed, she breathed in and out until the agony receded a bit. She knew she would have to watch for a concussion for the next day or so.

When she felt up to it, she opened her eyes—and saw the motionless bulk of a man lying in front of her. Startled, she recoiled for a moment, then relaxed when she saw who it was. The bullet hole in his cheek distorted his features into a smeared caricature of what he had looked like when alive.

"Lernik finally got his. Good." She had been careful to never be alone with the pig, not since the first time she'd made that mistake and he'd drunkenly tried to rape her in a club bathroom. She had fended him off then, aided by his throwing up and passing out, and kept quiet about what had happened when he didn't seem to remember later. She had also made sure to encounter him in a group from that point on.

Looking at the mussed bed and open window, it all

started coming back to her: the masked assailant holding a knife on Sevan…grabbing the vase and throwing it…listening to their conversation from under the bed… coming out and attacking him…seeing his face after hitting the floor, all black hair and ice-blue eyes…and then blackness… She looked around for other bodies, but didn't see any. The usually security-locked door to the bedroom stood open, and she couldn't hear any noise from the rest of the house.

Jesus, who was that guy? Did he take Alexsandr? Did Alexsandr kill him? All questions she'd have to find answers to later—assuming she stayed alive long enough to ask them.

However this turned out, she was pretty sure her mission was screwed. "Evie" was really Dina Finigian, a deep-cover operative with the Armenian Police, Combating Organized Crime Main Department. Finigian was half Asian, half Romanian. Her parents had moved to Armenia before she'd been born to help care for some distant relatives and help with disposing of a business. They'd ended up buying it and living in the city of Martuni. Finigian had grown up here, and considered the country her home.

Recently a new police chief had been appointed by the president. He had risen to prominence due to his dismantling of several smaller crime families in the southern part of the country, despite threats against his life, an assault and two assassination attempts. Those operations had brought him to the prime minister's attention, who had nominated him to coming to the capital to oversee a concerted push against the rest of the organized crime in the nation.

Finigian, along with her superior, had scheduled a

meeting with him during his first week to present their deep-cover proposal. All previous attempts to infiltrate the Armenian mob had been tried using male agents. All of them had failed, with the undercover agents disappearing or getting killed in gruesome ways. Finigian had presented a compelling case as to why a woman might be able to accomplish what the male policemen couldn't. The crime families, with their patriarchal, honor-based systems, wouldn't look too closely at a woman in their organization—especially an ordinary prostitute.

The prime minister was interested but apprehensive, fearing the public opinion backlash that might occur if the operation went wrong and Finigian was injured or killed. It was the riskiest operation they had ever undertaken—Finigian would be entirely on her own, with no backup, since they didn't know whom they could trust among the police force. However, she had told him she joined the force to fight all criminals, no matter what it took. That speech, along with her exotic appearance—all but guaranteeing the locals wouldn't think she was a plant—and the carefully orchestrated plan, was how she had ended up here, after being planted in Romania and "recruited" by the Armenians.

Since then she had found out exactly how callous they could be to the women they trafficked, dispensing casual brutality every day. Physical abuse, rape and even cold-blooded killing were normal facts of life here. Finigian had tried her best to minimize the brutality among the girls without blowing her cover, but it had been nearly impossible. Everything she'd seen, however, had only made her more determined to take these wolves in human form down once and for all.

She thought she'd gotten her chance when Alexsandr Sevan had seen her on a tour of the brothel and selected her to accompany him on the trip to Italy. That week had been spent charming both the Italian and Armenian mobsters while feeding her "clients" knockout drops to keep them out of her pants. She had been worried when the trip had been unexpectedly extended, but they had returned last night without incident. Fortunately, Sevan had been tired from the travel, so there had been no need to drug him before bedtime. Although that might have made the unknown intruder's job even easier, she thought.

But all that wouldn't matter if Sevan was dead. And it would matter even less if Finigian didn't make it out of here to report and eventually testify about what she'd seen during her time in this region of hell. No matter what, she had to make sure that no more women were fed into the grinder of what amounted to sex slavery.

First things first, however. She crawled over to Lernik's dead body and patted him down, breathing through her mouth to avoid smelling the stench of blood, sweat and feces wafting from the body. Finding a .45-caliber SW-1911 Pro pistol, black with gold filigree and ivory grips, still in its holster, she pulled it out and checked the action to find it fully loaded. Under his other shoulder were two full magazines, which she also took.

The rest of his pockets revealed a cell phone—broken—and a thick wad of 1000- and 5000-dram notes. She also noticed three unusual shell casings nearby. Picking one up, she saw it wasn't made of brass, but nickel, from an American ammunition manufacturer. *Hornady .40 caliber...definitely not a local.*

Only when she tried to put a casing, the extra ammo and cash somewhere did she look down at the sheer, plunging, satin cream negligee barely covering her body and shake her head. "Definitely need something else to wear," she muttered.

Opening the walk-in closet door, she began riffling through the endless men's tailored suits and leisurewear. The only women's clothing she found were either sluttier variations on what she was already wearing or expensive, ornamental dresses that would be absolutely no use to her now.

Finally she settled for the smallest pair of khaki trousers she could find, belting them around her waist with a five-hundred-dollar Armani leather belt. At least the length was decent—she had long legs. And now I have pockets, she thought, slipping the two magazines, money roll and shell casing into them. Selecting a navy-blue button-down shirt, she put it on and buttoned it up, rolling the sleeves to her elbows.

Finding proper shoes was impossible, as everything in the closet was too big. She didn't even think about trying to use her cheap, four-inch heels. Taking a deep breath, she hurried over to the doorway and peeked out, pistol held firmly in two hands. The weapon's thick grip made it difficult to hold in her smaller hands, and she knew it would kick hard, so she was hoping she wouldn't have to fire unless absolutely necessary.

She stepped out onto the landing and listened again, trying to figure out what had happened after the bedroom door had opened. Only silence greeted her. Pointing the pistol at the floor, she started down the stairs, every sense alert for any sign of Sevan, the intruder, or any of the eight to ten people who were normally around the house at any given time.

At the bottom of the staircase she found more of the nickel shell casings, along with three bodies in the large living room. Sevan's former bodyguards were all sprawled out in various lifeless poses. When she stepped forward, she saw the gunshot wounds to the chests and head of all three—accurate shots in the same places on each one. Her assessment of the masked intruder rose a notch. Maybe he was a policeman or military operative?

There was no sign of where the action had gone after that, so Finigian walked to the massive front door, which was steel-cored. It was impossible to hear through, so she opened it and peeked outside.

The morning sunlight nearly blinded her, making her shield her watering eyes as they adjusted. By the time they did, the nearest of several people milling around the lawn was only a few steps away. A woman whom Finigian thought might have worked as a maid, but wasn't sure. She didn't look very well, however. Her dress was only half on and she was missing a shoe. Also, her hair wasn't in the typical bun and she was sweating profusely, as if she had just run from the hotel, almost a kilometer away, to here.

"Oh…hello," Finigian said in Armenian. "What are you doing—?"

The second she spoke, the woman looked up, her face making Finigian recoil. Her eyes were red-rimmed and had a yellow cast to the whites. Her face was flushed, her thin lips parched and cracked. For a moment the two women stared at each other.

"Are you all—" she tried to ask when the woman opened her mouth in a terrifying snarl. With a scream, the villager rushed at her, fingers curled into claws on her outstretched hands.

Startled, Finigian backpedaled inside and tried to close the heavy door, but the woman thrust her arm between it and the jamb, blocking it while continuing to scream. The hand that was inside the room clawed at the policewoman's face and neck.

"Stop!" Finigian shouted while trying to keep the door closed. Over the woman's screams, she could hear others running to the door. "Help me! Stop her!"

The next thing she knew, the door flew open so hard it shoved her backward. Surprised, she stumbled into the middle of the room and tripped over one of the dead guards, landing on her buttocks. She had the presence of mind to hold on to the pistol, which she brought up when she saw the insanity in the eyes of the men and woman bursting through the door and heading straight for her.

"Stop!" was all Finigian said as she realized if she didn't kill them, they were going to tear her apart.

Scrambling backward, she was forced to hold the pistol with one hand as she squeezed the trigger. The pistol bucked and roared, firing heavy .45-caliber rounds that plowed into flesh and bone. She dropped two, but more surged forward from behind them. The two wounded ones didn't slow much, but their going down caused a knot of several more people to get jammed up in the doorway, with a third tripping over a wounded villager and falling on them, as well.

The others still charged forward, stepping over and on their fellows, but the break gave Finigian the chance she needed to get to her feet. Shooting until the slide locked back, she ejected the magazine and grabbed another one from her pocket while backing toward the stairs. Slamming it into the grip, she chambered a round and kept shooting, now using both hands as she reached the stairs and began climbing.

The bullets tore into arms, legs and chests, but when the second magazine was exhausted, three of the original half dozen or so were still coming at her. When she reached the top of the stairs, she loaded the last magazine, aimed down at the last of them and fired into their heads until they stopped moving.

A cloud of smoke from the pistol surrounded her, and she felt as though her ears were stuffed with cotton from the repeated booming reports in the enclosed room. Peeking over the railing, she saw a line of dead Armenians leading back to the door.

Retreating to the bedroom, she ran to the window and peeked through the curtain at the grounds. "God-*damn* it!"

The gunshots had attracted more villagers, who were running through the open gate and into the house. Finigian ran back to the bedroom door, closed it quietly and hit the keypad to lock it. Nothing short of a battering ram would be able to get in now.

The only problem was that she was now trapped in a room surrounded by a town whose inhabitants had apparently gone homicidally crazy. But how? Airborne virus? Contamination through the water system? It's like a bad movie come to life, she thought, sliding the magazine out of her pistol to check her ammunition. Three bullets left.

Regardless of what was going on here, she had to escape, at least to warn people about what was happening. But how the hell was she going to get out of here?

Creeping back to the door, Finigian put her ear to it and listened. She didn't hear anything on the other side, but when she tried the door, she also realized she didn't know the code to open it. Sevan hadn't trusted her enough to let her know what it was. She knew he had a wall safe next to his bed, but didn't know how to open it, either. However, there was one other thing she could take from this room. Trotting to the nightstand on Sevan's side of the bed, she grabbed the bottle of water and drained it. Opening the drawer revealed a stainless-steel dagger with an eight-inch blade in a black leather sheath. Finigian unbuckled her belt, threaded the knife onto it, and arranged it so that it hung at the small of her back.

The curtain blowing near the far window alerted her to the only possible way out. She walked over and pushed it aside, then stepped out onto the roof. The slate tiles were cold on her feet, but that was the least of her worries. In the distance she could hear shouts and screams, along with the occasional gunshot. Without checking the front, since it was probably overrun anyway, she headed to the back of the house, figuring she could climb the fence and get to an alley for cover. She just had to avoid being seen.

Reaching the edge of the roof, she peeked over at the ground, scanning left and right. The whole backyard was clear. It was about ten meters to the fence, and at the rear of the yard was a large flower garden with a small recirculating fountain ringer by large rocks. Sevan said it helped him relax from the stress of the day. What he hadn't realized was that one of the rocks was tall enough for a person to stand on and probably be able to reach the top of the wall.

Probably...

It was her only chance. Checking both ways once more, Finigian tucked her pistol into her belt, swung her legs over and carefully began lowering herself to the ground. Once she was hanging by her fingertips— still a few feet above the grass—she let go, falling into a shoulder roll as she hit the ground.

Coming up into a crouch, she looked around to see if she had attracted any attention—right as a man walked around the corner, only a couple meters away. She saw him as his head began rising, and pushed off, charging at him as she drew the pistol.

He was already moving forward, as well, opening his mouth to scream when she brought the butt around in a roundhouse shot to his temple. The man collapsed as if poleaxed, limbs twitching as he fell to the ground. She immediately turned and ran for the rock garden as a loud shout pierced the air.

Glancing over her shoulder, she saw two from the other side of the house running at her. Turning back, she found herself at the rock garden and leaped onto the closest ones, scrambling for the tallest rock. She could hear her pursuers closing in, one apparently falling into the pond, judging by the loud splash. Finigian didn't look, however, she just kept climbing. She had just reached the top of the tall rock when a hand grabbed her ankle, almost making her fall.

Still on her hands and knees, the policewoman put the gun between her legs and fired twice. The pull turned into a deadweight and she had to drop the pistol so she could hang on with both hands. Frantically she kicked the hand off before it dragged her down from the rock. Springing to her feet, she crouched and leaped at the fence wall, putting every bit of remaining strength she had into it.

She sailed through the air and caught the top edge of the wall with her fingertips, the rest of her body slamming painfully into it. She hung on, though, and began hoisting herself up.

Hearing a low growl from behind her, Finigian grabbed on to the iron bars and kept pulling, trying to get a leg up before—

The impact hit her back like a freight train, the villager's hands grabbing her legs and holding on tight. Finigian was in tremendous shape, but the extra seventy-five kilograms felt as it they were going to tear her arms from their sockets. She could feel the crazed person trying to bite through her pants, pressing the sheath of the dagger there into her back—

The dagger! Knowing she would have only a few seconds to do it, she let go with one hand. Whipping it behind her, she grabbed the dagger handle, drew it and stabbed blindly toward the face of her attacker. She connected once, twice, the blade skittering off a bone, then felt the point pierce skin and sink deep into something before she was released, tearing the knife out of her hand. And just in time, for the remaining arm holding her up had been about to give way. Getting her other hand up there, Finigian slowly pulled herself onto the top of the wall and looked down.

Two villagers were there. One unmoving, with a bloody hole where his eye would normally be, the second thrashing on the ground and making odd gobbling noises, the hilt of the dagger sticking at an odd angle out of his head.

Although exhausted, she knew she couldn't stay

there. Every second in the open risked discovery by more of these—people. Checking the empty street on the other side, she began climbing over the spikes and making her way down to the rough stones.

When her bruised, bloody feet touched down, she looked both ways again and then ran for the nearest alley, trying to watch everywhere at once as she moved deeper into the town now apparently populated by the insane.

CHAPTER THIRTEEN

Dr. Gerhardt Richter's cell phone chirped while he was overseeing a CAT scan of one of his latest test subjects. "Dr. Richter, please come to laboratory two immediately. There's activity at the test site."

"Gerry, take over here, would you?" Richter strode out of the laboratory, heading next door. He hit the double doors to the lab several meters down the hall and came up behind the video tech, an A/V whiz named Elden Clay, sitting at the bank of flat-screen monitors. "What's going on?"

"The place is turning into a madhouse. See for yourself." The drone, a lightweight, jet-black automated model that could be programmed to "fly-and-forget" had been launched and set to loiter by Firke before leaving. It had been transmitting high-definition images from the town via satellite for the past two hours.

Richter watched the devastation slowly take over the town. From isolated incidents—such as what looked to be a hooker killing two men in an alley to entire infected families emerging from their homes to spread the virus to others—the process was swift and exponential. Richter estimated from first contact, more than sixty percent of the population had been either exposed or killed in the first three hours. "I should be there observing this first-hand. Perhaps we can conduct further experiments on an isolated village nearby. I'll have security conduct some sweeps to locate a likely target. What's that?"

Richter pointed at one of the main streets. Clay zoomed in on a black SUV lying on its side in a street in front of the hotel where Firke and his team had spiked the water.

The resolution on the small cameras mounted on the rooftops was clear enough for Richter to notice what looked like dents on part of the car and even a smear of crimson across the chromed letters on the hood. "What caused the damage?"

"That's even more interesting," Clay replied, his fingers flying over the keyboard. "Watch monitor two."

Richter stared at the footage of the Range Rover speeding down the street with villagers running out to attack it, only to be thrown aside. Even so, every one tried to get up and resume their hunt, either limping or even crawling after the SUV or wandering off in a different direction in search of new prey.

"Fascinating," he said. "We haven't had the chance to experiment with subjects attempting to perform learned skills yet, although from what we've observed, they haven't proved capable of much beyond relatively mindless destruction. Therefore, I must assume that the driver is uninfected. Apparently they do not need to be within close contact to tell when another person is not infected."

"Yeah, then watch this." Clay switched to a new perspective on the street. "This happened while the subjects on the street were trying to attack the vehicle as it was moving."

Richter watched the man in black on top of the SUV

as he moved to the back door, which opened to admit him. "Now who is that? He looks like he would be one of Mr. Firke's employees. But I'm sure no one was left behind..." Richter paused as a thought struck him. "Perhaps a bodyguard or fellow soldier with the driver?"

"Maybe, although he didn't seem inclined to want to stop and let him in," Clay replied. "Plus, the SUV swerves here, and overturns, all without hitting anything, indicating that there may have been a struggle for control right before the crash."

"Keep an eye on it. It will be interesting to see what reaction the subjects have if there are any survivors inside."

"Yes, sir." The long, narrow fingers of one Clay's hands danced over his keyboard while the other manipulated a trackball with unconscious ease. "Hold on, what's this?" He glanced at another monitor. "One of the cameras has picked up what sounds like several loud reports. If I had to guess, it seems to be about a kilometer away."

"Gunfire?" Richter mused. "Maybe police?"

"Could be," Clay said. "But it seems like the virus hasn't gotten all of them."

Richter pulled out his cell phone and speed dialed a number. "Possibly," he replied as the connection was made. "Mr. Firke?"

"Yes?"

"You are in position?" Richter asked.

"Of course."

Richter peered at the screen. "The test is well under way."

"Then why are you calling me?"

"There are pockets of unaffected people still around.

I'm just checking to ensure that you are ready to enact the contingency plan once it is activated."

If the Englishman was annoyed by Richter's questioning of his ability, it didn't come through in his tone. "Rest assured everything will be handled as per our employer's instructions."

Richter leaned in over the monitor, watching an old man slowly approach the SUV. "Regardless, I want you and your team to remain on standby until I say otherwise. It is imperative that no one leave the area before it is cleansed."

"Works for me."

Richter hung up and straightened again, but didn't take his eyes from the SUV, which was attracting more and more villagers. "Looks like we're going to find out just how determined they can get. Be sure to get as much footage as you can on this. Notify me if anything else unusual occurs." His phone vibrated and Richter looked down with distaste at the reminder: Phone conference in 10 minutes.

He stabbed another button. "Prepare backups of all the data we have and send them to headquarters. I'll be in my office, dealing with lesser minds."

DESPITE WHAT APPEARED to be initial success with the field test, Richter's day went steadily downhill from there.

The preliminary test results on the latest run of the compound they had been using, including the batch that had gone to the Armenian village, revealed adverse affects on the surviving test subjects. The artificial adrenaline had apparently chemically lobotomized more than half of the survivors and Richter wasn't sure why. Previous tests on their isolated subjects had not produced this result and he couldn't explain the cause. His initial theory was that perhaps the dose had been too large, despite careful calculations of the proper amount for the village, which had caused overstimulation and damage of the lobes, but it would take more experiments to test and verify it.

But he wouldn't be able to start that work right now as he was currently participating in a video conference call with the board members of his company, answering pointed questions about what they perceived as his lack of progress. This was the part of his job Richter hated—trying to explain the delicate processes of science to men in suits who were only concerned with the bottom line: how they were going to make money from it. For the thousandth time, he cursed the recent recession that had caused Stengrave to have to sell shares of the company to ensure its survival. Now he was beholden to these men, who didn't understand anything of what he was trying to accomplish with his research, but were only interested in how they could best profit from it. He took a deep breath and pressed his hands flat on his desk to stop them from shaking before speaking.

"Gentlemen, please let me remind you that perfecting a process like this takes time and resources, and while we have some of each, we do not have unlimited access to both. The effects are not lasting as long as we had hoped. My point is that we have made tremendous strides in synthesizing our artificial adrenaline, but to achieve the results you are demanding will, quite simply, take at least one to three more years of rigorous testing and modification of the existing lines."

"Doctor, no one here is disputing your tremendous

discoveries while working on this project," the chief executive officer, a forgettable man in a thousand-dollar suit that hid his paunch and with a hundred-dollar haircut over his bland face, said. "However, if we do not have a viable adrenaline serum to begin human tests on within the next six months, I don't see how we can continue to fund this project. Our research—"

Corporate espionage, Richter thought.

"—shows that several other companies are also developing similar products and, although the current conflicts are still viable, we're concerned that we will miss our window of opportunity to market the stimulant for greatest effect—"

You mean the greatest profit margin, Richter thought, but only nodded as the man continued. My people are already working fourteen hours a day as it is.

"—so what resources do you need to achieve this proposed timetable?"

Richter sighed. "This is not a matter that money or more personnel can solve. Tailoring a virus to ensure that it has the desired effect without side effects or the possibility of mutation involves painstaking trial and error, not to mention multiple dead ends. It's like playing a biochemical lottery and trying to select the right numbers to hit the jackpot. Although you could have multiple experiment streams going at the same time, we would have to pull everyone off all of the other projects they're working on, which, given the secrecy this project has been kept under, poses a risk that we cannot afford to take, particularly in light of the potential profits of the other product revenue streams for the firm."

As much as he disliked this process, Richter also knew how to choose his words for maximum effect.

"I'm afraid, gentlemen, that we simply need more time. You've seen the results when the most recent version of the serum was released."

"Yes, and they've been very impressive." This came from Stengrave, who had been sitting at the end of the table in silence while Richter had sparred with the board members. Now he leaned forward, his deep, quiet voice demanding attention from everyone present. "I've been reviewing the doctor's notes on his trials with great interest, and think that perhaps we may be looking at this from the wrong perspective. What if this tailored virus was marketed as a limited-area effect group pacifier? Destroy an enemy by making them destroy themselves, with little fallout on surrounding groups?"

"That may be fine for areas with a high concentration of blood relations, but what about a disparate group of terrorists, for example?" a board member asked. "You can't tailor one virus to each separate member of a non-related group."

"That's the beauty of it, Mr. Seiver," Stengrave replied. "If the virus works, any uninfected stand a high chance of being destroyed by the infected—two possible ways that they are removed from the equation. Even the mental effects Dr. Richter claims can be presented as a positive, as anyone who survives is impaired enough to no longer be a threat. Doctor, how much trace evidence is left in the victims afterward?"

Richter blinked at the calm assessment and then found his voice again. "It's hard to say, since we haven't run the entire gamut of tests yet. There are no obvious traces of the serum itself, just an abnormal build-up of lactic acid in the muscles after so much activity in so short a time frame and, as mentioned, the mental impairment. I need to do more tests to provide an accurate baseline, but so far physical traces of the ingested drug itself have been minimal at best."

Stengrave nodded. "There, you see, gentlemen? It's very possible that the good doctor may have stumbled on the best weapon to eradicate potential enemies of the state. Need to wipe out a terrorist cell? Slip this into their water supply, and they'll kill themselves for you. Drug or sex smugglers running roughshod over the border? Give them a large cocktail of our special blend, and we could eradicate the fragmented growers, and even the cartels overnight with the right insertions."

"I don't know," A board member named Ari Tomas replied. "Given the current administration, I can hardly see the U.S. government going for this."

Stengrave chuckled. "It doesn't necessarily have to go straight to the top. I am aware of several black-bag programs at the Pentagon that would find this tailored virus very intriguing. But if they are not interested, we have other customers all over the world who will gladly take advantage of it. I can think of a half dozen who will be very interested in this weapon right now. We can begin recovering our expenses on it immediately, and when the refined version comes out, we'll simply market that one to the government. We'll have two revenue streams from one experiment line that could reap millions, even billions of dollars, and it would save lives in the process, since our customers wouldn't have to send their men in to neutralize enemies, when this would do it for them."

Richter nodded; the man's line of reasoning paralleling his own. For this particular experiment, he didn't care what they did with it, as long as he could sell it as enough of a success so that he could get back to doing what he wanted to be doing: his own experiments into rewriting the genetic code of the human body.

"With all due respect, Chairman, I have serious reservations about this line of procedure." The new speaker was one of the recently elected board members, Forbes Taney, a younger man with styled, black hair who also wore expensive suits. Richter had pegged him as a relative of one of the major shareholders, so he was surprised to see him taking this adversarial stand. "From what little findings have been made available—" Stengrave stiffened at this, but the other man didn't seem to notice "—is it true that you're performing tests on an indigenous population there?"

"Yes, but all test subjects are volunteers who are cared for and well compensated for their time," Richter lied.

"Including the ones suffering from these mental issues of... and I quote '...impaired thinking, judgment and motor skills'? And now you're actually proposing selling the virus that made them do this as a biological weapon? Not only would that violate several accords of the Geneva Convention, but we also have no indications of the long-term effects of this organism on the test subjects or the environment."

"Mr....Taney," Richter said. "We have been careful to select those subjects who do not have family, so any adverse effects will not harm them or potential relatives. Also, there is no danger to the environment, as the virus cannot survive on its own for longer than twenty-four hours. It is a built-in fail-safe that results in the virus killing itself at the end of its allotted lifespan if it has not found a suitable host."

"Yes, but what about mutation?" the young man

asked. "Look at the SARS virus, which leaped to humans. The fact that this is based off a virus present in roughly half of the human population around the world greatly concerns me."

Tomas didn't even acknowledge his words with a glance. "You let me worry about those details. We've invested a great deal of money, time and effort into creating this on-site facility and it has to produce tangible results. Some of the greatest inventions of mankind have been created accidentally, and this may be one of them. If there is a practical use for what Dr. Richter is working on—one that can save lives while eliminating an enemy—then we should find it."

Stengrave hadn't said a word during the exchange, instead just listened to the various members make their points. Now he leaned forward. "Mr. Tomas, Mr. Taney, I want proposals from each of you on the pros and cons of your positions regarding this program. Dr. Richter, continue your tests for now, but be prepared to have your staff evacuated on twenty-four-hour notice."

"Yes, sir." Richter kept his eyes on Tomas and wasn't surprised to see the man move his hand back and forth on the polished tabletop, the gesture clear. *Eliminate all potential witnesses.* His acknowledging nod was barely perceptible, but the other man replied with a minute nod of his own.

"Gentlemen, if you'll excuse me, I have much to do here," Richter said, then signed off.

Even though it was cold in his air-conditioned room, the doctor wiped his forehead and found the back of his hand covered in beads of sweat. *And the sooner I can get out of here and back to civilization and my true research, the better,* he thought.

He was just about to dive back into the problems with the latest tests when his phone rang. "Yes?"

"Very good, Doctor, you handled them quite well."

"Thank you, sir."

"You received the email with the new lines I wish created?"

"Yes, sir, my people are already working on it." Early that morning, the doctor had gotten a message about beginning to develop large batches of the virus tailored to a fairly specific genome type. "This version has the capacity to impact a sizable portion of the population, sir."

"Indeed it does, Doctor, indeed it does," Stengrave replied. "I want reports as to the quantity of the virus created 'round-the-clock."

"And you will have it, sir."

"In return, I will keep the board off your back. Just keep on doing what you are doing, Doctor, and I will take care of the rest."

"Thank you, sir." Something struck Richter when he hung up the phone. Everything Stengrave had said was supposed to sound reassuring, but somehow it didn't.

Instead it sounded as though he didn't care if this product ever made it to the market.

And for some reason Richter found that strangely ominous.

CHAPTER FOURTEEN

"Striker, come in. Striker? Are you all right? Over."

Bolan regained consciousness to find Akira Tokaido talking urgently in his ear. The soldier was crumpled on the bottom window of the sideways Range Rover, with his legs and feet on top of the rest of his body. Untangling slowly and pulling himself to his feet, he found that his head hurt and his right shoulder was numb from lying on it, but he didn't think he'd suffered any real damage in the crash.

"Striker here. I'm okay, Akira, just a couple of bruises."

He heard a relieved sigh on the other end. "About time. I've been trying to raise you for five minutes. What happened?"

"I let Sevan drive." A groan from the front seat alerted Bolan that he wasn't alone. Pushing himself up, he found the Armenian still buckled into the driver's seat and clutching his head. He looked around for a weapon, but both pistols had disappeared. He did have a combat blade on him and drew that to put to the other man's throat.

When he felt the cold steel on his skin again, the Armenian grunted. "Son of a bitch. You really don't give up, do you? I'd heard Americans are tenacious—almost as tenacious as we are."

"You got that right," Bolan replied. "Since you've

broken our ride out of here, I've got to go find another one, but you're coming with me."

"Fine, fine, just let me get out of this—" Sevan stopped talking as the Range Rover creaked and shifted a bit. The two men exchanged glances.

"Probably just settling. Let me—" Bolan stopped again as metal creaked again, louder this time and from the back of the SUV.

"That wasn't settling." Taking another zip tie from his pocket, Bolan grabbed Sevan's hand and lashed it to the steering wheel.

"Hey!"

Bolan held a finger to his lips. "Don't want you going anywhere," he whispered. "I'll be back."

He had just turned to see what was going on at the back door when a blurred shape leaped at him from around the top of the backseat. Bolan was shoved backward, against Sevan's seat, as a sweating, snarling, spitting, scratching old man tried his best to claw Bolan's eyes out.

The sideways back passenger seat of an SUV wasn't the best place for fighting, but Bolan had incapacitated a lot of people in a lot worse places. Sweeping the man's hooked fingers away from his face, he followed up with a ram's head punch to the man's chest, just to the right of his breastbone and into the heart. Normally an incapacitating wound, it usually stopped a person in their tracks.

This old man, however, was made of stronger stuff. Even as he gasped for air after the blow had emptied his lungs, he continued trying to get at Bolan, staring at him with red-rimmed eyes while clutching at his arm and snapping his toothless mouth.

"What the hell is going on here?" Bolan drove a

short punch into the man's jaw, making his gums click together as he dropped, unconscious, to the bottom of the compartment.

"Do you have everyone in town on your payroll?" Bolan asked.

The mob leader looked down at the old man in surprise. "Hardly. That was Hanes Palatian, the town butcher. I hope you are satisfied, American. You just assaulted an innocent citizen of Armenia. I will be happy to let your superiors know about this once we get to wherever you think you are taking me."

"Apparently you weren't watching the same fight I was. He came at *me* first, or did you conveniently miss that?" Bolan asked. "We're leaving."

He reached over and cut the man loose. "Follow me, and don't get any stupid ideas."

"I wouldn't dream of it." Rubbing his wrist, the Armenian stayed behind Bolan as he climbed over the body and headed for the rear of the Range Rover. Through the open back door he could see people moving around farther up the street, but there was no crowd gathered as there normally would be at the scene of an accident. Bolan also couldn't see any police on the scene, which made him frown. What was going on here?

The moment he appeared at the back of the SUV, however, Bolan attracted a lot of attention. Practically everyone on the street looked at him at the exact same time, making him think he'd stumbled onto a wolf pack in human form.

"Hello, is there a—" Bolan began to say as everyone began to move toward him. But they weren't approaching in any way that looked helpful. Instead they ran at him with outstretched arms, faces twisted in snarls of rage. As they got closer, he saw that they looked like the old man, with sweat running down their faces and red-rimmed eyes glaring at him.

Grabbing the handle of the back door, Bolan pulled it shut, just as the first of his attackers, a teenage girl, slammed into it and bounced off. She was followed by two more, each of whom hit and spun away.

"What is happening? What's going on out there?" Sevan asked.

"I've seen people act like this before, but I doubt it's the same thing. Your fellow villagers are under the influence of something," Bolan said.

By now a small group had clustered around the back of the Range Rover. Most of them were just screaming and pounding on the glass, but a clever one had found the back door handle and was trying to pull it open. Bolan held it closed, but the one pulling on the door was joined by another, both yanking on the handle with all their might.

"Akira, lock the doors!" Bolan snapped as he held the door closed with everything he had.

"I can't, Striker, I lost my connection to the vehicle!" Tokaido replied.

"Well, get it back!" Bolan ordered as he looked at his prisoner. "Sevan, get up front and lock the doors before they find another way in!"

The normally unflappable mobster actually seemed taken aback by what was happening outside. "All…all right." Slipping past the rear passenger seat, he was able to reach the driver's seat just as the SUV rocked back and forth and Bolan heard footsteps overhead.

"Hurry up, one's on top of us!"

Sevan stabbed at the lock button just as a hand scrabbled at the top rear door and pulled on it. When it didn't budge, the crazed man let out a howl of rage and began slamming his head and hands into the bulletproof glass over and over.

"What is happening here?" Sevan shouted.

"You tell me— These are your people!" Bolan yelled back. "What could have affected all of them like this?"

"I have no idea!" Sevan replied. "For all I know, it was something you did!"

Bolan eyed the crazed mob beating on the windows of the SUV. There were so many of them here now that he couldn't see the street. "I get in, I get you, I get out."

"Yes, and that's gone exactly as you'd planned so far, hasn't it?" Sevan asked.

"I wasn't doing too bad until your crazed mob came after us," Bolan told him. "We'll figure out what happened later. Right now we have to figure out a way out of here."

"Striker, what the hell is going on over there?" Tokaido asked through his earpiece.

"I'm not sure," Bolan replied. "My first instinct is that some kind of mind-altering chemical has been introduced to the population. I can't think of any other explanation for such homicidal mania occurring so quickly in such a concentrated area."

"Are you saying that someone used a bioweapon?"

"Based on the evidence, it's the hypothesis that fits best so far," Bolan replied.

"What can I do to help?" Tokaido asked.

"Right now, inform the bosses. If I'm right, we're going to need to bring in specialists to get a handle on this. Also, get Bear and the two of you go over all the footage from the past twenty-four to forty-eight hours.

Find anything out of the ordinary, or whatever you can about how whatever this is began so we can figure out a way to stop it."

"What about notifying the Armenian police or maybe the European Centre for Disease Prevention and Control?" the hacker asked.

"Good thought that it might be a disease, but we can't contact them until I'm out of here. I don't want to be caught in a quarantine or detained for questioning," Bolan said. "Someone set this chaos in motion, and I want to find whoever's behind it. Any questions?"

"Hey, I'm with you, but if this *is* a disease, shouldn't we be concerned about either or both of you already being infected?"

Tokaido's question brought Bolan up short and he glanced at Sevan, who was staring at the frenzied mob outside the SUV.

"I mean, if you don't get help from somewhere pretty soon, they might get there to find your dead body."

The SUV was starting to rock back and forth from the constant pounding. "I think you've been spending too much time with Bear," Bolan said. "There's always a way out of these situations."

"If you say so," Tokaido replied. "But you know if Bear feels differently about this, which I bet he will, you might be out of luck. At least let me contact Jack. Having someone closer on-site might be able to help with your exit strategy."

"Negative. I want him on the plane, ready to go the second we reach the tarmac," Bolan replied. "If he comes in and gets wounded or taken, then that's one more variable I'd have to deal with, and this mission is already so beyond FUBAR I'm not sure what to classify it as anymore. Radio in when you've got something for me, otherwise I'll call once we're out of the SUV."

"Got it…and good luck, Striker. I'll be in touch the second we find anything. You be sure to call in when you've reached safety, okay?"

"I will. And don't worry—I've been in tougher spots than this. Striker out."

"You have?" Sevan eyed the crowd of sweating, wild-eyed people hammering on the windows. "When?"

Bolan looked around at the sea of manic faces filling every window, scrabbling at the glass with their fingernails and teeth. "A while back, on a beautiful island." Searching himself for usable equipment, he came up with a knife and the tranquilizer gun.

"What is that?" Sevan asked.

"Trank gun," Bolan replied. "What I used to get past your dogs."

"Great! I'll open the door and you start shooting them." The mobster reached for the front passenger door, but Bolan grabbed him before he could pull the handle.

"The only thing it'll do here is guarantee us a quick death," he said. "It's aerosol, not darts. Besides, even if I did try to spray them, there's a good chance we'd inhale some, too, so that won't work. What does this thing have for equipment?"

"How the hell should I know?" Sevan said as he looked around. "I just get chauffeured around in it."

"Great…watch him." Bolan pointed at the old man as he moved to the back of the Range Rover and pulled the rubber protection mat off the cargo area floor. Underneath was a large hatch, which he opened to reveal a collapsible jack and handle and a small plug that, when pulled up, revealed a large nut.

"Hey, I found a flashlight on the door." Sevan held up a sleek black 3-cell flashlight. "Now I have a club at least."

"Great." Bolan was reading a sheet of paper that gave him instructions for releasing the spare tire underneath the SUV. "Well, that's fairly useless."

"Why don't you use your knife to cut up that mat you're holding and the ones in the foot wells to cover yourself in rubber using the zip ties? It might keep them off you long enough to get away."

Bolan blinked and turned to look at the other man, who stared back at him with an equally serious expression. "You weren't kidding about that, were you?"

"Absolutely not. We often had to improvise using whatever we had around here when I was growing up." Sevan shrugged. "It was just a thought."

Bolan picked up the mat again and studied it. "Too thick to really be of any help. It would slow me down more than anything. Good thought, though."

"So, do we open a door and come out swinging?" Sevan asked.

"Not just yet," Bolan replied, although he was currently stuck as to exactly what to do. Over, under, around or through was typically one of the four basic solutions to obstacles in the military, however, each choice here was unfeasible for one or more reasons.

Sevan pointed at his ear. "Why don't you call for help, then? I heard you talking to someone else through that thing."

"Even if I did, they wouldn't be here for hours." Bolan crouched on the wall of the vehicle. "Make yourself comfortable. We're going to settle in and wait them out. Eventually they'll find other, easier prey."

"You hope." Sevan grunted as he settled against the back of the rear passenger seat. "Very kind of you, by the way. They will leave us alone to find and kill other defenseless people."

Bolan scanned the mass of people surrounding the Range Rover: adults, teenagers, children, men in business suits and women in housedresses. "From what I can tell, most of the town has already been infected."

He turned back to Sevan, who was still keeping an eye on the old man. "But not you. Why not?"

"How should I know? Maybe everyone else has that mad-cow disease, but since I was gone, I didn't eat the tainted meat."

"First, mad cow takes decades to reveal itself," Bolan replied. "Second, if that were the case, your guards wouldn't have had it, either, but they were showing the same physical symptoms as these people."

"Yeah…I saw that when I was ordering them to get upstairs and kill you." A rueful grin crossed the Armenian's face. "If you hadn't tried to be such a goddamn cowboy, I already would have escaped, and this would all be your problem."

"Now who's being ruthless?" Bolan asked.

Sevan shrugged. "As you said, it appears that the majority of them are already affected by whatever is going on around here, which makes the choice fairly simple—my survival." He glanced at the raging mob around them. "I don't think either of us is getting out of here alive. You ever see *Day of the Dead*? Or *28 Days Later*? *World War Z*?

With a frown, Bolan shook his head. "My schedule doesn't leave a lot of time for movie watching."

"You should." Sevan nodded at the crowd outside. "They remind me of those things. Voracious. Unstoppable. If I could call my men, they could probably get us out…but like you said, they're probably turned into those things, too. That's how it happens in the movies. First one, then it spreads to everyone else, until there is no one left—"

The sound of breaking glass caught both men's attention, along with the plume of flame that sprouted at the back of the Range Rover, among the struggling, screaming villagers.

CHAPTER FIFTEEN

"What the hell are you doing?"

Gary Alcaster and Siranush had grabbed William Scott and yanked him back inside as the first crazies had barreled at him. They'd slammed the heavy, wooden door closed just in time, locking it as hands beat a frenzied tattoo outside.

"Jesus, that was close." Scott looked sheepish under his companions' glares. "Sorry about that. It won't happen again." He listened to the constant pounding outside. "They just won't stop."

"Windows?" Alcaster asked. "Do you think there are any open windows on this floor?"

"No, it is too cold now," Siranush replied. "Windows are all locked at night. If no one is up to open them, they will still be closed."

"Okay...okay." The screech of tires down the street made the three all look toward the direction of the sound. "What was that?" Alcaster asked.

"Someone's driving something—" William was interrupted by a louder screech this time. "Fast." A loud crash sounded close to the front door, followed by the scrape of metal on stone for several seconds.

"What the hell?" Scott started for the window next to the door, but Alcaster grabbed him.

"No, don't reveal yourself. We don't want to make ourselves a target."

"Don't you want to find out what's happening out there?" Scott asked.

"Yeah, so come on." Alcaster started for the stairs, but was stopped by Siranush.

"Wait! The master key to rooms is behind the desk."

"So what?" Scott asked.

Alcaster's thoughtful expression was similar to hers. "She means for us to lock all of the doors up there from the outside."

The woman nodded, her face pale.

"But we don't know who's turned or who's alive in them," Scott said.

"Right, but we can find out later," Alcaster said. "Look, if anyone took a...turned one with them last night, they're as dead as dead by now. If they are okay, they'll bang on the door, or they can let themselves out with their own key. Either way, they're safer inside for now."

Alcaster ran for the main desk and rummaged around in its drawers until he came up with a ring of keys. "This it?" Siranush nodded, and he hefted his club over his shoulder. "Then let's go lock some doors."

The three crept back up the stairs and began moving down the left hallway, stopping at each door. The men would both hold the door closed, with Siranush turning the key. At three out of the first five, fists began banging on the other side, but there was either silence or frenzied moaning along with it. The other two rooms were dead silent.

"Got to move faster, they might get others riled up," Alcaster said.

"Going as fast as I can."

"Be sure to mark the quiet ones. We'll check them later."

"Uh, I think we'll be able to figure out which ones those are." Scott nodded toward the other doors, shaking in their frames under the rain of blows.

"Yeah. Good thing this place was built nice and solid," Alcaster said as they continued down the hall. They had just locked both doors at the end when they heard a knob rattle near the staircase, followed by a door on the right side swinging open.

Alcaster started forward, but his friend stopped him. Putting a finger to his lips, he held up his free hand. *Wait.* The two men stood together in front of Siranush, holding their clubs at the ready.

A shadow appeared in the hallway, followed by one slender figure, then a shorter, rounder one. They looked around, as if sensing the air, then both heads swiveled toward the three at the other end at the same time.

"Shit, they've spotted us!" Alcaster said.

The two immediately broke into a run, heading straight for the trio.

"Stay where you are, Will." The Canadian stepped forward and raised his club. "I've got left, you take right. Siranush, take out whoever's left if we go down."

Then the two were on them. Cocking his club, Alcaster didn't take his eyes off his target—a balding, portly man in striped pajama bottoms—as he lumbered closer. He felt Scott tense behind him, and heard a small squeak he thought might have come from Siranush, but it might have been the Brit, too.

When they were only a meter away, Alcaster swung from the shoulder as if he was swinging for the fences back home. The heavy end of the makeshift club smacked into the side of the man's head and knocked him right off his feet and into the wall. The med student followed up with an overhead swing and crushed the top of the man's skull, making him stop moving immediately.

Hearing meaty thwacks from behind him, he looked over to see his friend beating in his attacker's brains. "Will...Will? *Will!*"

Finally the Englishman looked up, gore and bits of bone dropping off the end of his club. "You got him, man."

"Oh...right...I did." Scott stared at the twitching body with its bashed-in head at his feet as Alcaster walked over to inspect his handiwork. "Yup, he's a goner, all right. You did great."

He glanced back at Siranush. "You okay?" Then, at her nod, he added, "All right, let's lock down the rest of the hallway."

They completed their sweep of the right side hallway and moved to the other side. This was much easier, since the young men already had three of the rooms and the two crazies had come out another, leaving it empty. That left just four others, all of which they locked without incident, save for loud, fast banging on the doors of two of them.

"Okay, that's that." Alcaster ran for the first room, where the two crazies had come out of. "We can see what's going on in the street from the window."

He ran in—and stopped cold in the doorway. The remains of a woman lay on the bed. Her chest had been torn apart and entrails covered the floor. Blood spatter was everywhere, patterning the walls and ceiling in dark red droplets.

Scott skidded to a stop behind him. "Uh—maybe not this room."

"Yeah…" The two backed out and closed the door, then went to their original room, which was right next to it. Throwing the window covers back, they looked out over the street.

"Look at that!" A large SUV lay on its side, only a few meters from the main door. It was surrounded by villagers, scrabbling against the glass in a vain attempt to get inside. Screams and hoots burst from the crowd, the din drowning out the ones now banging on the hotel room doors.

"There must be someone trapped inside," Alcaster said. "Otherwise they'd go off and find someone else to kill."

"Yeah, but what can we do about it?" Scott asked. "One step out there and we're crazy food."

"We'll have to find some way to get them away from the vehicle…" Alcaster thought for a bit. "I've got an idea. It's a bit risky, but I think it will work. Come on."

He led the other two down toward the bar. No sooner did they hit the bottom step than three men dressed in white came running at them from behind the staircase, where the kitchen was. Alcaster and Scott both took one down, then turned to Siranush, who stood over the spasming body of the busboy who had cleaned their table the previous night. A spike heel jutted from one of his eyes.

"Damn! Nice job!"

She reached down and pulled the heel from the body, then ran to the bar door. "Open it."

Inside, Alcaster found a box and began to fill it with liquor bottles, mainly vodka. With a nod, Siranush ran to help.

"I fail to see how getting smashed is going to help anyone," Scott said.

Alcaster didn't stop packing the box, nor did he look at his friend. "Molotov cocktails. We'll throw them down and the flames should drive them away."

"Oh!" Scott grabbed a box and began selecting more bottles from behind the bar, as well as several packs of matches from an ashtray.

When both boxes were full, they took them back upstairs. "Make wicks from the curtains?" Scott asked.

His friend nodded. "We'll stuff them in and just make sure they stay upright. If we knock one over—especially a lit one—we're screwed."

Siranush had already torn down the faded curtain and was ripping it into long strips. The three worked steadily, all trying to ignore the frenzied howls and thumps coming from outside, and soon had a dozen Molotov cocktails ready.

Alcaster picked up a bottle with a wick hanging from the top. "All right, here's what's gonna happen. You two head down to the front door, both to watch each other's backs as well as help if someone's injured and can't move by themselves. When you're ready, give me a shout and I'll start dropping bottles. I'll try to not get too close to the SUV, but I may have to throw one on top to clear them out. The moment it is clear, or you see someone come out, get them over to the doors and inside. We lock it back up and go from there. Any questions?"

Scott and Siranush exchanged a glance, then both shook their heads.

"Make sure you have the keys, and holler when you're in position," Alcaster said. "Good luck, and be careful."

"Damn right about that," Scott said. "Let's go."

"Close the door on your way out, just in case," Gary said.

The two left, closing the door behind them. Alcaster heard their footsteps recede, then nothing for a minute, until Scott's voice floated up the stairwell. "Okay!"

"Sure hope there weren't any floaters on the main level," the Canadian muttered as he cracked the window open and leaned out. "Jesus Christ…"

There had to be at least thirty people trying to batter their way into the SUV, making it rock back and forth on the street. After placing four bottles on the windowsill, he studied the scene for a few seconds, figuring out where to place the bottles for both maximum effect and to minimize the risk of someone inside getting hurt.

Finally he picked up a matchbook. "Okay, here we go." Striking a match, he held it to the cloth wick of the first bottle until it flamed up. Picking it up, he aimed and tossed it onto the street at the back of the SUV, where a knot of Armenians struggled to claw their way through the back door. The bottle smashed on the ground and the resulting puddle of alcohol immediately bloomed into flames.

It caught the people at the rear of the group first, the fire rapidly spreading to shoes and pants. At first the crazies didn't seem to notice, but when the flames spread to the skin of their legs, first one, then more began feeling the heat. They tried to ignore it, slapping clumsily at it with their hands, but soon the heat grew too intense, sending the crazies scampering away, batting at the flames licking up their bodies.

However that had only cleared a few of them away. But it had worked. Alcaster tossed three more bottles around the vehicle, each one shattering into flames that forced more of the blood-crazed crowd to retreat. But there was still about a dozen left, with half of them on top of the SUV, now ringed in flames. Alcaster noticed the fire at the rear of the SUV was dying down, and a few on the outskirts were already moving closer. He tossed another bottle onto the street to keep them away, then held his breath.

"Okay, now's the time to make your move, guys…" he said as he threw a bottle on top of the SUV. The glass shattered and the entire side was covered in flames, along with the suddenly panicked crazies standing on it.

He watched for any sign of movement from inside the SUV, but nothing seemed to be happening.

"Come on…get out of there…come *on*…"

CHAPTER SIXTEEN

Exhausted and unarmed, Dina Finigian stuck to the shadows as much as she could while sneaking through the village toward the main gate. Once outside the walls, she wouldn't care if she had to walk all the way back to the capital city, she'd find some way to get help. Above all, whatever had happened here, she had to make sure it didn't spread beyond this place.

She'd been on the move for about ten minutes and had already hidden twice from roving groups of villagers searching for more prey. She had spotted the tell-tale signs of each cluster being infected with whatever everyone else had here—sweating, red eyes, jerking movement and shambling walk. Both times she'd been near alleys with garbage cans and had huddled near the refuse, hoping the stink would cover her own scent. It had seemed to work, but she knew she only had to be spotted once for it to be all over.

After the second group had passed, Finigian crept back out and began heading down the street in the general direction of the main gate. Passing what looked like a bakery, now on fire, with broken windows and overturned shelves littering the floor inside, she smelled burning bread.

At the corner, she heard glass shatter behind her. Glancing over her shoulder, she saw a large, balding man wearing a white apron and with a face resembling a demented clown—equal parts sweat and gummy flour—look around from the front of the ruined bakery. Spotting her, he broke into a run, snarling and reaching for her.

Finigian took off around the corner, which was a mistake, as the group she'd just avoided was still in the middle of the road. She skidded to a stop as they all whirled at the same time and began running back toward her.

Scanning left and right, she saw a narrow alley between the ruined bakery and what looked like a house behind it. She bolted for it, thinking it would either come out on the other side, or if she had to fight in the tight space, she could take them on one by one.

A dozen steps in, she encountered a dead end, strewed with more bags of garbage. Approaching footsteps pounded behind Finigian as she searched for a way out. A small window above her head was cracked open, and she leaped for it. Grabbing the sill with her fingers, she pulled herself up with strength fueled by fear.

With her arm on the sill, she shoved the window higher and hoisted herself into a dark room. The policewoman had just gotten her waist over the windowsill when she felt hands grab her leg, fingernails dig into her skin. With a strangled scream, she spread her arms to anchor herself while wriggling and kicking to get free. Sharper pain flared in her calf as Finigian fought, and she tried not to scream as she felt the back of her leg being savaged.

Flailing with all her might, she felt her other foot smack into something and lashed out as hard as she could with it, driving off the maniac trying to pull her out. The grip slackened, but she felt other hands trying to grab her, and pulled herself away from them with one last effort.

Finigian lay on the bare floor, panting with terror. She felt warm blood running down her leg and rolled over to get a look at the injury. A large chunk of flesh had been torn out of the muscle, which was bleeding freely, and hurt like hell.

About to examine her injury, her attention was drawn to a shadow falling across the window. She looked up to see one of the crazies scrabbling to climb up and through.

Scrambling to her feet, she looked around to find herself in a small, dark pantry or laundry room, with shelves of canned goods and various items all around her. Grabbing a white plastic container, she unscrewed the cap and splashed the clear liquid at the woman's face. Screaming as the bleach burned her skin and eyes, she fell back out of sight. Finigian hobbled to the window, slammed it closed and locked it as someone else tried to leap up, but couldn't get a grip on the narrow ledge and fell to the ground again.

Leaning on an ancient washing machine, she grabbed a couple of flour sack dish towels, tied them into a large bandage and wrapped it around the wound. The pain was so great when she knotted it that she thought she was going to pass out. Breathing hard, she rested for a minute, then tested her injured leg. It throbbed with agony every time she put any weight on it, but she could manage a limping walk. She was going to have to, if she wanted to survive this.

Looking around for some other kind of weapon, the policewoman found a plastic container of lye and took it with her; it was dangerous, but was the best thing she could find. With each left step burning like fire, she opened the door and walked into the house.

The stench here made her stomach clench and her bowels tighten. The walls of the living room were so dark that at first she thought the family that had lived here had painted them black, but upon closer inspection, she realized that the thick liquid smeared and spattered on the walls was clotting, drying blood.

She fought to control her gorge while her eyes adjusted to the dimness. The interior was a shambles, with shattered wooden furniture everywhere, including the remnants of a table sticking out of the back wall.

Looking down before she went any farther, she froze as she realized that she had almost stepped on the small, motionless arm of a child, a girl, maybe nine or ten years old, torn almost into two pieces while she'd tried to run away from whoever had slaughtered her family. She was only a step away from the front door, from the outside and survival. Her arms were twisted in the dirt, her legs bent as if she had tried to keep moving even after her face had been savaged and her throat torn out. Blood had coagulated on her shoulders, arms and back, coating her in a thick, red-black layer as it had spurted out to stain her skin, her pajamas and the wooden floor.

Finigian tore her gaze away from the small body, but wherever she looked, she saw more death. The slumped body of a woman lay near the table, her dangling arms and legs still slowly dripping blood. Her head had been attacked so severely that the pale yellow-white of her skull could be seen through the savage bite marks crisscrossing her ruined scalp and face, one ear dangling by a strip of skin, twisting and turning in the thick air.

But the worst was yet to come. In a corner of the room was what looked like a pile of blankets, the middle of them dark and sopping wet. Finigian took a step closer, then another. With a trembling hand, she reached for a corner and pulled it back, letting out a long, shuddering breath as she saw what was underneath.

In front of her was an even smaller child, maybe five years old, still clutching a handmade woven doll to her breast. Her killer had impaled her with a butcher's knife, stabbing her with such force that the blade had driven through the doll, the child's chest and pierced the back of the chair, where a small pool of blood had gathered. Of the father, there seemed to be no sign, giving Finigian a good picture of what had happened.

He went crazy, slaughtered his family, then ran off into the village to kill more people, she thought. *But what would possess him to do such a thing?*

Knowing there was nothing she could do, she made for the doorway leading to the kitchen on unsteady legs. The weak sunlight through the window had never seemed more welcoming.

She took several deep breaths to try clear her nose and lungs, although a part of her knew she would never forget that thick, sickly sweet odor. Hawking up saliva, she spit in the sink, then grabbed a glass and filled it with water, which she raised to her mouth, but stopped just before starting to drink.

Contaminated water? Placing the glass on the counter, she limped to the small refrigerator and opened it to find a container of milk and a small one of watery apple juice, which she drained. Rinsing out the small bottle, she filled it with water from the tap, sealed it tightly and tucked it into her pocket.

Heading for the front door, she stopped when she noticed a row of shoes by the front door. Among them was a pair of sneakers that looked close to her size. She sat on the first step and tried them on. They were a bit large, but still felt like heaven on her battered feet.

As she got up, she heard a noise from the second story. Finigian looked at the narrow staircase along the wall as she strained her ears to try to catch it again. *There*—a board creaked. Someone was walking around up there.

Grabbing a chair leg from the remains of the furniture littering the room, she climbed the stairs, each step making her wounded leg flare with pain. At the top, she wiped away the sweat that had suddenly appeared from her forehead with the back of her hand. There were three doors on the small landing. She listened again, trying to figure out which room the noise had come from. A rustle came from her left and she walked to that door and opened it, club raised high in case she had to defend herself.

This room was relatively untouched, with a child's bed and small dresser illuminated in light coming in from a window on the east wall. A young boy, maybe nine years old, was half under the bed, staring at her with wide eyes like a trapped animal. Unlike the others, he appeared unmarked by the slaughter that had swept through his home.

For a moment the two stared at each other. Finigian lowered her club and held her other palm up, not daring to move. "It's okay," she said in Armenian. "I'm not one of them. I'm not going to hurt you." She smiled in what she hoped was a calming gesture. "Can you tell me what happened here?"

"Dead...all dead... I hid in here...away from the screaming...everyone was screaming so much..." The boy trembled as the words tumbled out. While he talked, Finigian edged closer. At her movement the boy edged farther underneath the bed.

She watched the boy, trying to hold his gaze with her own. "What's your name?"

"A-Aram."

"My name is Dina, Aram, and it's very nice to meet you. I want to take you away from here. Would you like that?"

"No!" He disappeared under the bed. "No, you'll kill me like the others!"

"Aram, listen to me, I'm not like them," she replied. "I want to take you away from all of this, to keep you safe from the people who did this."

"No, he—*he* did it to them!" the boy cried, huge tears welling in his eyes. "I don't know why Father killed them—he wouldn't stop...and they just kept screaming..."

Finigian walked over to him and pulled the screaming boy out from under the bed, enfolding him in her arms as his cries turned to sobs. "It's all right, it's going to be all right. You're safe now." Even as she mouthed the platitudes, she knew his life would never be the same again. She picked him up, the boy's skinny arms wrapping around her neck and clinging tightly to her as she headed for the stairs. "Come on, let's get out of here."

A part of her screamed she was crazy, that bringing this child with her in her injured state was probably going to get them both killed, but she knew she couldn't leave him here. Once she was out of the village, there would be no coming back, not without serious reinforcements.

"Just close your eyes and put your head on my shoulder, Aram," Finigian said as she hobbled down the stairs. "I'm taking you somewhere safe." Just as soon as I find out where that is, she thought.

At the front door she put her ear to it and listened for any movement outside. Hearing none, she took a deep breath and slowly opened the door just enough to peek out.

The street was deserted again, with no sign of any crazies around. Finigian looked up and down the lane carefully, then sniffed the air. Something…burning?

She also heard a commotion—what sounded like dozens of animal howling in the distance. Unfortunately it sounded as though whatever was happening was in the direction she had to go—toward the main gate.

"Are we walking out of here?" Aram mumbled on her shoulder. "We should take the car."

"Car? What car?"

"Our car." He raised his head and pointed at a small key rack on the wall next to the door. Finigian's breath caught when she saw a key fob with a small VW symbol on it. Snatching the key off the hook, she peeked out the front window to see a decade-old Volkswagen hatchback parked on the street outside. For the first time, she felt a ray of hope.

"Yes, Aram, we are definitely taking the car."

CHAPTER SEVENTEEN

At the back of the Range Rover, Bolan and Sevan both watched the fire drive the crazies away.

"Looks like we're not the only normal people left here," Bolan said.

"Yes...where do you think it's coming from?" Sevan asked.

A blur of motion caught Bolan's eye and he looked behind them to see another burst of flame sprout at the front of the SUV, sending a cluster of villagers dancing away as the flames caught them. "I think they're being dropped from the building right next to us."

"The hotel?" Sevan glanced out the driver's window at the two-story building next to them. "Makes sense. Some of the guests must still be okay. At least, okay enough to try and help us."

"Right." Bolan looked around. Most of the villagers were gone, driven away from the pools of guttering fire around three sides of the vehicle. But there were still a half dozen on top, hammering at the glass and shouting their rage at being denied what was inside. Bolan glanced toward the back of the Rover, which was mostly clear. "If they could get these guys—" he pointed up "—off the roof, we'd have a shot at getting inside."

As if the incendiary-thrower had heard his request, another flaming bottle crashed onto the top of the SUV.

The resulting fire ignited the people there, forcing them to run or fall off the side, their screams now of fear and terror as they tried to beat out the flames consuming their clothes and skin.

"Move your ass!" Drawing his dagger, Bolan leaped for the back door and opened it—just as another bottle smashed on the stone street a few meters away. The burst of flame forced a group of approaching Armenians to back away, still staring at Bolan with wide, vacant eyes. Unlike other fuels, the alcohol burned clean, with no smoke, enabling Bolan to see all around him.

"Anyone inside the SUV come to the hotel doors *now!*" a voice shouted in English.

Bolan looked back at Sevan, who was extricating himself from inside. He had just reached the back when a mottled, liver-spotted hand grabbed his ankle. Bolan tried to find an angle where he could help, perhaps throw his knife as a distraction, but the crazed old man was behind the Armenian, almost completely blocked from sight. He began climbing back in to free Sevan, aware that every second of delay meant more of a chance of being trapped in here again.

"Damn it!" Still clutching the flashlight, the mobster brought it down on his attacker's arm, snapping it, and then moved to his head, the anodized aluminum flashlight rising and falling until the end was dripping red.

"Come on, Sevan!" Bolan snapped, still watching for attackers. The other man pulled his foot free, got to the rear of the vehicle and stepped out. "This way!"

Bolan shoved him toward the large wooden door, which was cracked open just enough to show a pale face peeking out from inside. He followed as Sevan ran toward the hotel entrance, but when he was only a few steps away, what felt like a freight train barreled into Bolan and carried him back to slam against the roof of the Range Rover with breath-stealing force.

Dazed for a moment, Bolan regained clarity to find himself dangling several centimeters off the ground, his left arm pinned to his side. A huge—easily 200 kilogram—man buried his face in Bolan's tactical vest and tried to chew through it while trying to squeeze the air from his lungs at the same time.

Bolan had lost his knife in the impact, but he raised his free right hand and boxed the guy's ear hard, once, then again. All it did was make the fat psycho squeal with rage and drop Bolan lower in his arms so he could get at his face with his teeth.

The man's visage was straight out of a nightmare. He was covered with sweat, slicking his hair and collecting wet, grimy dust under his eyes and around his mouth. Mucus flowed from his nose in a constant stream, but he didn't seem to care. His eyes were rheumy, red and constantly watering, adding to the mess on the rest of his face. Opening his cracked lips revealed tobacco-stained teeth and truly foul breath that washed over Bolan's face like a stream of airborne sewage.

Getting his free arm under the stinking man's throat, Bolan levered gnashing teeth away from his face. But with that hand occupied, he had no way to get free. He drummed his heels against the man's legs, trying to crack a kneecap, but to no avail. He even raked a heel down the guy's skin and smashed his foot, but where that made a normal release him, this guy just whiffled mucus and sweat into Bolan's face and redoubled his efforts to chomp on him, squeezing him even harder around the ribs.

Bolan's vision was starting to gray at the edges, and he knew he was on the verge of passing out. He tried to get better leverage to force the man's head back, but his arm slipped, letting the snarling mouth get a little closer. He groped for something, anything, with his left hand, and touched something that felt vaguely gunlike in a side pocket.

The trank gun! With the guy's teeth just inches away, Bolan scrabbled to open the pocket and pull the gun out. He didn't both shooting it, but brought it up as far as he could, almost to within reach of his right hand. The two were just an inch away, and with a final push, Bolan grabbed it in his right hand.

Raising it high, he smashed the bottle of tranquilizer into the man's open mouth, breaking a tooth off as the glass shattered—releasing the remaining drug. The man instinctively bit down, his teeth crunching on glass. The tranquilizer began taking effect almost immediately, making him drop Bolan, who stumbled for the door as he pulled air into his lungs with a wheeze.

"Come on…almost there…!" Bolan heard glass shatter and another whoosh nearby as an alcohol-fueled blaze lit the street again. Reaching the door, he was pulled inside and it slammed shut behind him. A second later, fists began pounding on the wood—a lot of fists.

Hands on his knees, Bolan took a moment to get his wind back. A shout and a blur of motion caught his eye and he turned in time to see Sevan aiming a kick at his chest. Bolan trapped his foot and pushed him backward to fall onto the floor. "Knock it…the hell…off!"

The mobster glared at him from the floor. "You just don't know when to die, do you, American?"

Bolan shook his head wearily. "Never have." He

glanced up at his saviors to see a whip-thin man in his early twenties, with shirt, messy brown hair and round glasses, holding what looked like a stained leg of a chair ready to brain either of them. "If he does that again, clobber him, will you?"

"Has either of you been bitten by them? Is either of you infected? Feeling sweaty or have red eyes?" the young man wearing the glasses asked.

"Not that I know of," Bolan replied.

"You're—you're American," the young man said.

"Yes. Matt Cooper, Justice Department," Bolan replied. His credentials were completely fabricated, but given the circumstances, it was unlikely that anyone here was going to bother to ask him for identification.

"What are you doing here?" the pretty young woman in a short skirt and blouse next to him asked.

"He's kidnapping me—" Sevan began.

"Shut up," Bolan said to him. "That's technically classified, but since you've already seen me and him—" Bolan waved at the Armenian "—I'm extraditing him."

"Against his will?" the man asked.

"You got that right, boy," Sevan said.

"He's the head of a large criminal syndicate, with outstanding warrants on him in several countries for crimes ranging from drug smuggling to murder." Bolan took a deep breath. "As you might imagine, he'd prefer to not go quietly. But enough about my problem. Who are you two and what are you doing here?"

"I'm William Scott and this is Siranush…" The man glanced at the woman, who shrugged.

"If it matters, my name is Siranush Tatilian."

Scott pointed at the ceiling. "My other friend—the one upstairs with the bottles—is Gary Alcaster. We came here with a third friend, Josh Tyrell, but he's dead. We're all medical students from London."

"Students backpacking across Europe?" Bolan raised his eyebrows. "I didn't think you guys went in for that sort of thing anymore."

"It was a special trip…" Scott trailed off and Bolan could almost see the thought in the young man's mind… *That got my friend killed.*

"Look, you guys had no way of knowing what you stumbled into here—" he began.

"Which was?" Scott asked.

"Right now, I don't exactly know," Bolan replied. "But my primary mission is to get out of here and inform some people who can find out and stop this— hopefully without too much more bloodshed. Now, I've got a small jet waiting at a private airstrip about thirty kilometers away that can take all of us out of here. Do any of you have a car?"

Scott nodded. "It's parked out back. It'll be a tight squeeze, but we'll all fit."

Bolan nodded. "Good. Let's grab your friend and get the hell out of here."

"Best damn idea I've heard all day," Scott said. "Come on, this way."

"Hang on." Bolan walked over to Sevan, who was still sitting on the floor. "Get up and put your hands behind your back."

With a groan, the mobster did as he was told. "Not again."

"Well, I wouldn't have to, except you tried to kick me in the face."

"I was aiming for your chest," Sevan replied. "Then

I would have left and either gotten another car to escape or holed up to wait all this craziness out."

"No chance of that now," Bolan said as he held the man's shoulder tightly. "Everything else may have gone to hell here, but I've gone through way too much to have you walk now. You're stuck with me." He nodded at Scott. "Go get your friend while I let my people know what's going on. Make sure he has the keys."

He pushed Sevan down into a chair. "Take a load off."

Scott took off up the stairs while Bolan activated his earpiece. "Base, this is Striker."

"This is Base," Kurtzman's voice said into his ear. "Akira filled me in on what's happening over there—sort of. Striker, what have you gotten yourself into?"

"Sure wish I knew, Bear," Bolan replied. "I've seen something like this before. The entire village has been affected by an unknown pathogen that causes decreased mental capacity and homicidal dementia. It's recognizable by increased sweating, red-rimmed eyes—and a strong urge to attack anyone who is not already a carrier."

"You're serious about this?"

"Yeah, Bear, I am. Whatever this is, it's the real deal. The transmission vector is unknown at this time, although I suspect it's mainly by bodily fluids. I don't think it's airborne, otherwise we'd all be snarling idiots by now."

"Right. Look, we need to bring in the European Centre for Disease Prevention and Control on this."

"Agreed. You might as well contact them now, since we're leaving soon and heading up there for a consult. Have the jet ready to go the second I arrive, heading for wherever their headquarters is."

"Stockholm, Sweden," Kurtzman replied.

"Inform them that we'll need quarantine facilities for observation for the next twenty-four to forty-eight hours. I'm bringing the package, plus three. They're civilians and I can't leave them here."

"Got it." Bolan heard Kurtzman's fingers fly over his keyboard. "You know I have to notify Hal about this, too."

"Of course, and have him kick it up the chain to the White House, as well as the CDC. I want everyone with any intel on this in the loop. There's a strong chance this is a man-made pathogen, and I want to know anything and everything they might know about it. I'm about to head out with the survivors, so I'll be signing off."

"Right. One more thing, although this kind of pales in relation—you said you reacquired the package?"

Bolan dropped a heavy hand on Sevan's shoulder. "Absolutely."

"Thank God for small favors," Kurtzman replied. "Jack replied to say he's going through preflight and will have the engines hot by the time you arrive."

"Good, Striker out." Bolan grabbed Sevan and hoisted him to his feet as Scott trotted down the stairs with another young man in tow, carrying a clinking backpack and a large chair leg similar to Scott's.

"Gary, this is Matt and Alexsandr. Matt and Alexsandr, this is Gary Alcaster," Scott said. "We all set?"

"What's in the bag?" Bolan asked.

"The rest of my bottles," Alcaster replied. "It worked pretty well so far."

"No argument from me," Bolan replied. "And thanks for the diversion outside. That was quick thinking. Does anyone know if there are any better weapons around here?"

"Narek kept a small revolver in the cash register in the bar," Siranush said.

"Show me," Bolan said to her. He nodded at the two young men, then at Sevan. "Keep an eye on him."

"Why?" he heard Alcaster ask as he followed the young woman into the bar. Bolan went behind it and sprung the cash drawer, finding a small revolver, just as she had said. He dropped out the cylinder and spun it. "Thirty-two caliber, loaded." Snapping the cylinder up into the gun, he checked the rest of the small compartment in the drawer. "No more bullets. Well, it'll have to do. Come on."

On the way back, Bolan grabbed an empty cardboard liquor box.

The two walked into the lobby to find Alcaster and Scott both staring at Sevan, who had leaned back in his chair as comfortably as he could. "Is this guy really a wanted criminal?" Alcaster asked.

Bolan nodded.

"And he's coming with us?"

The soldier nodded again as he handed the box to Alcaster. "Put the bottles in there—better access and less chance of breaking them."

He crossed to Sevan, grabbed his shirt collar and pulled him upright. "Soon as Alcaster's ready, we're leaving."

"We're going out the back way to the parking lot," Scott said, pointing behind the staircase.

"Siranush, was it?" Bolan asked. "Please carry the box, if you don't mind." The young woman took it in her arms without a word.

With the two men and their chair legs in the lead, the group walked around the staircase to the double doors leading to the kitchen. Another body was sprawled in the doorway between the two rooms, a worker in kitchen whites. His mouth and forehead were both bloody and a heavy, cast-iron frying pan lay on the floor next to him.

"This must have been the one who bit Lusine," Alcaster said. "At least she took him out."

Bolan leaned down to check his pulse. "Yeah, dead. Let's clear the kitchen, then stay in there for a moment. I've got some packing to do before we leave."

Pistol steady in both hands, he nodded at Alcaster. "Push the door open, but stay to one side."

The young man did so and Bolan entered, checking everywhere for movement. The kitchen was still, with various spices and ingredients out next to stainless-steel bowls that were going to be used to begin that day's menu. A trail of blood led to the open freezer, but there was no body inside.

"Clear. Everyone inside," Bolan said as he dragged the body into the kitchen. Shoving the pistol into his belt, he grabbed a meat cleaver and several plastic bags from the counter, then went back to the body. "Everyone look for a small cooler or insulated bag, like something that keeps a pizza hot."

"Why—" Scott began to ask as Bolan raised the cleaver. The resounding thunk as he cut off the body's hand answered the question.

"What the hell are you doing?" Scott asked.

"I'm sorry for having to do this, but I need samples from an infected person for analysis," Bolan replied as he double-bagged the hand, making sure each seal was tight. "Unless, that is, one of you wants to volunteer to be infected."

"No!" the three survivors said as one.

"That's what I thought." Bolan moved to the head of the body and tipped it up, pushing against the rigor mortis that was setting in. "You may want to stand back for this."

Scott paled as he realized what was about to happen. "Uh, yeah…"

"Is there no limit to your depravity?" Sevan muttered.

"Tell that to whoever unleashed this on your people," Bolan replied. "They're the real villains here. I'm just trying to stop it before it goes any further."

"Here." Siranush held out a large insulated bag. "Will this work?"

"Perfect. Turn away from this, young lady."

Bolan raised the cleaver again and brought it down with all the strength he had "As grim as this is, it's much easier than trying to capture a live one."

"Good thing I already threw up earlier," Scott said, looking slightly green.

Double-bagging the head, as well, Bolan nodded at an industrial freezer. "See how much ice is in there."

Alcaster opened it and hauled out a ten-pound bag. Bolan nodded as he put the hand and the head into the insulated bag. "Fill the rest with ice, Gary." Once that was done, he sealed it and regarded his handiwork critically. "Maybe not lab-approved, but it should do the job. Thanks for the help, everyone. Now let's move out."

At the back door he checked to make sure the parking lot was empty. It appeared to be. "Which one is yours?"

"The brown Peugeot, at the end." Alcaster pointed to the small, four-door car the farthest from the door.

"Figures," Bolan replied. "All right, here's how it

works. Gary, you and I are going out there to get the car. Everyone else watch for any kind of movement from the road. We come back, everyone piles in and we're out of here. Got it?"

After everyone nodded, he tapped the young man's shoulder. "Let's go."

The two eased out into the small parking lot and headed for the car, reaching it without incident. The paved yard was eerily silent compared to the rest of the village, but Bolan attributed that to there simply not being any viable prey here.

At the car Alcaster unlocked all the doors and looked at the bigger man. "You want to drive?"

"Go ahead," Bolan said as he got into the passenger seat. "I'll handle crowd control."

"Right." The med student got in and buckled up, then started the car. Pulling out, he drove to the door and stopped. The second he did, the other three came out and piled into the backseat.

"All right, let's go," Bolan said. "Turn right at the road. We don't want to try to drive past the crowd out front."

Knuckles white on the steering wheel, Alcaster nodded as he turned onto the street and accelerated away from the hotel and toward an intersection.

"Well, the good news is there shouldn't be any other cars—"

Scott's words were cut off by a dingy red blur that rocketed out of nowhere from their left and smashed into the car.

CHAPTER EIGHTEEN

Dr. Richter was finishing a conference with his top researchers on yet another instance of bad news with the virus.

"So, the instances of homicidal mania can be held to the two to three percent, we believe?" he asked.

Nods all around confirmed that. "Also, the tighter we can tailor the virus to certain genetic codes, the less chance it will have of occurring in the field," Dr. Estvaan said.

"Great. We can limit the chances of a target going into a berserk rage, but not eliminate it." Even as Richter said that, a part of him got the impression that Stengrave might not care all that much. After all, given their discussion at the board meeting, apparently he didn't really care how the targets eliminated themselves, as long as they did so.

"We've known from the start that working with such a combination of factors from the two viruses would lead to trade-offs in certain aspects of how it operated in a real world environment," Ronald Ricards, his chief oncologist, said. "Given the communication vectors we were given, that percentage is, quite frankly, incredible."

Richter nodded. "Right, right. I'm not spreading blame or saying it's an issue. You've all done superlative work in a—" he spread his hands to encompass the room, and moreover, the laboratory they had all been working in for the past year "—less than optimum conditions."

His phone vibrated in his pocket and he rose from the table. "All right, good work everyone, that's all for now. Just keep synthesizing more batches of the virus using the latest genetic code we've received as quickly as possible. Our employer could want an up-to-the-minute report of our progress at any time, and I would like to be able to assure him that we are still ahead of our estimated schedule."

Walking into the hallway, he pulled out the phone and saw that Clay had sent him a video file with a brief note.

Subjects in test zone trying to leave. Thought you'd like to know.

Richter brought up the file and watched the two men escape the SUV, aided by the incendiary devices thrown by an unseen person from the adjacent building. "Clever, indeed." Then the picture cut to a shot down a side street showing a car pulling out of what had to have been a parking lot behind the building. "That cannot be allowed." He speed-dialed a number, waiting for the man on the other end to pick up.

"Yes?" Reginald Firke said.

"You are still in position?"

"Of course. I assume that you're not calling because you don't have anything better to do. What's up?"

"There is a small group, at least two to four people, trying to leave the village. That must not be allowed to happen."

There was a brief pause as the news sank in. "Are you authorizing full contingency?"

"Yes, I think that would be best. Also, procure me a complete full-body sample for research. Alive would be ideal, but dead would work just as well."

"Judging by what we've been hearing from inside recently, you're gonna get a body."

"I am sure that Mr. Stengrave would compensate you for the trouble of acquiring a live specimen."

Firke paused and Richter figured he was probably doing cost versus potential profit calculations. "He probably would at that. I'll see what I can do."

That wasn't the answer Richter was prepared for and he found himself surprisingly gratified. "Thank you. Be sure to notify me when it's done."

"Don't worry about that. By the time we're finished, there'll be nothing but ashes."

"Excellent." Richter hung up, then texted his boss.

Contingency plan activated. Test site will be cleansed in the next 2 hours.

FIRKE LOOKED AT his men, who had been busy preparing for his next words over the past twenty-four hours. "All right gentlemen, time to clean up the mess we made. You all have your assignments, so let's get to it."

With that, the six men split into three two-man groups. Two teams got into the cab of a panel truck and began driving toward the walled village, while Firke and his sniper got into the SUV and headed toward the gate to set up a position to take out anyone trying to leave.

Over the next half hour Firke received regular radio

contact from his men in the truck, who had parked outside the walls and climbed into the guard posts. From there they used the wall perimeter to set improvised incendiary napalm devices near as many flammable buildings as they could. Once they were done, they would take up positions on each side and the back of the wall, and watch for anyone trying to leave the village, taking whatever steps necessary to ensure that they did not do so. As they worked, they reported smelling something already burning from somewhere inside, but couldn't see any smoke. Firke frowned at this news—it would have been convenient if the town had burned itself down without any help from them, but needs must and all that, he knew.

Meanwhile, Firke and his sniper were set up on a small hill three hundred meters from the gate that gave them a perfect view of the half kilometer of road leading up to it. They were guaranteed to be able to take out anyone trying to leave. It was the perfect setup—either the uninfected survivors would be burned to death in the coming inferno, suffocated by the smoke, or they would die the moment they tried to leave through the gate.

Firke's thin lips curled up in a mirthless smile as he settled in behind the scope of his custom 7.62 mm Les Baer Monolith sniper rifle. Everything was in place. It was only a matter of which version death would claim any unlucky bastards still alive inside....

THE IMPACT SPUN the Peugeot and sent it spinning toward another building. Alcaster fought for control, twisting the wheel as he tried to avoid hitting anything else. In the back Scott and Siranush both screamed, while Sevan braced himself for another impact.

As quickly as it had started, the car came to a halt with a bang, smacking into a telephone pole hard enough to activate the air bags, which quickly deflated while the engine sputtered and died.

Jolted hard against his seat belt, Bolan got his bearings first and made sure he was still holding the revolver. Gripping it a bit more tightly, he glanced around. "Is everyone okay?"

Nods came from everyone. "How're the bottles, Siranush?"

She opened the flap of the box on her lap and nodded again. "None broken."

"Can you start it?" he asked Alcaster.

He turned the key, but didn't even get a click from the engine. He tried twice more, but with the same result. "Nope. We made it—what?—a whole block."

"Yeah." Bolan had spotted the other car, which had come to a stop behind them, its grille and fender crumpled, but looking like it might still be drivable. "I'm going to check on the other car. Gary, William, you guys get out and watch for villagers. At best, we probably only have a couple minutes before they come investigate. Keep those bottles handy."

"Right." Scott grabbed two from Siranush and handed one to his friend, who had opened his door with a screech of metal and stood on the car seat so he could look farther down the street.

Bolan got out and cautiously approached the small red hatchback, watchful for any crazed villagers who might have been attracted to the crash. Steam hissed from its crumpled hood, making him reevaluate his previous idea about using it to escape. A woman was slumped over the steering wheel, long, black hair covering her face. A young boy sat in the passenger seat next to her, staring at Bolan with wide eyes and his mouth hanging open. Putting a finger to his lips, Bolan then opened the driver's door and felt for a pulse on the woman's neck.

"No!" With a start, she jerked back in her head, arms flailing to bat his hand away. "Get off me!"

Bolan reached in to restrain her, pushing her back into the seat with his forearm and clamping a hand over her mouth. "Quiet! I'm not going to hurt you! Shut up!"

His words finally pierced her fog of terror and she looked up at him with familiar blue eyes. Bolan stared back in disbelief. "You're the woman in Sevan's bedroom!" He put the gun up to her head. "Where are you going?"

She didn't answer, but her gaze flicked down at his hand still over her mouth. "When I release you, talk quietly, okay?"

She nodded and he did so. "Something's gone wrong in the town and I'm taking this boy out of here—or I was, until I hit you people. Who are you, and why is an American trying to kill Sevan?"

"Not kill. I'm taking him on behalf of the American and European governments—or I was, until all this happened. You, however, don't exactly look—or fight—like a prostitute. Who are you really?"

"Dina Finigian, Armenian police. I was on the inside, working undercover, which you blew wide open, thank you very much."

"The Department of Justice and the FBI had no intel on anyone inside Sevan's organization," Bolan replied.

"That's because it was on a need-to-know-basis, and we felt you Americans didn't need to know," she retorted. "After all, you certainly haven't given much attention to other crimes in our country or the surrounding region."

"That you know of," Bolan countered. He was pretty familiar with this region of the world, having battled organized crime and terrorists from this area more than once. "Besides, if you don't tell other police forces, they can't really be blamed for not knowing, now, can they? Look, there'll be plenty of blame to pass around later. Right now we all need to get out of here. Does your car run?"

She turned the key and it started, but when she shifted it into gear, the car didn't move. "Something's wrong with the transmission, it's going nowhere."

"This day is just getting better and better," Bolan said. "Are you hurt?"

"I was bitten by one of those—things—earlier today, but I'm okay so far. I can walk. Aram!" She turned to the boy, who had watched the whole exchange without saying a word, and checked him over. "He's fine. We need to find transportation and get out of the village as soon as possible."

"Yeah, not to mention the other four in my car." Bolan nodded at the Peugeot and heard a low whistle from it. "Come on, let's get under cover until we can figure out a plan. Let me grab him—" He reached for Aram, who shrank away from his hands.

"No, I'll take him." Gathering the boy in her arms, she pulled him out of the car and hobbled over with Bolan to the wrecked Peugeot, where the other four were huddled behind it.

"What's happening?" Bolan whispered as he rejoined them.

"Couple of crazies at the far end of the street," Alcaster whispered back. "I don't think they've seen us yet."

A low scream sounded, rising to a high screech. "On second thought…" Scott began.

"Fire, now!" Bolan ordered.

The two students lit their Molotov cocktails and heaved them over the car. The bottles burst in a whoosh of flames.

"Everyone else, follow us!" As he said this, Bolan scanned around for other villagers and, sure enough, saw a couple round the corner of the hotel, followed by several more. As soon as they saw the group of people down the street, they all broke into a run.

"Gary, a bottle over here!" Bolan said. Alcaster lit another one and hurled it as hard as he could down the street. The flaming missile exploded only a few steps from the vanguard of the pack, and he couldn't slow down or change course in time to not run through it. Fire caught at his boots, making him run faster, which only fanned the flames on his body, until he was busy slapping out the conflagration even as he moved forward. Several people behind him were able to avoid the patch of flames and kept running relentlessly toward them.

Bolan and the others were already moving by this point, away from both the hotel and the direction Dina Finigian had come from. "Head for the wall!" Bolan shouted, pausing just long enough to grab Sevan by his shirt collar and haul him forward. "We might have to climb over and make our way on foot."

"I don't advise that as an escape route, Striker," Kurtzman said in his ear. "In fact, I suggest that you do not approach the walls under any circumstances."

"Why not? Have they made it outside?" Bolan asked.

"No, but we've got a visual on armed teams that have been setting what appear to be timed incendiary devices along buildings," the Stony Man computer genius replied. "It looks like they're going to burn the entire place to the ground. No doubt they will repel anyone trying to leave with lethal force."

"Damn!" Bolan swore. "That must be the team that introduced the pathogen in the first place. Track them and make sure you don't lose them! I need to know everything about them we can."

"Already on it," Kurtzman said. "They won't be able to fart without us knowing what they had for lunch. What are you going to do?"

"Get wheels, first and foremost." Bolan veered left at the first intersection they came to, heading deeper into the village.

"Where are you going?" Siranush asked. "The nearest wall is that way." She pointed in the direction they had been heading.

"Change of plans." Still trotting along, Bolan informed them of what he'd just heard.

"But that—that's monstrous!" Finigian exclaimed. "Surely there are other people here who may be uninfected! They'll need help, too!"

"You're right, but how do you propose evacuating them?" Bolan asked. "Between the psychotic villagers roaming the streets and the armed men on the walls, we can't help them, not without risking ourselves. And we have to make it out of here to tell people what we've seen. A lot of these houses are made of stone. Hopefully anyone who's taken shelter is in one of those. They should be safe enough from the fire to survive."

"That's just as heartless—" Finigian began.

"That's what I've been trying to tell all of you," Sevan said.

"But he's right." The policewoman shook her head, as if she couldn't believe what she had just said. "Everyone I've seen except for you people has been affected by whatever is here. Searching for others will be dangerous, and most likely fruitless. We need to go *now*."

"We're going to need a sturdy vehicle to get out of here…" Bolan sniffed the air. "What is that smell?"

Finigian lifted her nose into the air, as well. "We must be near the waste collection depot. USAID distributed garbage trucks across Armenia in 2008. This village probably received one."

"That could work," Bolan said. "Let's find it."

They followed their noses to where the smell was coming from—a squat, cinder-block building that took up half a village block, with the other half encircled by a chain-link fence. On the inside was what Bolan was looking for: a dirty, dingy but relatively new garbage truck, painted red and blue. And even better, it still had a large, dirty green metal bin on the front hoist.

"This should take us where we need to go," Bolan said. "All right, Gary, William, let's get inside, get that thing started and get the hell out of here! The back should provide enough protection for everyone in case we're shot at."

He handed Finigian the pistol. "Since you're carrying the boy, please watch Sevan until we get back out here, okay?"

Setting the child down, she took the revolver and aimed it at the mobster, who stared at her in disbelief. "You're seriously leaving her in charge of me?"

Bolan had already begun climbing the fence. He glanced back at them. "Yeah. She'll just kneecap you if you try to run, and we'll leave you for the villagers."

"It would be my pleasure," Finigian said, her grip on the pistol rock-steady.

Sevan's face paled and he looked around nervously. "Well, hurry up and get the truck out here already!"

By the time he was finished speaking, Bolan had hit the top, swung over and landed on the ground inside the fence. Alcaster and Scott were right behind him, leaving Sevan, Siranush, Finigian and Aram still outside.

"Normally, I'd be concerned about leaving this still working for the village after we're done—" Bolan grabbed a piece of thick steel rod from the ground as he climbed up on the step to the driver's door and tried it, only to find it locked "But since that probably won't be an issue…" Holding the rod so a couple inches jutted from the bottom of his hand, he drove it into the safety window. It starred under the first blow and shattered on the second.

Bolan swept the glass pebbles off the seat and checked the glove compartment and visor for a key, finding it as it fell into his lap. He unlocked the passenger door and started the vehicle as the two men began to climb in. "No, you guys are going into the back."

"Why?" Scott asked.

"Because the men on the wall are probably going to be shooting at the cab, and I don't want any of you getting hit." Bolan maneuvered the rear door controls, and listened as the back door began rising. "Get in there so you can help the others when we pick them up. Signal me on the wall when you're both inside."

The two men headed to the back of the truck and

once Bolan heard the signal, he put the truck in gear and headed straight for the gate, managing to get it up to about thirty kilometers per hour before hitting the wooden-slatted, metal-framed gate.

Even going that slow, it was no contest. The heavy sanitation vehicle smashed the gate wide open and sent it spinning off its hinges. Bolan pulled to a stop outside and watched in the side-view mirror as the others climbed into the back. He heard two thumps on the back wall, and was about to pull out when the passenger door opened.

Bolan turned, ready to repel boarders, but stopped when he saw Finigian climb in. "You know the cab is going to attract the most fire, right?" Behind her, he saw the first of the crazies appear at the end of the street and quickly got the truck moving again.

"I know. That's why I'm here!" she replied. "You can't drive and shoot effectively at the same time."

Bolan locked the doors again. "That popgun doesn't have the range to reach anyone!"

"Maybe not, but they won't know that—gunfire is gunfire. If this makes them duck their heads for even a few seconds, it'll be worth it!"

"Okay. Hang on and keep your head down," Bolan said as he downshifted.

"Turn right at the next intersection," Finigian said. "There's a side street you can take that's flanked by buildings. Follow it to the end and you'll practically be right in front of the gate."

"Great," Bolan replied as he cranked the wheel. "Hopefully we'll have enough power to smash through the gate without breaking anything vital."

"I'd think that—" the policewoman pointed at the

metal bin, which blocked the top half of the windshield "—should do the job."

"We'll find out soon enough." Bolan shifted into fourth gear and put the gas pedal down, feeling the truck lumber forward on the stone streets toward freedom.

CHAPTER NINETEEN

"They're heading for you right now."

Firke spoke into his headset while still sighting on the main gate, which was constructed of thick wood banded with metal strips at the top and bottom. The sound of automatic weapons fire could be heard from behind the walls. "Can you stop them before they leave the city?"

"Negative! They're...a—age truck!" The explosives team leader, a normally unflappable German, sounded as upset as Firke had ever heard him.

Firke tapped his earpiece even as he heard the growl of a diesel engine growing louder in the distance. "Say again? Your last transmission was garb—"

A large truck with a big green bin in front of the cab burst through the gate with a deafening crash, sending wooden splinters and entire boards flying everywhere. The driver punched the gas, making the heavy truck lurch forward in a cloud of black exhaust.

"Never mind, we have acquired the target. Leader out." Firke settled his eye back behind the scope and his reticule on the front tire and fired. The 7.62 mm jacketed hollowpoint round exploded the tire in a cloud of rubber shards. The truck swerved to one side, but the driver wrestled it back into the middle of the road and kept going.

"Target the rear tires, I'm taking the driver," Firke said, adjusting his sights to the driver's window. He could just make out a shadowy form trying to sit as far back as he or she could in the cab, but it wouldn't make any difference. The Winchester rounds he was using would have enough power to punch right through the cab wall and into them.

"You're not getting away that easily, I'm afraid," he muttered as he squeezed the trigger.

"RIGHT! A LITTLE MORE right! Ten degrees more! Straighten out! Okay, punch it—"

Hearing a *ponk!* above him, Bolan looked up to see a hole in the cab fuselage right where his head would have been if he'd been sitting upright.

"Left five degrees! Hold it!" Finigian shouted from her perch on the outside of the passenger side of the cab, holding on to the side mirror as they barreled down the road. "Keep it straight!" She was guiding him on the road by sight, since Bolan couldn't see anything where he was, crammed in the leg compartment of the driver's seat.

Warned by Kurtzman about the two-man sniper team positioned outside the main gate, he and Finigian had come up with this improvised solution. They had to go a little over a kilometer before they'd reach the cover of the foothills. Bolan was hoping the marksman wouldn't turn his attention to the engine, or their escape plan would come to an abrupt end.

A second tire blew on the driver's side and Bolan wrestled with the wheel as the truck slewed again. It was already running rough from the loss of the front tire and another one gone didn't help very much. Just then another bullet pierced the cab, this one flying astray upon impact and shattering the glass of the half-lowered passenger window.

"You okay?" he shouted at Finigian.

"I've been better," she shouted back. "Right ten degrees! You're coming up to a left-hand turn! Start turning…now!"

Bolan turned the steering wheel as directed, leaning with the truck as it lumbered into the turn. He figured they were more than halfway to the hills and if their luck held out a little longer, they just might make it.

"Ditch, ditch, ditch—right fifteen degrees!" Finigian shouted at him. Bolan corrected, just enough to feel the tires on the passenger's side grab the dirt road again.

"Hills coming up!" Even as the policewoman said that, Bolan heard another *ponk!* but didn't see a new hole appear in the cab. It was followed by another one and again he heard the impact, but didn't see any damage. This time, however, the truck lurched and slowed a bit. "Damn…" he said as he realized the engine wasn't running as smoothly as before.

"We made it!" Finigian opened her door and gracefully swung inside. "I can't believe it! Out of the village and into the hills!" She glanced at him with a wide smile. "You can come up now, you know."

Bolan unfolded himself and emerged from his hiding place, feeling the distant tingle of blood returning to his legs and feet. "We're not out of trouble yet. Hear that?" He paused while Dina listened to the grumbling engine.

"Sounds rougher now," she said.

"Yeah, the engine's been hit. I don't know how much

farther it's going to go." As if hearing him, a loud bang sounded from the somewhere under the hood and the garbage truck began decelerating even more. Bolan pumped the gas, but to no avail—the truck began slowing just before the crest of a shallow hill where the road descended for a good half kilometer.

"Take the wheel!" Bolan said as he punched the back hatch open and opened the driver's door.

"Where are you going?"

"To push it over the top." By now the truck was down to a crawl and Bolan was able to step down and run to the back, where the rest of the group was clustered near the open hatch.

"What's going on?" Alcaster asked.

"We're all dead if you don't get out and push," Bolan snapped as he grabbed the rear bumper and shoved with all his strength. Alcaster and Scott jumped out and lent their strength to the effort. Even Siranush hopped down and heaved at the slowly stopping truck.

"Just a few…more…meters…" Bolan grunted as the front of the truck reached the top of the hill. It hesitated, as if gathering strength, then started slowly rolling forward again, gathering speed on the noticeably downward slope.

"Everyone back inside!" Bolan helped Siranush into the rear compartment as Alcaster and Scott scrambled back up and in. The soldier pointed at Sevan. "Make sure he doesn't go anywhere!"

"Don't worry, he won't!" Alcaster replied, but Bolan was already sprinting forward to the cab again.

Leaping onto the step, he pulled himself up and into the driver's side. "Move over!"

"Gladly!" Finigian said as she scooted out of the way. "How far do you think we'll get?"

"Maybe a half to three-quarters of a kilometer, if the blown tires don't slow us down too much," Bolan replied. "But the airfield's still about twenty-five klicks away. If we don't find some other transportation—or stop them from coming after us—we're as good as dead."

"We could always try going overland, as the crow flies," the policewoman suggested.

"If we can maintain enough of a head start to truly lose, them, I'd risk it, but if they spot us on foot, we're sunk." Bolan could already feel the truck slowing as they reached the bottom of the hill, and cursed under his breath. "Whatever we're going to do, we've got maybe a minute to figure it out. After that, we're sitting ducks."

"I DON'T CARE what you think!" Firke said into his headset. "My orders stand—capture at least one alive before you leave the village." He cut off his subordinate's protest. "Well, if you had stopped them, then another team would be getting this assignment, but you didn't. For God's sake, it can't be *that* hard. I said alive, not uninjured. Just find one near the truck, shoot it in the knee, club it over the head, tie its hands and feet, and toss it in the back."

He interrupted himself to point ahead. "They should be just around this bend," he said to his driver, who nodded. Firke turned his attention back to his conversation while pulling the charging lever back on a HK MP-7 A-1. "I don't care what you have to do, just get it done, or I'll hand you over to the scientists for research!"

He cut the channel just as they rounded the turn and saw the garbage truck in the middle of the road. Firke's driver pulled to a stop about ten meters away. The back door was up and they could smell the stench of rotten garbage. There were no signs of life in or around the battered vehicle.

"We'll both take it on my mark, DiMera." Firke made sure his bulletproof vest was secure, then nodded at his partner. "You take the left side, I'll take the right. Go right for the cab. And don't forget your keys. Now!"

He caught DiMera's eye roll, but didn't care as he got out and ran toward the cab, staying low and looking around for anyone to try to come at him. The only sound he heard was the crunch of his combat boots on the dirt road and his rapid breathing.

At the side of the cab he put his back to the truck for a moment, ready to shoot anyone who stuck his or her head or a gun out. When there was no movement, he reached up, grabbed the door and opened it. When no gunfire or movement came from inside, he leaped up on the step and covered the interior.

There was no one inside. A moment later the passenger door opened and Firke's partner appeared framed in the entrance, his gun covering his side of the cab. "Clear," he said.

"Clear," Firke answered just as he heard a gunshot from behind him and felt an impact on the back of his vest. Immediately he dropped to the ground, rolled onto his stomach and aimed at where the shot had come from, letting off three 3-round bursts. He could hear his other gunner firing from the cab itself.

"Get out of there!" Firke shouted as he rolled away

from his original position and stopped moving and firing, waiting to see if the gunman would shoot again. A moment later he heard a crack of gunfire again, a bit farther away this time, and sent a dozen bullets toward where he thought the shot had come from.

"What the hell are they doing?" DiMera asked from underneath the truck.

It was a good question, one that was answered a moment later when Firke heard breaking glass, followed by a whoosh of flame. He turned in time to see another flaming bottle crash against the windshield of his SUV, enveloping the vehicle's front in flames.

"He's on top of the goddamn truck!" Firke shouted. "Cut him off on the other side!" He was already up and climbing, not caring if he got shot again. Scrambling onto the roof of the cab, he leaped on top of the garbage truck and found—no one.

"You got him?" Firke shouted down.

"No!"

Firke ran over to the side and saw DiMera looking up at him with a shrug. Pointing to the rear, Firke stepped as quietly as he could over to the top, stuck his gun over the side and sprayed the rest of his magazine inside the interior. Slugs pinged and whined off the thick metal. He reloaded, then jumped down, rolling on his shoulder, and came up covering the back next to DiMera, who was already there with his submachine gun pointed at the refuse container.

There was no one inside. Firke walked all the way around the truck, looking for any sign that someone had been there, but came up with nothing. The scrub grass didn't hold any tracks, and there were no footprints on the road to indicate where the Molotov cocktail thrower might have gone. It was as if they had been ambushed by a ghost.

"Teams Two and Three, regroup on my signal, on the main road one-point-five klicks from the main gate," Firke said. "Team Four, continue with your additional mission, then evac and blow the place."

There was a muffled whump as the gas tank under the SUV detonated.

His gaze icy, Firke stared at the burning wreck, thinking about what a pleasure it would be when he caught up with whoever did this, and killed the bastards.

"I STILL CAN'T believe you made that shot!" Alcaster said as he led the group over the hills toward where Bolan said the airfield was. "With a .32-caliber revolver, I mean—it was one in a thousand!"

Finigian shrugged. "My grandfather and father both hunted all their lives. They taught me how to estimate range and wind. I took my best guess, and it paid off. What sucks is that I didn't hurt him."

Scott glanced back where a greasy column of black smoke rose into the sky. "You think Cooper made it out of there?"

"I can't think of anyone who's more likely to," Alcaster said. "Besides, even if he didn't, our marching orders were clear—get to the airfield and tell this pilot guy who we are and have him get us the hell out of here."

Scott looked at Finigian next. "You sure you're okay? Your wound looks pretty bloody."

"I'm fine, thanks." She glanced at the blood-covered rags. "It hurts—a lot, but I'll go as far as I have to be clear of that place.

"Yeah, still…no sweating or fever?" He peered closely at her face. "No red around your eyes?"

"Will, for God's sake—" Alcaster began.

"No, it's all right. I'd be asking the same questions if I were in his shoes," the policewoman said. "He's got every right to be suspicious. If this disease or—whatever it is—is transmitted by bodily fluids, then I'm infected. But honestly, I feel fine. Well, other than being tired, and every time I take a step, the chunk missing from my leg throbs."

The young men chuckled and even Sevan managed a thin smile. "I bet—" Scott's reply was drowned out by a series of loud explosions from the village. Everybody stopped where they were and listened to the blasts echo off the hills around them. "Jesus… Cooper wasn't kidding. They blew up the whole place."

"Covering their tracks," Sevan, who was marching ahead of Finigian and Aram, said. "Whoever was behind this was organized and well-armed. It makes me think of a certain foreign government who was probably behind all of this."

"If they were, I wasn't informed," a familiar voice said behind them.

Everyone turned to see a filthy Bolan walk toward them. All except Sevan crowded around him for a moment, until he held up his hands. "All right, everyone did great. But we got a long way to go and no time for a stop. Those men are still out there, and since they know we escaped, they'll be searching for us, so let's get moving."

"Yeah, but the plan worked!" Scott said.

Bolan nodded. "It required split-second timing, but yeah, I used the last three bottles to disable their SUV, then slid out and underneath the truck while they were going topside. When they went to the back, I scooted out under the engine and made it to the ditch right before the leader came back around. It was close—if he'd walked a few more paces out, he might have spotted me. Once they headed back to the burning SUV, I slipped away and circled around to find you."

He nodded at the policewoman. "Great job on the distraction, by the way."

She smiled. "Just glad to help."

Bolan looked around the sparse, steep hills. "However, we've still got at least twenty klicks to go, and the terrain isn't easy. I hope everyone's up for a long walk in the countryside."

He glanced at Finigian, who looked at him defiantly. "Don't worry about me. I'll keep up."

"All right, let's move out."

THREE HOURS LATER they reached Bolan's bivouac site and rested for a few minutes while he changed into cleaner clothes and distributed the last of his food and water among the group. Aram was flagging by now, and with a little encouragement from Finigian, Bolan was able to convince him to climb onto his back and clamp his arms around his neck. Supporting his legs, they set out again, with Bolan estimating that they were about halfway there.

Thirty minutes later, as the group was picking its way down the side of a ravine, the soldier heard a faint, familiar buzzing noise overhead.

"Everyone move as fast as you can to the bottom of the ravine," he said, still holding on to Aram. "Once there, crouch down or lie on the ground."

He joined them a few moments later, set the boy down and scanned the sky for the source of the noise. "There." Bolan didn't point to the small black speck overhead. "They've got a drone."

"Think they spotted us?" Alcaster asked.

"There's no way to know for sure right now," Bolan replied, turning to look along the winding ravine. "It's more luck than anything that we ended up in here. However, if they did, we'll find out the moment we come out of the ravine. Everyone take five and give them a few minutes to chase their tails, then keep moving. They'd have to be right on top of us to see us in here."

They all sat and caught their breath for a few minutes, and sure enough, the sound of the drone faded. Bolan rose and picked up the sleeping Aram. "Time to go."

They followed the ravine for another few hundred meters, until it tapered off into a crack. The sides were steep, but climbable, even for Sevan.

"You know, I could move faster if you would free my hands," he said, puffing as he labored up the hillside. "If I fall and hurt myself, we'll move that much slower."

"Yeah, but that's not going to happen, is it, Sevan?" Bolan asked. "You don't want to be stuck out here. Besides, you're a fit guy. You're doing fine. Save all that breath for walking instead of complaining."

ANOTHER TWO HOURS of hard walking brought them to the edge of the small airfield. It wasn't much—just a straight, two-kilometer-long dirt strip carved out of the landscape. A small hangar that looked ready to fall in the next storm stood off to one side. The entire place looked forlorn and deserted.

All of which made the brand-new Cessna Caravan turboprop airplane sitting near the hangar a bit incongruous at best.

"Sure glad we brought the bigger plane," Bolan said as he tapped his earpiece. "Flyboy, this is Striker, do you read?"

"Striker, this is Flyboy, about time you got here. I was almost starting to get worried."

"We thought we'd take the scenic route back. When can you be ready for takeoff?"

"Ready? Hell, I've been ready for the past two days," Grimaldi replied. "Come on in and get situated, and we'll get out of this godforsaken country."

Bolan frowned at the pilot's bluntness. "Roger that. Striker out." He turned to Finigian and shrugged. "I'm sure he didn't meant it quite that way."

She smiled. "I've spent enough time in the north country. He's not too far off."

"All right, we're heading in," Bolan said. "Sevan, you're with near me. Everyone get aboard and find a seat as soon as you can, and we'll be out of here in no time. Let's go."

He got up and led the way across the runway to the aircraft, whose turboprop was already started. Grimaldi stood with the main door open, waving them in.

Bolan stopped at the door and shoved Sevan ahead of him. "Get in and head back."

The rest followed, the small parade making the Stony Man pilot whistle. "Did you forget we only sent you after one guy?"

"Long story," Bolan replied, turning to scan the hills one last time. A cloud of dust in the distance made his brow furrow. "Company's coming, Jack, and they aren't friendly."

"All the more reason to get into the air. Come on." The pilot waited for Bolan to climb into the copilot's seat, then got in and closed the door. "Everyone buckle up and hang on."

The Stony Man pilot taxied onto the runway and drove to the far end. "This tarmac is just long enough for this baby to get airborne," he said as he ran through his final preflight check.

Bolan's eyes were on the approaching vehicles that were getting closer and closer. "Time to go, Jack."

"You don't have to tell me twice." The pilot hit the throttle and the turboprop began picking up speed, faster and faster until the ground blurred underneath them, and before Bolan knew it, they were in the air.

"Whoa!" Grimaldi banked left, still climbing, a frown on his face. "We just got shot at. Whoever was after you, they weren't dropping by to wish you a fond goodbye."

"You got that right," Bolan replied. "And I'm going to find out exactly who's down there."

FIRKE WATCHED THE plane disappear into the sky, tasting the bitter flavor of something he had never experienced before—defeat.

He pulled out his cell phone and hit the first speed-dial number. "There's been a problem…yes, at least four escaped… I do not have any idea where they are going at this time…yes, sir. Yes, sir, that was accomplished. And— I understand…it will be done."

He ended the call and turned to his team. "We're heading to the Congo."

He looked past them at the wild-eyed woman sitting alone in the rearmost seat. She was bound and gagged in duct tape, and she stared at him when not whipping her head back and forth in a futile attempt to attack someone. "You've got an appointment to keep."

CHAPTER TWENTY

"And that, along with the samples provided upon arrival, is all of the information I and the rest of the witnesses can provide at this time."

Mack Bolan leaned back in his chair and drained his water glass, feeling the events of the past day—and of the past several hours—catch up to even him.

After securing Sevan to his seat, he'd sacked out for several hours of much-needed rest, and had awakened to find Jack Grimaldi bringing them down at L'viv Danylo Halytskyi International Airport in western Ukraine.

Based on his conversation with Aaron Kurtzman and Barbara Price, Stony Man's mission controller and coordinator of the American response to what Bolan had found in Artakar, they'd all agreed that faster transportation was needed to the European Centre for Disease Prevention and Control in Stockholm. A fueled and stocked Learjet 85 awaited them on the tarmac, and Bolan had wasted no time transferring the passengers and his grisly cargo onto the jet, which had been wheels-up in twelve minutes.

They had touched down at Stockholm Arlanda Airport less than two hours later, where a contingent from the ECDPC had been waiting for them, along with several large container trucks. The jet had been guided into a warehouse, where the doors were closed behind them. Bolan had found out later that the entire building had been sealed off and placed under armed guard.

The passengers and pilot had all been escorted off the airplane by hazmat-suited men and women and each one taken into a separate truck for medical examination. From there, they had all been chemically decontaminated and allowed to shower. There had been only one slight disagreement, when Bolan had said he would need to leave as soon as possible to pick up the trail of the professional soldiers who had unleashed the pathogen on the village and then destroyed it. The doctor in charge of the operation, a short, slender Frenchman named Jean-Pierre Bellamy, had said he could not be allowed to leave until it was confirmed that he was not a threat to the general populace.

In a very polite tone, Bolan had told him what he could do with that suggestion, and also told him that when he did leave, Alexsandr Sevan would be leaving with him. It had taken a hurried conference of Barbara Price, Hal Brognola, the doctor and both his counterparts at the CDC in Atlanta, renowned epidemiologist Harriet Marks, as well as the lead scientist at the Army Medical Research Institute of Infectious Diseases, Colonel Marvin Gorman, to work out a solution to expedite the tests on Bolan's blood work to clear him for departure ASAP. That had required a call from the U.S. President.

The team was working on all of the samples, including the ones taken from the kitchen worker, as well as those drawn from the rest of the survivors. The samples from Sevan, Finigian and Aram were all of particularly high value, since they were taken from live exposed subjects. Meanwhile, all of the survivors were being interviewed separately—and exhaustively.

Dr. Bellamy leaned back in his chair, rubbing a hand over his bleary eyes. "I do not wish to alarm anyone here, but this could be the beginning of the epidemic we've been fearing ever since the SARS outbreak of 2002. I cannot overstate how important it is that we locate and lock down the source and contain it as soon as possible."

"Agreed, Doctor, which is why I need to be back in the field, tracking that team," Bolan replied. "Other than the witnesses I brought here and whatever your people find in Artakar, they're the only surviving link to this event, as well as who's behind it. My people already have eyes on them, and we know where they're headed—"

"Matt, we have that intelligence, up to a point," Price said, maintaining Bolan's cover. "They also left the area right after you did, and headed west to Shirak International Airport, where they boarded a private jet that we're currently tracking over the Mediterranean Sea. Preliminary indications are that they're heading into Africa, but we're not sure as to their final destination yet."

"Why would they be heading there?" Dr. Marks, teleconferenced in from the U.S. along with the Stony Man team, asked.

Gorman grunted. "Besides the nonexistent oversight there, I would imagine that if you tossed one of those tin-pot dictators a few million dollars, they'd let you do whatever you want in their country, no questions asked."

Bellamy cleared his throat. "Believe me, I'm just as concerned about tracking the source as everyone else here is, but first we really must find out what we're dealing with."

"No argument there, Doctor," Marks said. I've cross-referenced the known symptoms with our database, but the hits are far too large to realistically narrow down the suspects until we have more data from your people—"

A knock at the door interrupted him. Bellamy sprang up to get it, accepting a tablet computer from the woman outside. "This should get us closer to that answer. According to our preliminary tests…" He read quickly, his eyes widening. "That's bloody ingenious."

"Hey, Doc, mind filling the rest of us in," Brognola said as he popped an antacid tablet into his mouth.

"Oh, right, sorry. Just let me…" He tapped on the tablet for a few moments. "Dr. Marks, Colonel Gorman, I'm forwarding all the data we have so your people are on the same page, as it were, with ours."

"Thank you, Doctor, I'll be sure this gets to our top researchers," Marks replied, with Gorman nodding in agreement.

"Basically, as Mr. Cooper surmised, and thanks to the samples both he and Ms. Finigian brought back with them, we are looking at a man-made pathogen," Bellamy began. "It is a particularly clever one, a modified version of the *Toxoplasma gondii* protozoan, that's carrying a particularly fast-acting strain of the rabies virus. The cellular structure of *T. gondii* is easily recognizable. It was the splice of the rabies virus into it that gave us a bit of pause."

"Okay, what does that mean?" Brognola asked.

"*Toxoplasma gondii* is a hardy, fairly harmless parasite found all over the world," Bellamy replied. "Its life cycle runs from mice or rats to cats, and can be passed to humans, but only rarely does it sicken them. Medical studies have showed that up to one-third of world's population may be infected with it. The interesting thing is that studies have showed that mice infected with it exhibit more impulsive behavior, for lack of a better term, causing them to be more likely eaten by cats—"

"Wait a minute," Bolan interrupted. "Are you saying that in effect this parasite rewires its victim to, in effect, make it go kill itself?"

"To a certain degree, yes," Bellamy continued. "Although *T. gondii* asexually reproduces within and can be transmitted by humans—as well as just about any other warm-blooded animal—it sexually reproduces only within the intestines of members of the *felid* cat family, so transmission to and among the cats is still paramount for its spread."

Marks was reviewing the data on her computer, as well. "Some studies have also showed the disease it causes, toxoplasmosis, to have an intensifying effect on suicidal behavior in humans, which might explain the advanced aggressiveness you all reported."

"What are the normal symptoms of this disease?"

"In a normal exposure, the infection typically causes a mild, flu-like illness or no illness in the first few weeks," Gorman said. "However, those with weakened immune systems, such as those with AIDS and pregnant women, may become seriously ill, to the point of fatality. The parasite can cause encephalitis and neurologic diseases, and can negatively affect the heart, liver, inner ears and eyes. Recent research—although this is still ongoing—has linked toxoplasmosis with attention deficit hyperactivity disorder, obsessive compulsive disorder and schizophrenia."

"So, very much a brain disease," Bolan said. "And combined with a rabies virus as fast-acting as the one we saw, it's deadly as hell."

"Yes, particularly if those symptoms of rabies that lead to abnormal behavior—confusion, excitation, agitation—are exacerbated by the *T. gondii*'s propensity to drive its host to engage in risky behavior to spread itself," Gorman added.

"I have a question," Bolan said, glancing at the French doctor. "From what you've seen, Ms. Finigian, although bitten by one of the infected, has not showed any symptoms of the parasite, even though it has been at least ten hours since infection, correct?"

Bellamy flipped through his notes. "That is correct, Mr. Cooper."

"Why not?" Bolan asked. "An effective bioweapon is designed to have the maximum impact across the broadest swath of the population. Once released, they do not discriminate. Yet she seems to be fine. So does Sevan, although to the best of my knowledge, he wasn't bitten, but he had fairly close contact with several of the infected. Why haven't they been affected?"

"We're working on that," Bellamy replied. "The simplest answer may be that in every population, there is a small percentage that epidemics simply do not affect, as they either have a natural immunity or their genetic makeup is such that they can contract the disease but are unaffected by it. It may be that she is one. However, we're working on figuring out if that is the case, *why* that is. She could be the key to a vaccine against it."

"Just to reiterate, ladies and gentlemen, this is the first outbreak we've seen of this particular pathogen, correct?" Gorman asked. Bellamy and Marks agreed with the AMRIID director's assessment. "Therefore, it is imperative that we lock this down ASAP, before whoever is creating it gets the chance to unleash it," he said.

"Agreed," Bolan said. "As soon as we're done here, I'm going after that aircraft and anyone they're involved with. If we're lucky, the lab itself may be there and I can wrap up the whole thing in one big bang."

"I'll send one of my top researchers to meet you at the landing point," Gorman said. "She'll be invaluable in assisting you with gathering onsite information."

"Thank you for the offer, Colonel, but I doubt she'll be able to get there in time," Bolan said. "Once I'm on the ground, I'll be moving fast."

"There's no need to worry about that, Mr. Cooper," Gorman replied. "Lieutenant Briggs is currently working at the Spiez Laboratory in Switzerland. It will be a simple matter to expedite her to wherever your final African destination is. Based on this evidence, you're going to need a qualified expert in case of accidental exposure or release of the pathogen."

"Speaking of accidental release, what's going to happen at Artakar?" Brognola asked. "Our intel confirms that the entire town was burned to the ground shortly after Cooper and the other escapees left. Is there any chance that the virus could still be on-site?"

"We dispatched a Biolevel 4 safety team to quarantine the site and work with local police and military forces to make sure that no surviving infected person escaped, and that the virus is contained at that location," Bellamy said.

"That's all well and good, but the best way to ensure that doesn't happen is to find the source and destroy it, which is exactly what I plan to do," Bolan said. "In the meantime, Hal, be sure to work with these folks on taking care of the others that came out with me."

"Again, no reason for concern, Mr. Cooper," Bellamy replied. "The two medical students have been very helpful already, and we will ensure that they and the other young lady will be well cared for. Ms. Finigian and her young charge will also be closely monitored until they can be repatriated."

"Matt, we've pinpointed where that jet wound up," Brognola said. "It landed in the Democratic Republic of the Congo."

"That's all I needed to hear," Bolan said as he rose from his chair. "You've all gotten everything I can give you. Now it's time I got back to work."

"Lieutenant Briggs will rendezvous with you in the Congo," Gorman said. "Good luck, Mr. Cooper, and Godspeed."

CHAPTER TWENTY-ONE

Kristian Stengrave finished his review of the biomedi-cal research laboratory's finances and rubbed his eyes. Running a company as large as Stengrave Industries required juggling several balls at once and being pre-pared to have more introduced into the mix at any time. After more than fifteen years at the helm of the com-pany, taking over as Chairman and CEO when he'd bought out his own father, he was adept at keeping things moving, even when certain side projects ran into unexpected snags.

His phone rang and he picked it up. "Yes?"

The voice on the other end whispered quickly, "This is Forty-Three."

Stengrave sat a little straighter in his chair. Although he deplored other companies using corporate espionage against him, he saw no reason not to deploy it himself. To that end, he had planted loyal employees at various companies and nonprofits across Europe to keep tabs on what was going on in various scientific fields of re-search. "Go ahead."

"I work at the Spiez Laboratory, in the city of the same name in Switzerland. Over the past several hours, there has been a lot of communication with the ECDPCS in Stockholm. It has all referred to the release of a man-made virus, and they requested access to all of our files on *Toxoplasma gondii*. I remembered the work our lab had done with the strain three years ago, and thought I should contact you, to see if it was something our company had been involved in."

"Possibly. Can you give me any more information?" Stengrave asked.

"The incident concerns an outbreak in a remote village in Armenia called Artakar. They're classifying the site as a biological hazard until further notice. Apparently the Americans are involved, as one of the visiting doctors here from the United States, a Lieutenant Cheryl Briggs, was ordered to the Congo with all haste. I happened to be the one who helped her process her flight on our end."

"Thank you, you've done very well," Stengrave replied. "Your company appreciates your diligence. Go about your usual routine and rest assured that this will be handled appropriately."

"Yes, sir. Glad I could help, sir."

"You have, more than you can possibly know," Stengrave replied, then disconnected the call. He turned on the flat-screen television in his office while dialing another number.

"Yes?"

"Mr. Firke, you should prepare yourself for company down there," Stengrave replied. "It seems that the fly in your ointment came from the Americans, and he's coming down to see what he can find out in the Congo. There's an American scientist who's joining him, a woman." Stengrave gave her name.

"Excellent—I'll make sure neither of them leaves here alive," Firke replied. "I know just how to get both of them, too. If you'll excuse me, sir, I have a few calls to make to prepare a warm reception for them."

"I'll leave you to it," Stengrave replied. "Let me know when it is done."

He ended the call as his attention was directed to a report on riots in France, where crowds of Muslims protested the continued police practice of banning the full-face veil for women in public. He flipped through other news channels, using an internet aggregator to cull the particular articles and topics he sought, and found more of the same.

> *...the German population is expected to be twenty percent Muslim by 2019...*
> *...ground breaking commenced on a new mosque in New York City, joining the more than 800 similar new structures built in the United States over the past decade...*
> *...emigrated Muslim population has formed its own enclaves, with their own businesses and insular societal networks, wherever they migrate to...*
> *...a lawsuit in rural England has brought the right of a Muslim girl to wear a full-body burka to elementary school. Proponents say that it is a religious right, and should not be restricted...*
> *...economists estimate that the percentage of money spent by Muslims in Europe over the next decade will grow from its current 7 percent to 17 percent...*

It is an ideological crusade, nothing less, Stengrave thought. The inexorable migration of Muslims into Europe and their fecund birth rates, combined with the declining ones all across the continent, had led him to this inescapable conclusion. At first he'd hoped the Muslims would succumb to the lures of a Western life-style, and indeed, some had, but the majority clung fast to their faith and their imported society. He had conducted several long-range population studies, trying to game the results with different scenarios, but, absent a world-shattering event, such as a pandemic or colossal war or natural disaster, the results had turned out the same every time.

They plan to take over the world by breeding out the other indigenous populations and installing themselves in their place, he thought. And nowhere did he feel this was happening faster than in his beloved homeland, Sweden. Drawn there by the egalitarian, socialist government, which welcomed them with open arms, and access to excellent education and health care, the northern nation had seen a rising influx of Muslims over the past decade.

Although the government claimed the actual number of practicing Muslims in the country at around 100,000, Stengrave didn't believe it. Census numbers estimated the number of Muslims, counted as those of Arab descent or having a Muslim name, at around 300,000. To the industrialist, they were all lumped into the same category; a blight slowly creeping unchecked across his country and the whole of Europe, slowly overtaking its nations and cities, and displacing the natives with the immigrants.

Stengrave had hoped to come up with a less-drastic idea to check this rising tide, whether through stricter immigration or reproduction laws, or even population caps. But the more he had tried to work through the official channels, the less attention he had received. It was as if everyone around him was blind to this stealth invasion occurring right under their noses, and even worse, content to sit idly by and let it happen.

But not Kristian Stengrave. As the evidence mounted regarding the increasing disparity in native versus immigrant population, and how that would only increase in future years, he realized that he would have to take more direct action.

At first, he'd thought of creating a eugenics program in which he would release a virus that would render only men and women with certain Arabic genotypes infertile, thereby slowing their reproduction. But when his population estimates revealed that even this admittedly drastic measure wouldn't be enough to reverse the population expansion, he used that genetic referencing data to embark on a different, even more radical path, one that would not only stop the incursion in its tracks, but ensure that immigration would cease not only in Sweden, but throughout Europe, as well.

It was a nearly perfect plan. Since most Muslim communities were relatively self-contained, they would primarily destroy themselves once the virus was unleashed. Yes, there would be some collateral damage to the surrounding populations, but Stengrave saw this as necessary to preserve the whole, not to mention, he admitted only to himself, a bit of punishment for not recognizing the hazard they faced. If Europeans didn't recognize the danger living next to them, right under their very noses, then someone had to make them see it. If that was to be him, so be it.

The violence would also have the added benefit of scaring the governments into passing harsh anti-immigration laws, to ensure that a repeat of what was only a few days away from happening would never happen again. Sweden—and Europe—would be saved, and Islam and its jihadist leaders would be dealt a serious blow. Stengrave was already considering the next phase of his operation: unleashing the virus in the heart of the most religious nations—assuming it wasn't going to be carried there naturally by fleeing refugees.

No matter, he thought. *It will arrive eventually—one way or another.*

His phone beeped and Stengrave looked at the message from Dr. Richter.

Final batch of product nearly complete. Will be ready for pick up in 24 hours.

Stengrave didn't text back; Richter would know he'd seen it. Instead he called Firke again. "Once you've disposed of that problem we discussed earlier, there will be a package for you to pick up at the laboratory. You know what to do with it."

AFTER RECEIVING HIS orders from Stengrave, Firke dialed another number.

"Good afternoon, Mr. Sambele. How are you? This is Reginald Firke... Yes, of Stengrave Industries... I'm well, thank you... I'm afraid that I am calling with some unfortunate news regarding an incoming visitor to your country... Yes, a medical doctor from America named Cheryl Briggs, associated with the United States Army Medical Research Institute of Infectious Diseases. We understand that she will be meeting another American here."

Firke studied the murky blown-up picture they had retrieved from the cameras in Arkatar. "He's over six feet tall, about two hundred pounds, very well built, black hair. What do they intend? Well, given the Americans' propensity to throw their weight around whenever they can, I wouldn't care to speculate what either of them might be doing here, but given that she is from the part of the Army that studies biochemical weapons, I wanted to pass this on so you could follow up if necessary… What did I have in mind? Well, it may be better for all concerned if you could arrange for them to be delivered into our hands… Yes, the jungle is a dangerous place, indeed… Very good, I will await your call with pleasure… Yes, we must certainly dine together when I am back in Kinshasa…I will be sure to let you know the next time I'm in the city… Thank you for your assistance in this matter, Mr. Sambele… I look forward to hearing from you shortly."

Firke disconnected and called Richter. "I'm coming in tonight to pick up everything you've got. Make sure it's ready."

"You'll have plenty, Mr. Firke. By the way, I wanted to thank you for the live subject your men dropped off earlier today. She's already proving very useful."

"Glad I could help," Firke replied. "Too bad I couldn't dump the interfering asshole who nearly fucked up the Armenian op on you, too. Apparently the bastard's coming here to snoop around."

"Really?" Richter's tone grew thoughtful. "Do you think you might be able to capture him alive?"

The security man's face darkened. "Why in the hell would I want to do that?"

"Because my testing has reached its limits on ordinary people—" Firke could almost hear the scientist's mind working "—and I would be very interested to see how the virus would work on more skilled people who have been trained to operate under difficulty, who are used to thinking under intense stress and hardship. Besides, wouldn't you love to lord it over the man who bested you once already?"

Firke smiled, his lips pressed together, tight and bloodless. "Yeah, but there's a limit. Easier just to put lead in his head."

"Well, unless one of your men wants to volunteer for the testing…given their genetic makeup, it shouldn't cause much harm…"

Firke scowled at that, although the thought of putting his two team members who had screwed up and let the American escape under the needle had crossed his mind, he dismissed it with a shake of his head. After seeing what had happened to the people of Artakar, there was no way he'd let any of his people undergo the doctor's tests. "Maybe…I'll see what I can do."

"Make this happen, Mr. Firke, and I'll reward you myself," Richter said. "That's a promise."

CHAPTER TWENTY-TWO

As her plane descended on its final approach into Kinshasa International Airport, Lieutenant Cheryl Briggs, M.D., was still trying to sort out the sketchy data she had received only a few hours earlier regarding her reassignment. Even the summary report read like something out of a Michael Crichton novel.

> New man-made pathogen released on civilian population in Armenia...infected subjects exhibit extremely aggressive and violent behavior toward others, with an end goal of spreading the pathogen to as many people as possible... Suspects involved fled to Democratic Republic of the Congo... Rendezvous with Matt Cooper, Justice agent assigned to investigate the incident, locate the suspects and arrest them. Pathogen samples are to be destroyed...any recoverable data on the pathogen should be obtained for further study if possible.

"Not exactly what I signed up for," she muttered, although she also couldn't deny a thrill deep inside her. Cheryl had joined AMRIID to help research and fight infectious diseases, and while a she had gone through the appropriate training, she had never been in the field in what could conceivably be considered a hostile situation. But this... Who knew what was really going on?

As her plane touched down and she saw the distinctive yellow-and-blue terminal building in the distance, Briggs was acutely aware of the strife and trauma the country had gone through over the past few decades. Ever since obtaining its freedom from Belgium in 1960, it had ben racked by a succession of internal strife, military coups and a twenty-six-year dictatorship under Joseph Mobutu, an army general who had named himself president in 1971.

After he was forced to flee in 1997 due to internal and external pressure, the indigenous group known as the Tutsi launched an invasion from Rwanda and Uganda, setting in motion a war that spread to envelop six other African nations. Sporadic fighting continued to this day among several groups based both inside and on the borders of the struggling country. It was particularly harsh for women, with an estimated 400,000 sexually assaulted each year. Briggs had looked out over the thick, verdant jungle on their approach and wondered how so much beauty could mask such depravity and destruction.

She had been warned about attracting attention to herself, and had her service pistol with her, although it was currently in her suitcase, as the fastest, as well as the least conspicuous way to get to the Congo, had been by passenger airline. Even so, she was acutely aware of being one of only two Caucasians on the airliner.

Briggs exited the plane, stepping out into the bright sunlight and suffocating heat. She walked down the mobile stairs, across the tarmac and into the terminal building. She headed straight for the luggage terminal, hoping that her suitcase hadn't been opened, or even worse, stolen. Tapping her foot impatiently, she waited at the antiquated luggage stand, keeping a wary eye out for pickpockets and thieves. She had spent just as much time reading up on the city of Kinshasa, as well as the country, and was familiar with the con games and tricks unscrupulous people tried on foreigners. She was prepared to resist with any and all means at her disposal.

Eventually her suitcase was trundled out and Briggs was relieved to see that it looked undamaged. Even so, she hauled it to a deserted corner, opened it and retrieved her 9 mm Beretta pistol, loading it and slipping it into her purse. Sensing eyes upon her, she turned, keeping one hand inside the handbag, to see a tall white man with black hair and piercing blue eyes striding toward her. He wore tan chinos, a white button-down shirt and a khaki tropical-weight linen sport coat.

"Lieutenant Cheryl Briggs?" he asked as he came close. His eyes flicked down to her purse. "Matt Cooper. You have good taste in guns, I see."

Briggs withdrew her hand and tried her best not to grin sheepishly or blush at the situation. "I believe in always being prepared, Agent Cooper."

"I couldn't agree with you more. And call me Matt." He smiled slightly, transforming his face from a serious mask into something somewhat less harsh. A moment ago he had been all business, but now he resembled another just adventurous tourist who had come to Africa. "Is this everything?"

"Yes, I was told to travel light, and did exactly that," Briggs replied as she wiped irritably at her pinned hair, which was already turning into a sodden, sticky mass at the back of her neck. "I trust you'll be able to fill me in on what is going on regarding the subject of our mission?"

"At the moment you probably know more than I do," Bolan said as he picked up her suitcase and they headed for the main entrance. "We're supposed to be meeting with a representative from the government, but keep your eyes open—in developing countries, corruption is a way of life. Often one can never tell how many payrolls a state employee is on."

"Right." Briggs's already jangly nerves twitched even more upon hearing that not-so-reassuring bit of news, but she quickened her pace to keep up with the taller man's long legs as they headed for the exit.

Near the doors, an impeccably dressed African man with fashionably short hair and wearing a neat shirt, sport coat and slacks approached them. "Mr. Cooper? Dr. Briggs? I am Evrard Kayembe, assistant to the governor of the city and province of Kinshasa, André Kimbuta. On behalf of the Democratic Republic of the Congo, we welcome you." He showed them an official-looking government identification, which Bolan scrutinized carefully and then handed to Briggs for her review.

Gratified that he hadn't just assumed she'd go along, she examined it carefully, and saw that everything seemed to be in order, finally handing it back to Mr. Kayembe, who had waited patiently during the process.

"I have been in contact with your Mr....Brog-nola," he said with a smile, pronouncing the Stony Man liaison's name with care. "And have made all necessary arrangements for both of you during your stay. If you will follow me, please."

He turned and headed toward the main doors. Briggs

exchanged a glance with Bolan, who was already talking into his earpiece. He listened for a moment as he followed the shorter man through the doors. "Confirmed that this is the guy we're supposed to meet, right down to his—" he pulled out his smartphone and looked at the picture "—mug shot."

"Okay then, into the woods we go," Briggs said.

Kayembe led them to a large, white Land Rover, complete with a roof rack and well-used front brush guard. "It is about an hour to the city proper. Just relax, and we will be there soon."

By unspoken agreement, Bolan took the front passenger seat and Briggs got into the back, on the driver's side. Kayembe pulled out into the sparse traffic and drove away from the airport, heading toward the city.

"When can we begin our search for the people we're looking for?" Bolan asked.

"That will be the first topic of discussion with our people," Kayembe replied. "We have some promising leads that should help you quite a bit."

"Good." Bolan's eyes narrowed as he saw flashing blue lights in the rearview mirror. Glancing behind them, he saw another Land Rover approaching fast. "Are you speeding?"

Kayembe checked the mirror and grimaced. "No, that is just the police escort I requested. Unfortunately they are not being as discreet as I would like. Just a moment." He pulled over onto the side of the road and the police vehicle followed, stopping a few meters behind them. Kayembe opened his door. "Let me reinstruct them as to what is happening. Wait here, I'll be right back."

He got out and walked back to the driver's side of

the other vehicle, while Briggs and Bolan watched the conversation, though neither could make out what was being said.

"What do you think?" she asked.

"He left the keys, so if it is an ambush or shakedown, we'd have a means of escape," Bolan replied. "His body language doesn't appear to be nervous or threatened, and most important, no guns have been drawn from the police, so it looks like this is on the up-and-up so far. Still, keep your purse open."

She smiled grimly. "It hasn't been closed since I got here."

"Good."

Briggs noticed that one hand was behind his back, as well. "I see you're not taking any chances, either."

"I try not to," he replied, still watching the conversation, which came to an end with Kayembe waiting for another man to emerge from the back of the police SUV. The two men walked toward the first vehicle again, splitting up to go to their respective sides.

"Looks like one of the policemen is riding with us," Bolan said. He did not remove his hand from the small of his back.

The doors opened and both men climbed in, Kayembe talking as he sat behind the wheel. "Officer Nestor Muamba, may I present Lieutenant Cheryl—"

As he spoke, both the police officer and Kayembe raised short-barreled pistols, each one aimed at the person in the seat next to him, and pulled the triggers.

Briggs jumped when the pistol next to her made a loud coughing sound, and looked down in disbelief at the brightly colored dart sticking out of her side. She suddenly felt weak and sleepy. She tried to pull her pistol, aware of some commotion in the front seats, but her arms and legs felt as if they weighed a thousand pounds each. Even her head felt too heavy to keep upright.

As it lolled against the headrest, she watched the man across from her take her purse and remove her pistol and her smartphone. She fought to keep her eyes open, to fight, to scream, to do anything, but she couldn't move, couldn't think, couldn't do anything but slip into the long tunnel of darkness that appeared before her.

The last thing she remembered hearing was the deep voice of her ambusher. "Where you're going, I doubt they'll care what your name is...."

At Stony Man Farm, Barbara Price had called an early meeting to update everyone on where they were with this rapidly developing new mission. In attendance were Hal Brognola and Aaron Kurtzman, with Akira Tokaido pulling double duty by both monitoring their computer network and attending via Skype.

"Good morning," she said. "First, I wanted to wrap up the tail end of the mission that uncovered this mess. I've just received word that Alexsandr Sevan was received into Department of Justice custody earlier this morning. In a rare show of interdepartmental cooperation, the DoJ and FBI are working together on his case. Sevan won't be going anywhere for a long, long time. Good job, everyone."

She opened the tablet in front of her. "Now, on to more pressing matters. There's been a rather interesting development regarding this pathogen mission."

"Only one this morning?" Kurtzman snorted. "Or perhaps you're referring to the Chinese definition?"

"Trust me, it's plenty big enough to complicate matters." Price's tone was so dry it could have parched toast. "Akira caught it during his analysis of the data and flagged it for immediate attention, hence this meeting."

Brognola frowned. "If it's that important, why wasn't I notified immediately?"

"It reached me only twenty minutes ago, and there is no immediate crisis regarding it at the moment, there's only the matter of how to proceed." She took a seat. "Akira, if you would, please."

The genius hacker cleared his throat. He had a lot to report, and some of it wasn't happy news. "Okay, so, we were able to track that second incursion team back to their airport—"

"Hold up, Akira, that reminds me," Brognola said. "I thought we had eyes on the Armenian village the whole time Striker was there. According to the after-action report, from the onset time of this virus, they would have had to plant it sometime in the twelve hours before his mission began. Why didn't we see them come in?"

"I'll answer that one, Hal," Kurtzman replied. "We had allocation for the drone for the original mission window, plus an extra twenty-four hours either way, as per standard operating procedure. As you know, the mission ran long due to the delayed arrival of the primary target. Striker made the call to wait him out, but the drone had to be recalled, as it was assigned somewhere else after that period. By the time we got another one onsite, a fifteen-hour period had elapsed where we did not have aerial reconnaissance capability."

"Fair enough," Brognola grunted. "I know that we can't always get what we want when we want it. There are protocols in place. But what about Striker? He was watching them like a hawk, but said he didn't see anything out of the ordinary, either."

Kurtzman and Tokaido exchanged a glance. "Extrapolating from our best data, we theorized that they came in through the sewer system, the outflow point of which is on the other side of the village," the young hacker said. "Striker couldn't have seen anything from his vantage point."

"Exactly," Kurtzman stated. "We're good, but even we can't work miracles all the time."

"Got it." Brognola twirled his finger in the air in the universal "keep going," sign.

Tokaido checked his notes again. "Okay, where was I? Right. The good news is that while we didn't see them, they didn't see us, either, and apparently assumed that once Striker and the others from the village left, that was the end of it. They were decidedly lax in covering their tracks as they went to the airfield and boarded a private jet, which took off and landed in the Congo, which everyone already knows. The interesting thing is who the jet was registered to. Although they tried to hide it, they didn't do it well enough. The plane belongs to a holding company of Stengrave Industries."

That got Brognola's attention. "Stengrave? The Swedish multinational corporation?"

"The same," Tokaido replied. "We've prepared a quick-and-dirty summary of their operations around the world. Biochemical, manufacturing, computer technology—they're into just about anything on the cutting edge of technology."

"Let's see what his company's been up to, as well." Brognola flicked through electronic pages. "They're working with just about everyone around the world, from landing contracts with State, Agriculture, NASA, even Homeland Security. They've also partnered with private businesses around the world, including a dozen Fortune 100 companies."

"Not to mention that they've diversified over the past decade." Price paged forward to a long list of the company's subsidiaries. "They own stakes in a military vehicle manufacturer as well as one that makes body armor, and even a bioresearch and development laboratory dedicated to perfecting the human body. Sounds a bit ambitious for a company that got its start manufacturing low-end medical equipment, don't you think?"

Kurtzman and Brognola scanned the page she was reviewing. "Depends on what they're doing with it," the computer expert replied. "There are two current research fields regarding improving the human soldier. The first is through external technology—exoskeletons, real-time adaptable camouflage, remote-piloted drones or robots to remove the wounded from the battlefield, that sort of thing. The second one is to improve from the inside, including artificial stimulants, selective genetic modification and much more. We've come across the latter a time or two."

"Hmm, curiouser and curiouser," Brognola said. "Looks like they're even hedging their own bets. Recent investments include purchasing a controlling interest in a robotics R and D lab in Massachusetts last year."

"That just seems like good business to me," Price said as she leaned back in her chair, arms crossed. "After all, why put your eggs in one basket? Whichever route proves most effective—and profitable—they're in a position to be on the inside track. And besides, just because one country goes one way, doesn't mean another country wouldn't be interested in a different approach."

"Be that as it may, the fact that they're involved *and* the head company owns a subsidiary that sounds suspiciously like it could be in the business of creating bioweapons means they deserve a closer look ASAP," Brognola said.

"Bear, Akira, you guys know what to do," Price said. "Also, what's the latest from Striker?"

"He checked in on touchdown and said he had made contact both with Lieutenant Briggs and a government official," Kurtzman said. "They were heading into the city to meet with other government officials."

"An afternoon yakking with government middle management?" Price and Brognola shared a grin, knowing full well the big man's disdain for bureaucracy. "Hopefully Striker will at least attempt to be diplomatic."

"Let me know the moment he checks in. I want to be sure he's updated on everything, Akira. Akira?" Price repeated when she saw the young man staring at something on another monitor.

"I'm afraid the enemy knows Striker is there."

Price closed the tablet on the table in front of her and gave him her full attention. "Go ahead."

"Reviewing the satellite communications traffic coming out of the region over the past forty-eight hours, I found this excerpt of conversation that was received by a deputy minister in Kinshasa three hours ago," Tokaido stated. "Just so you know, this is raw data."

He touched a screen next to him and a sound file played back, completed with the jagged green bars of a voice stress analyzer. Price heard an unfamiliar voice discussing the arrival of the Army lieutenant, and providing the description of an unnamed man who sounded like Bolan, with a Mr. Sambele, who promised to follow up with the volunteers. The unnamed man suggested that when the pair was apprehended they be turned over to him.

"Who's the speaker?" Price asked.

"It matches the radio transmissions from the team leader at Artakar. The speaker is still unknown. We're cross-referencing the voice pattern with other possible matches, but haven't come up with a positive ID yet. What I can't figure out is how they knew about the involvement of AMRIID?"

"Tell me you've contacted Striker about this," Brognola growled.

"I tried every way I could think of. We've called three times on his red line, emailed him, texted him, everything but smoke signals, but so far there's been no answer."

"Damn it! Bear, get back in there and retrace Striker's steps out of the airport—" Brognola began.

"With all due respect, Hal, I've already got it." Tokaido tapped another screen and a picture appeared of the airport with a time-date stamp indicating it was thirty-three minutes old. The analyst zoomed in on Striker with two smaller figures, one in front and one behind him, as they headed to a Land Rover, got in and drove off. "So, that satellite continued in its orbit, and the next one picked up this…"

The picture changed to a nondescript four-lane highway. The same SUV was now parked by the side of the road, with another SUV with flashing blue lights on top pulling to a stop behind it.

"What the hell's going on?"

"It's a common trick played on lone drivers at night—men pretending to be police pull a victim over, take him into the jungle, rob him and leave him there," Kurtzman replied. "Something's seriously wrong if they're hitting a group in broad daylight."

"It actually looks like they're legitimate—at least, at first," Tokaido said. "Keep watching."

Price, Brognola and Kurtzman watched as the government contact got out of the first SUV and headed to the driver's door of the second. There was about a minute of conversation, then he and another man headed back to the first vehicle and both got in. There was a few seconds' pause, then both vehicles started up and got back on the road again.

"Two minutes after that, Striker's smartphone signaled that it was being tampered with before it suddenly stopped broadcasting. All attempts to raise him have been, as I mentioned, unsuccessful."

Price nodded, her voice calm even though her heartbeat had sudden sped up. She knew Bolan had been in tight spots before, and had the devil's own luck in getting out of them. Hopefully this time would be no different—and neither was her reaction to the news of him being in harm's way.

"Keep trying, and tell me the moment you find out where those vehicles are going." Her eyes never leaving the screen, Price opened a channel to Grimaldi. "Jack, Striker has gone off the grid, and we have reason to believe he is in enemy hands. I'm expediting air assistance, along with Charlie Mott, down to the Congo... Yes, I have every expectation that you'll need both before you're through there..."

CHAPTER TWENTY-THREE

Bolan regained consciousness slowly enough to keep looking as though he was still out cold. He gathered his wits, replaying what he knew in his mind. The last thing he remembered was being shot with a dart, but he'd still tried to draw his pistol while going for that smiling bastard Kayembe's throat. Their betrayer's eyes had gone as wide as saucers as he'd beat at Bolan's steel-hard grip, but then the tranquilizer had taken hold and everything had gone black afterward.

Now, his eyes still closed, Bolan extended his other senses, taking stock of the situation as much as he could.

They were still in a vehicle, but the soft leather seat had been replaced by bare, hard wood. The purr of the Land Rover was also gone, traded for the thunderous rattle of a diesel engine. Sweat soaked his body and he felt hot, damp wind swirl around him as they moved, but not blowing directly into his face. *The back of an open transport truck.* Also, his feet were bound together, and each hand was lashed to what felt like a chair arm on each side of him.

Catching flashes of sunlight, even through his closed eyelids, Bolan cracked an eye as he swayed with the jouncing truck. His impressions were correct—he and Cheryl Briggs, sitting with her head slumped forward beside him, were both lashed to seats on a bench in the back of what appeared to be a secondhand military transport truck. Although they were both tied, there were no guards in the back, which meant their captors were confident or careless. Judging by how they had captured both of them, as well as when he realized that just about everything he could have used as an improvised weapon had been taken from him—right down to his shoelaces—Bolan wasn't betting on the latter.

Opening his eyes fully, he looked around, trying to figure out anything else he could about their predicament. It was dusk, but he couldn't be sure it was still the same day, although it probably was. Administering continuous doses of tranquilizer to an unconscious victim increased the risk of something going wrong. Plus, his internal clock just felt as if no more than a few, maybe several, hours had passed at the most.

The setting sun threw his shadow onto the back wall of the truck cab, so they were heading roughly due east. The real question is where? Bolan wondered.

A low moan from his right made him turn to see Briggs coming out of her drug-induced unconsciousness. "My head…" Her voice trailed off when she tried to move her hands, then her feet. Only then did she look up to see the back of the truck around them, and Bolan sitting next to her. "Where do you think we are?" Her voice was surprisingly calm.

"At least five or six hours away from Kinshasa," Bolan replied. "We're in the deep jungle, heading east. Obviously we were transferred during some part of this whole operation." He glanced at her, as much to see how she was handling this news as in assurance. "How do you feel?"

"Like someone stuffed my head full of cotton, then pulled it all out through my nose and mouth," she replied.

"Yeah, the tranquilizer will do that do you," he said.

She regarded her zip-tied hands and then looked up at him. "So, what now?"

"Well, they obviously want us alive for a reason, but I've been trying to figure out what that is, and haven't come up with anything yet," Bolan replied. "Best thing we can do is to go along for now, figure out where we are and what's going on, and wait for an opportunity to escape. They obviously have vehicles, so if the right opportunity arises, we can commandeer one, get back on the trail and go as far as we can before either finding someone or running out of gas. The important thing will be to put as much distance between us and them. That way they'll have to waste more time searching for us. Then we figure out how to contact your people or my people, and they come in and pick us up."

All through his instructions, Briggs had been staring at him with a befuddled expression on her face that had slowly changed into disbelief at his matter-of-fact tone. "You sound like you've done this before."

He looked at her, a faint smile on his lips. "I've been in some tight spots, yeah. You'd be surprised at what you can accomplish if you stay alert, keep your wits about you and are willing to exploit any opportunity that may arise." He watched her steadily.

Briggs didn't get what he was referring to at first, then she dropped her gaze to her trim, lithe body, covered but not hidden by her blouse and slacks. "You don't mean…"

"All I'm saying is that if the opportunity arises and

your choice is between using your wiles enough to get an edge and death, I know the one I'd choose."

"Yeah, I'll bet that scenario comes up for you all the time," she muttered.

"You'd be surprised," came the quick reply. "Look, I'm not saying it will, but it's best to keep as many of your options open as possible. That reminds me, if the situation is that one of us gets free and can't get to the other, the free one has to leave, no hesitation, no going back. Whatever they're doing out here can't be allowed to continue. It's vital that one of us gest back to our superiors and report. You understand?"

"Perfectly," she replied.

The engine's tone changed and the truck began slowing as it turned right. "Looks like we're going to see what's behind the curtain. Be ready."

"I am." As she replied, they drove into darkness lit by electric lights. "What the—"

"I don't know," Bolan replied as what looked like a large section of rock wall slid over the opening they had driven through. Their truck turned again, and he could see several other vehicles parked in the large, rock-walled garage, along with several people moving around. "Wherever we are, they've been here a while, in order to do all of this."

"Should we feign being unconscious?" Briggs asked.

"I don't see the point," Bolan replied. "We're outnumbered and outgunned anyway. Best to meet them on the best terms we can and make a later strike."

The truck stopped and two men holding FN P-90 submachine guns walked up to the rear and covered both of them. Bolan heard the truck doors open and close, and footsteps come around to the back.

"Ah, good, you're awake," their captor, a trim, slim man in pressed fatigues and flanked by two more men, said in a precise English accent. "It would have been most annoying to have to carry you both inside. I assume that you both know the drill, so don't be stupid, and you won't force us to be, as well."

He nodded and the other two men jumped into the back of the truck and drew combat knives. They cut Briggs's hands free, but not her feet, then made her kneel on the truck bed while they zip-tied her hands behind her back. Only then did they cut her legs loose and allow her to stand, bracing her so she didn't fall over as the circulation returned to her aching feet.

Then they turned to Bolan and repeated the procedure. He noted their professionalism and efficiency, one of them always staying far enough away to not be easily attacked. Even so, he considered the odds against him and knew a better opportunity would arise later.

"You were the guys in Armenia," Bolan said as they hauled him to his feet. He didn't react as the blood rushed back into his toes, making them tingle painfully.

"We were indeed," the leader replied. "Apparently we passed each other in the night at some point. I must say, it was quite engaging watching you get out of there. You're very good." His tone left the second part of his statement unspoken: *but not good enough to avoid capture.*

So, they knew about me after the village, Bolan thought as the two men marched him to the edge of the truck and he jumped down. Makes sense, since they were able to grab me so easily.

"It is a pity you got as far as you did, however." The man shook his head. "If you had simply died back in the village, you and the young lady wouldn't be in this situation now."

Bolan and Briggs were led into what had appeared to be a tunnel carved into the side of a small mountain. They walked past stone walls for several yards, until they were replaced by stainless-steel panels on the wall and floor that led to a set of thick metal-and-glass double doors that slid open at their approach.

"Keep moving." One of the guards prodded Briggs in the back with the muzzle of his rifle, earning him a glare from Bolan.

The second guard noticed his scowl and poked him in the back. "Knock it off, asshole."

"Cut the zip tie off and I'll be happy to."

Crushing agony exploded in Bolan's kidney, sending him staggering into the airlock door. The pain radiated through his back, making black spots dance in front of his eyes. It was so intense he couldn't breathe for a moment, but was reduced to vainly trying to suck in air, his lungs wheezing with the effort.

"Stop it, all of you!" Briggs ran to Bolan, but bound as she was, there was nothing she could do.

"I'm…okay," Bolan gasped. He straightened with an effort, fighting to keep the wince from appearing on his face. He looked back at the guard, noting his face, but said nothing.

"All right, stand still and breathe normally." The other guard hit the door button, sealing them all in the airlock. A white vapor plumed from jets in the ceiling and walls, bathing the group in a slightly acrid mist.

"Vaporized disinfectant?" Briggs asked.

"Someone likes their James Bond toys, that's for

sure." Adding after Briggs's frown, "Well, what else would you call this?"

"A concealed laboratory designed to continue its research without suffering the ridiculous oversight of ignorant governments and regulatory organizations?"

Bolan and Briggs turned at the new voice behind them. Out of the cloud of antiseptic appeared a tall man dressed in a white lab coat, with a wrinkled, button-down Oxford shirt and shapeless brown slacks under-neath. His face was v-shaped, long and lean, with a small, almost snub nose, high, hollow cheekbones and a jutting jaw. His black hair tapered to a widow's peak on his broad forehead, and below that were bright-blue eyes glittering with dispassionate intelligence.

"Good afternoon. My name is Dr. Gerhardt Richter, and you—" he indicated Bolan with a nod of his chin "—are Matt Cooper, and the lady is Cheryl Briggs. I expect your names are probably both aliases, but it doesn't really matter at this point. I don't offer either of you any regrets for what has happened, or how you have been treated so far. I assume that both of you were both poking your noses where they didn't belong, which is why you ended up here."

"Yeah, and where exactly is that?" Bolan asked while massaging his lower back.

"This is a small copper mine that was excavated twenty-five years ago and abandoned during the local civil war of the early twenty-first century. Its location was suitable for our research and, with the proper mod-ifications, has served our purposes well for the past three years."

"But the power grid required…the energy… Where does that all come from?" Briggs glanced at the other set of doors that slid open, revealing more of the complex. "How do you supply it?"

"That's a long story, and one I won't bore you with, since we have much to accomplish. Come along." His request was punctuated by more prodding from the two guards. Bolan and Briggs were escorted down a large, low-ceilinged hall with side corridors every few meters. At one point they came to a large T-intersection with several people walking to different destinations, including a young black man escorted by two guards.

Richter stopped them and briefly examined their captive. "Good, he's recovered nicely. Have him ready to go in two hours." Nodding at Bolan and Briggs's guards, he directed, "Take these two to holding and get them prepared."

Bolan and Briggs exchanged quizzical glances, but Richter was already walking away. They were led to a small room that was little more than a hollow cube hewed from the rock of the mountain, with a very sturdy steel door as the only exit.

"Up against the wall." One of the guards held his submachine gun on them while the other expertly frisked Bolan, then Briggs, even removing and examining their shoes and socks. He searched Briggs's hair for pins or picks and even took a look in Bolan's mouth, after warning him that any attempt to bite would cost him teeth. After a glance at the second guard, who already had the butt of his subgun poised, Bolan submitted without any protest.

Afterward, they cut the zip ties, letting Bolan and Briggs massage life back into their aching joints. "New clothes are on the bench. Food will also be coming, and don't worry, it's not drugged. The doc prefers you both to be fully alert and ready for the tests." They both chuckled at that.

Bolan turned to ask what they were talking about, but the guards prodded them inside and then closed the door. He immediately turned to examine the barrier, checking its seams along the frame and the door. "No luck getting through this without a few ounces of C-4, which would blow us to pieces, as well, unfortunately. I imagine the rest of the cell is just as impregnable, unless you know how to tunnel through a few hundred yards of solid rock."

Briggs walked to the metal bench bolted to the floor along one side of the room, picking up a T-shirt and looking at it, then letting it drop. "I can't believe you're so calm about all of this. We have no idea who these people are, or what they're doing out here in the middle of nowhere, yet you're acting like we're taking a tour of the place, as if our lives aren't at stake here."

"We're still breathing, aren't we?" Bolan walked over to her and gently took her by the shoulders, his back to the door. "Look, they obviously want us alive for some reason, we just have to play along—"

"Shh." Her eyes flicked to the wall above the door, where the unblinking eye of a camera lens was watching them.

Bolan lowered his voice. "I know, that's why I'm standing here. I'm sure the room's wired for sound, as well. My point is that we're being kept in one piece for a reason, and we have to play along until we can figure a way out of here."

With a disgusted snort, Briggs twisted out of his grip. "I'm not sure what kind of ridiculous games you play at, but this is real life—real guards, real guns, real bullets. I don't see any possible way out of this except our deaths. I mean, really, why do you think he was so quick to introduce himself to us?"

Although her words weren't lost on Bolan, he kept his tone light as he replied. "Who knows? Maybe he's lonely out here. Perhaps months out here looking at research charts and the other lab coats made him friendlier than your average mad scientist. Just keep your chin up. Don't give them a reason to come after you, but you can't go catatonic on me, either. You're stronger than that. I can see it in you. Keep your eyes and ears open, and watch for opportunities. Something will come along, and I'll need your help to take advantage of it."

"You really think we'll be able to break out of here? I don't even know where the hell we are right now."

"Out the door, down the corridor, left at the large intersection, right at the second one down, back through the airlock, and we're in a truck and home free. Fear and despair only work if you allow them to. Trust me, we can get through this, but we'll have to work together, all right?"

Briggs nodded. "All right… I'm with you."

"Good. Why don't you change? Dressing in the assigned clothes gives captors the impression you're cooperating and willing to work with them. They're more inclined to believe that you're accepting your position." He picked up the shirt and loose knit pants and held them out to her.

Briggs snatched them out of his hand and crossed her arms. "Face the wall, please. And if you can find a way to cover that camera lens, I'd appreciate it."

Bolan took the larger set of clothes and turned toward the opposite corner. "Unfortunately it's too high up, set into the wall and covered with wire mesh, so there isn't much I can do about it."

"That's all right, I'll be quick. I wonder when they'll serve dinner. I hate to say it, but the mention of food made my stomach rumble."

Bolan pulled the T-shirt over his head. "Yeah, mine, too. Just take it when they bring it in. No need for any kind of tantrum or display, and it probably won't get us anywhere anyway. Besides, I'm betting we'll need our strength before this is all over." He walked over to her and sat on the bench, patting the cold metal beside him. "We're going to be all right. I promise."

She regarded Bolan warily, then sank onto the bench and leaned against him. "I hope so. I'm just so scared right now."

"I know," Bolan said as he tried to figure out just exactly how they were going to escape their captivity.

CHAPTER TWENTY-FOUR

Barbara Price sat at her desk and tried to remain busy—mainly to keep her mind off Bolan's situation.

Unfortunately she had done everything she could at the moment. Charlie Mott and *Dragonslayer,* Jack Grimaldi's state-of-the-art combat helicopter, were on their way overseas at that very minute. Also, with Hal Brognola's assistance, she had initiated a sting operation with the CIA to take down Sambele and his minions; no one sold out American agents and got away with it on her watch.

With nothing on her plate until they uncovered more intel, she'd been reviewing after-action reports on recent Phoenix Force and Able Team missions for analysis and feedback.

Her monitor flashed, indicating a call from Tokaido. She answered quickly, since he hardly ever contacted her unless he had pertinent news. The computer hacker's boyish face appeared on screen. "What did you find?"

"A lot of interesting coincidences," he replied. "That all add up to something seriously weird going on down there."

"For example?"

"That recently acquired Stengrave subsidiary, the Michelangelo Corporation, has been sending equipment and supplies to the DRC—a lot of both. However, once it gets there, it all just magically disappears."

"Disappears?" Price frowned. "Explain."

"For starters, there's no official Michelangelo project in the country, not even the hint of a company presence. Whatever's happening down there has been going on since 2009, and their overall budget for this mystery operation has reached more than one hundred million dollars."

"That's an awful lot of money to sink into the jungle with nothing to show for it."

"That's what I thought," Tokaido replied. "Also, the company itself has been *really* shady about logging the money. Invoices and payments were routed through subsidiaries and shell companies, shipments of building materials and computer systems were sent to Europe and Asia and then written off as 'lost' or 'stolen.' This happened far too often to be simply isolated incidents. It's almost as if they don't want their corporate owners to know what's going on. I'm still tracking the money, as I'm sure this goes deeper."

"All right, good work, and absolutely stay on it. Any update on Striker's location?"

"We're still working on it. Twelve kilometers outside the city, he was transferred from the government employee's vehicle into a deuce-and-a-half truck, which then headed deeper into the jungle."

"Okay, so where did it stop?"

"That's what we're still triangulating. It reached a series of jungle-covered hills and then disappeared. Vanished right before our eyes."

Price's shoulders slumped. Without a target, she

couldn't send in a strike team. Even though she tried not to show it, Tokaido still noticed.

"We'll find him, you can count on it. Besides, Striker's been in plenty of tight spots before and he always finds a way out of them. Hell, Jack and Charlie will probably get there and find he's already taken the place out by himself."

Price smiled again, gamely this time. "You're probably right, Akira—and thanks." She squared her shoulders. "Okay, so what do we know about the area where the truck disappeared?"

Now the young computer hacker was the one frowning. "Topographically speaking, not a lot. Congolese building and development records are fluid, to say the least, when they exist at all. However, one of our satellite monitoring programs has been tracking encrypted burst transmissions from a region within thirty klicks of where the truck disappeared. They're being bounced off several satellites, but I've tracked those kinds of communications before. The path the truck was taking headed pretty much toward where the bursts are coming from."

"Now that's promising," Price said. "Try to narrow it down as far as you can, then send those coordinates to Jack and have him scout the area. If we can get any kind of fix on Striker, we're that much closer to finding him. Let me know whatever else you turn up."

"You got it. I'll be in touch as soon as I've determined the best position for Jack to start his sweep. Akira out."

The call window disappeared.

Price sat back in her chair, pondering everything that had just happened. Something about it just wasn't fitting together, especially this uncovered information about the Michelangelo Corporation—information that their owner company didn't seem to know about. The mission controller had never been one to believe in coincidence, and all of the evidence uncovered on the heels of the biochemical assault on the Armenian village smacked of something larger in the works. But how was something that like not popping up on any law-enforcement radar?

Of course, it wouldn't be the first time a terrorist group had managed to carry out their plan, despite hints of the operation being uncovered, she thought as she accessed Stony Man's top-secret list of back doors into just about every major law-enforcement organization around the world. That's why Stony Man existed, after all—to make sure they didn't get away with it again.

FIRKE STARED at the rows of dozens of ampoules of oily black viscous liquid; each nestled in its own foam cutout inside the stainless-steel briefcase. "How many are there?"

"Sixty," Richter answered. "If applied properly, each one has the potential to infect a minimum of four to six thousand of the target genotype. After the initial contact, it will take care of further transmission, of course."

"Of course." Firke closed the lid and made sure the locks were secure before picking up the case. "Incredible work, Doctor, as usual."

"We do what we can." A smile played around Richter's lips. "Are you sure you have to go so soon? After all, thanks to you, we are about to begin the latest round of tests on the man who almost ruined the Armenian operation. I thought you would be interested in seeing how he fares."

Firke regarded the doctor coolly. "The only way I'd be interested in seeing that bastard again is in the sights of my pistol right before I put a bullet into his face. Besides—" he raised the briefcase "—you have your orders and I have mine."

"Which must be carried out as soon as possible. I understand," Richter said. "Safe travels."

"Very kind of you, Doctor." Firke walked to the door, then paused as if he had just remembered something. "I think you should know that on my last trip here, I was ordered to arm the fail-safe system in this complex. In the event of discovery or an accident—"

"I have all of the proper codes," Richter patted his lab coat. "Do not worry, it will be taken care of in the event circumstances require it."

"Good. Goodbye, Doctor."

Carrying the briefcase firmly in his hand, Firke left the compound, strode to his waiting Land Rover and got in.

"To the airport," he said, resting the metal case on his lap. "It's time to begin remaking the world."

DR. RICHTER CAME for Bolan and Briggs ninety minutes after they had been placed in their cell. He entered the cell, accompanied by three guards.

"Brought the entire welcoming committee, I see." Bolan rose wearily to his feet. His back had stiffened after the kidney shot, but he wasn't about to give any of them the satisfaction of seeing him in pain.

"It's time. Both of you will come with us."

Leaning against the wall, Bolan crossed his arms. "What if we refuse?"

The doctor's neutral expression didn't change. "Then you both will be shot with a stun gun, no matter if only one of you resists, and you'll be taken regardless. I think you'd both prefer to walk under your own power...especially you, Mr. Cooper. I don't think you'll want to be suffering from any residual muscle spasms in the next few minutes."

"Well, since we don't seem to have a choice...." Bolan turned to Briggs and nodded toward the door. "Come on. It'll be all right."

Briggs rose from the far end of the bench and approached warily, as if ready to bolt at the first opportunity. She crossed her arms and fell into step beside Bolan as they left the room.

Richter set the pace, with one guard beside him. Bolan and Briggs followed, with the other two guards behind them. "So, what do you have planned for us?" Bolan asked.

The tall scientist, his head bowed to avoid the low ceilings, glanced back with a sardonic look on his face. "I must admit, I'm torn between telling you, to see if you can comprehend my work, or keeping it from you to better judge your natural, unbiased reaction."

"Why don't you let me be the judge? I'm sure I can handle whatever you plan to throw at me."

"We will see, Mr. Cooper, we will see. I can tell you that this installation was originally built to research and develop medicines from the rain forest. Did you know that there are thousands of plants in these jungles around the world whose properties are barely known?

Lately, however, our employers have assigned us a different direction to pursue."

They came to another airlock door and Richter produced a small key card, which he inserted into a slot at the side of the entrance. Walking into another airlock, they went through the decontamination process again before stepping out the other side into a large laboratory. The guards remained alert and close at all times.

The room was at least fifteen yards wide by twenty-five yards long, and filled with lab tables, computer monitors and other complicated machines Bolan didn't recognize. It was ringed on all three sides with large windows, each of which looked into a separate room. To the left was a room just as large, filled with at least a half-dozen large, listless, black-furred apes, all being monitored by white-coated scientists. Ahead was what looked like some kind of large observation room that had been transformed into a jungle habitat, with a tree sprouting in the middle and, as they approached, Bolan saw dirt and tall grass covering the floor. Behind the windows of the entire right wall was another kind of laboratory, where silver-suited people, covered from head to toe in environmental safety suits worked among centrifuges, more computer monitors, glass test tubes, beakers and pipettes.

"This is impressive," Bolan murmured, though he had no real idea what he was looking at. What he was sure of, however, was that he had found the origin point of the virus outbreak in Armenia, and it had to be stopped, one way or another.

Briggs, however, was not nearly as interested in their surroundings. "What are you doing to those apes? They look ill."

"Unfortunately this species does not thrive well in captivity. We've been extracting samples from them for experimentation, but that is of no concern to either of you."

He turned to Bolan. "You, Mr. Cooper, are going to be the test subject for the latest variation of our biggest success to date."

That got Bolan's full attention. "What?" As he said that, the guards around him snapped to full alert, pointing their weapons at him. "The virus you used on Arkatar?"

The scientist passed off his concern with a shrug. "Not that precisely—a more refined version of it that should have less negative side effects. I would think a man of your capabilities would be intrigued at the opportunity to be turned into Superman for a short time. Now, we need to get some basic measurements from you, blood type, resting pulse rate, that sort of thing."

"Not a chance." As he spoke, Bolan measured the distance between himself and the scientist, evaluating whether he could reach the man without getting shot first.

Richter regarded him with a speculative expression. "Let me tell you what you're thinking right now. 'If I can take a hostage, can I escape from here?' I can assure you that there is no chance of that happening. My guards will kill both of you in an instant rather than risk an escape." Even as he said that, Richter edged a step backward.

As Bolan listened to the scientist, he sensed that the man was perfectly serious. "Right."

"Of course, I hope it won't come to that," Richter continued. "I mean, we could always strap you down before injecting you. There is also the hostage we hold—" his gaze flicked toward Briggs, who was hugging herself as she looked around, shivering in the scientist's lair "—but rather than resort to such crude tactics, I would prefer that you simply allow us to run your test in peace and quiet."

"But if I don't, you also have the guys with the guns." Bolan glanced around one last time, but failing to see an avenue of escape, he sighed. "Okay, let's get this over with."

"Matt, you can't seriously go along with this!" Briggs had snapped out of her daze.

"Again, I don't see that we have much choice in the matter." *Also, it's a given that my refusal would probably mean a quick death instead of a slow one,* he thought. "Besides, the doc here will make sure I come out of it in one piece, right, Richter?"

"Mr. Cooper, you'll be pleased to know that my entire hypothesis depends on it. I have high hopes that a more disciplined mind will be able to handle what I have in store for you. Now, if you would step over here, please."

With a shrug, Bolan walked to the table, covered by the guards at all times, both careful to remain at least ten feet away from him. Richter's assistant attached a blood pressure monitor to the Executioner's finger, then drew two small test tubes of his blood. He then attached an electrode to Bolan's temple. "This is to get a baseline of your brain wave patterns. Just remain calm and silent, and try not to think about anything in particular."

Bolan sat for a few minutes, busy contemplating just how he was going to get himself and Briggs out of there, and coming up empty.

After a few minutes the tech removed the electrode from his head. "We've got it."

"What's next, Doc?"

"Since we have enough for a baseline comparison—it's hardly what I would call a complete workup, but I imagine we can get your physical records back in the States—we might as well begin the actual experiment. Stand and roll up your right shirt sleeve. Remember, please don't do anything you might regret."

When Bolan did so, he was grabbed by the two guards, one to each arm, and held fast. "I said I'd co-operate. What's with the goon squad?" he asked as they marched him over to the thick steel-and-Plexiglas door that led to the jungle observation room.

"That, actually, is for our own protection, Mr. Cooper." Richter was fiddling with a pair of small gray devices that looked like futuristic pistols, fitting a small ampoule containing some kind of thick black liquid into the reservoir. "Hold still, this might sting a bit." He pressed the tip to Bolan's upper arm, and he heard a brief hiss. Richter immediately followed that up with the other gray tube, pressing it against the same spot. "Start the timer now. Get him into the room."

"What am I supposed to do in there?"

"Another man will join you shortly. When you see him, you will know what to do."

"What the hell does that mean?" Bolan asked as the guards pushed him toward the door, which slid open as they approached. They shoved him through, the door closing on its own behind him.

This room, approximately the same size as the main laboratory, was hot and quiet. Somewhere, Bolan heard the steady drip of water, but other than that, all sound had been cut off. He couldn't hear anything from the outside lab. He took a cautious step into the area, hands held away from his sides, ready to defend or attack as necessary. Coming across a stained patch of dirt, he knelt beside it, touching it with his fingers. He scratched off a bit and lifted it to his nose, smelling the unusual loamy scent of the jungle earth, along with a familiar odor he'd smelled too many times before—spilled blood.

Bolan rose, every sense on sudden alert as he looked around, trying to gauge where an attack would come from. However, as he stood there, he realized he could now hear *everything* inside the room. From the soft hiss of the air-recirculator to the minute noises his shoe made as it brushed across the dirt, to the faint rustle on the far side of the room—

Someone's over there—

My enemy—

Must be destroyed—

Bolan shook his head. Where did that come from? His mind had suddenly filled with overwhelming images of finding the other man in the room and attacking him—no, *destroying* him. Bolan put a hand to his temple, his pulse pounding in his ears.

What the hell is happening to me?

The rustle sounded again, a bit louder now. Focusing on the area where the sound was coming from, he found with some astonishment that he could see individual blades of grass moving on the far side. Tentatively he lifted his nose and sniffed the air, finding it redolent of decaying plants, fresh bark, feces, that same hint of blood—and sweat, coming from the corner to his right, which was overshadowed by the tree in the center of the room.

He's on the move—

I'd better check it out, just in case—

Bolan took his hand away from his face to find it clenched into a fist, just like the other one at his side. He felt great, every sense preternaturally aware. His body had stopped hurting, even his back, and every inch overflowed with energy, as if he could run a dozen marathons back-to-back. But above all, his mind was filled with an overwhelming predatory instinct, as if he had reverted to the base responses to conflict—fight or flight. But it was difficult to consider flight as a viable option anymore. Instead there was only the burning need for combat, to dominate his opponent—any opponent—and leave the person bleeding and defeated in the dirt.

Almost unaware that his lips had peeled back from his teeth in a feral grin, Bolan stepped farther into the room, his eyes wide and searching.

Hunting for his prey.

CHAPTER TWENTY-FIVE

Shivering in the chilly laboratory, Briggs noticed she was pretty much ignored by the staff bustling around her and the experiment. One of the technicians oversaw a bank of monitors that showed several different angles of the room Bolan had just been shoved into. Another one watched what looked like a heart rate monitor, while a third kept an eye on another machine that showed a range of constantly fluctuating numbers even she didn't understand.

"Despite your opinion of me, I'm hoping that your friend Mr. Cooper will prove this latest variation a success," Richter said. "Indeed, I have no wish to see him killed. His survival is vital to my experiment."

Briggs started and turned to see Richter standing beside her. "What are you talking about? Tell me that the black stuff you injected into him wasn't the same as what was inflicted on those poor villagers in Armenia."

"Not exactly. Even in the short time frame between that field test and what we're doing right now, we have greatly refined the virus." Although the doctor appeared calm, Briggs sensed he really wanted to talk about the experiment.

Might as well give him the chance, she thought. Besides if he's so confident we won't make it out of here, then I should be able to get him to talk more about it.

"Look, we already know that you've spliced the *T. gondii* parasite with a fast-acting rabies vaccine, but its effects turned people into crazed killers. How did you refine it?"

"You might be more aware of the local fauna out here, since you're more familiar with the region," Richter said. "Have you ever heard of the Goualougo chimpanzees?"

Briggs thought for a moment. "Aren't those the tool-using chimps located somewhere in the Congo rain forest?"

"Correct." Richter actually smiled, as if Briggs had been a student who had given the correct answer. "Their habitat is in a region known as the Goualougo triangle, the western border of which is about ten kilometers from here. Not only are those chimpanzees tool-users, but they can also kill a full-grown leopard. My company directed us to set up shop here, as it were, to try to discover what made them so formidable. I'm pleased to say that we have, for the most part."

"That's why you have them in captivity?" Briggs's voice dripped disgust. "You're experimenting on them?"

Richter's bushy brows knit together. "Hardly! We've given them the best accommodations, treated their diseases and injuries, and have provided them with a better life here than they ever would have in the wild. Naturally, that comes with a price. We needed the samples from them to create our virus, but rest assured, they have been treated like honored guests. Them and a number of gorillas."

"Says the man who just injected a man with an unknown substance and locked him in a room. Given how you treat humans, I don't think I'd care to be an 'honored guest' here." Briggs walked around him, ostensibly to get a better view of what was happening in the next room. "The black liquid—what is it exactly?"

Richter smiled indulgently. "That 'black liquid' as you refer to it, is the latest version of the viral cocktail, but with an additional twist. We've added synthesized chimpanzee adrenaline, modified to be absorbed by the human bloodstream. It gives the user superhuman strength, reflexes and senses, turning them, in effect, into an apex predator. Faster, stronger, better than human."

Briggs frowned. "That must take an awful toll on the test subjects, I suppose." Richter gave her a sidelong look and she mentally kicked herself.

"An astute observation. The subject suffers both physical and mental impairment after prolonged use, or if the dosage is too high. However, given his training, I expect that Mr. Cooper will come through the test in better shape than our usual subjects."

Briggs walked to the table where Richter had injected Cooper. The air-hypo and several of the black ampoules were still on the table. She'd watched the scientist do it; it hadn't looked difficult—just insert the ampoule, place the end against the subject's skin, pull the trigger... She crossed her arms, staring at the thick glass. "But if this also contains the Artakar virus, then he's going to exhibit those signs in a few hours."

"Oh...you and your colleagues haven't figured that out yet." Richter shook his head. "Perhaps you are not as capable as I had first thought."

She raised her head to glare at him. "Well, why don't you fill me in, then?"

The doctor nodded, as if indulging a wayward child.

"This experiment has two components to it. The first, as I stated, is to study the effects of the virus on a trained individual. The second is to verify that the programmed virus does not activate in an improper genetic host."

Briggs blinked as the ramifications of the man's statement sank in. "You've programmed the virus to only attack targets that meet its preselected genetic criteria."

Richter nodded. "Exactly. That is why we needed to test the sample on a localized and isolated group. The village population served that purpose well." He stated this with no more emotion than reciting the results of an experiment on lab rats. "Mr. Cooper will benefit from the artificial stimulus in his system, which, in a real-world environment, would serve to spread the virus further, but if we've done our job, the virus will otherwise lie dormant in his system until it dies, twenty-four to forty-eight hours later, and is expelled."

My God, he's created a genetically defined eugenics system, she thought. The ethical scientist in her was appalled at his methods, even if she could admire the scientific breakthroughs he had made. The benefits of such a system were incredible. After all, it could be used to deliver whatever someone wanted to deliver to a particular population—antibodies, vaccines, vitamins. But to use it so callously...

To hide her reaction, Briggs turned away from him. "So, what happens now?"

As if reading her mind, Richter nodded at one of the guards, who walked over to her, his flat, dark gaze staring right through her, as if daring to her make a move. "As I told Mr. Cooper, there is another man in there.

When one of them sees the other, the experiment will begin in earnest."

"Doctor, both subjects are now within ten yards of each other."

Briggs felt a pressure on her elbow and allowed Richter to lead her to a position between the monitors and the window.

"We've introduced cover to see whether the affected subjects will utilize their natural surrounding to maximize their position before attacking, or simply strike once they've sighted their target. The foliage can often obscure what happens, hence the cameras."

"The other person has been injected, as well?"

"Of course. If he hadn't been, Mr. Cooper would tear him apart within seconds. He's not the usual test subject, either, for what it's worth. He's a criminal from the worst slum in Kinshasa, delivered to me by specific request. I've been studying his reactions to the virus and adrenaline, evaluating whether the environment he's been raised in has given him any particular advantages. He's been through two of these trials already and I'm curious to see if that gives him any advantage over his opponent. Ah, there's Mr. Cooper right now."

Briggs followed his pointing finger to a monitor in the lower corner, and saw Bolan moving through a patch of waist-high grass, intent on someone or something she couldn't see. But the expression on his face made her hands rise to cover her mouth in shock.

Bolan's handsome features were twisted into a mask of pure feral hatred, his forehead wrinkled as he stalked forward, his blue eyes wide, the pupils dilated, his jaw clenched; teeth bared in a silent snarl as he moved closer to his target. He looked as if he was an instant away from killing anything in his path, whether that be a chimpanzee, a human or an elephant. He looked as if he would take anything on, even if he destroyed himself in the process, as long as he got the chance to tear into his enemy.

No, it wasn't just that, Briggs realized with a frisson of horror as she watched him stalk the other man, now on camera, whose features bore a similar expression.

He looked as if he was enjoying *himself.*

TRANSFORMED INTO a pure predator, Bolan advanced on the other man.

His world had been revealed as though he'd never known it before. Every color, every sound, every disturbance of every air current around him was as distinct and individual as if they had arrows pointing to them telling him everything he needed to know. Every sense—eyes, ears, nose, even taste and touch—was wide open, gathering the myriad data surrounding him. Instead of being overwhelmed by the flood of raw sensory input, his mind categorized it with ease, discarding all useless information and channeling the vital facts he needed to execute his hunt.

His muscles were loose yet strong, bursting with energy just waiting to be unleashed on his enemy. His nose told him the man was now only about six yards away, and his preternaturally sharp vision confirmed that when he saw a shadow move on the other side of the tree.

Waiting for me to come to him, he thought, lips peeled back in a silent snarl. *I don't see why.*

Shaking his head, Bolan mastered the sudden impulse to stalk the other man. *If he's anything like me,* together we could take the guards. With that thought in mind, he stepped out into clear view and raised his hand. "Hey—"

The moment the other man heard him, he charged forward. Bolan was surprised for the barest second, taking in his rage-filled face, narrowed eyes and snarling mouth. The man looked just like the people back at the village, arms reaching out to tear into him.

Although every fiber of his being wanted to meet the man headlong and tear him apart, Bolan resisted the urge enough to jump up and grab a tree branch over his head, levering himself up into the foliage. But the funny thing was that everything around him seemed to be happening in slow motion, while he moved through it all normally. He was already on the other side of the tree and ready to swoop on his prey before the branches he'd disturbed during his passage had stopped swaying.

If I can get the drop on him, I can incapacitate him without having to kill him, Bolan thought.

A branch cracked below and the man came into view, searching the thick branches for his prey. Without hesitation, Bolan swung off the branch and pounced down onto his target, only to find the other man already rolling out of the way as Bolan plummeted down, hands outstretched to tear into whoever was underneath him—man, animal, it didn't matter anymore. Any rational thought had been replaced by the collection and processing of all data aimed toward one singular goal: to destroy his enemy.

As he hit the ground Bolan shoulder-rolled away from the other man. A shadow loomed over him and a thick tree branch slammed into the dirt where his head had been a moment before. Springing to his feet, Bolan turned to see the blurred form of his opponent coming at him, the branch cocked high overhead, about to be brought down on his skull.

The Executioner bared his teeth in a grimace of fury. Instead of dodging again, he rushed at the man, closing to inside his club's range before the slender black man could drive it into the top of his head.

Just before they would have collided, with the man fully committed to his blow, Bolan sidestepped his opponent. The man passed by so close by he felt breath on his face. Bolan threw his right elbow into the guy's nose, while his left fist sank into the man's side below his ribs with every ounce of magnified strength he possessed. He felt cartilage and muscle tear at the impact and knew he'd weakened him, but the man wasn't down by a long shot.

When he turned to face his enemy again, Bolan found the African coming after him, the wiry man's mouth open in a silent scream of rage, blood pouring out of his crushed nose to stain his teeth crimson. He swung the branch like a baseball bat toward Bolan's shoulder. The soldier ducked while deflecting the blow with the edge of his hand, pushing the branch up and away. His opponent didn't even seem fazed by the blows he had taken; he was moving just as fast as if Bolan hadn't tagged him.

The man whirled and lashed out with the limb again, going for Bolan's midsection this time. Again, the soldier stepped into the flying limb—which still looked as though it was coming at him in slow motion—and as it came closer to his ribs, swept up his right arm, redirecting the branch over his head. As soon as it cleared his hair, he stopped it with his left hand and then brought his clenched right fist down on the branch, snapping it in two. The wood had barely finished cracking apart when Bolan flicked out the piece in his left hand at the man's head, just missing him. He felt a solid crunch in his side, and looked down to see the shorter piece pull away from his ribs as the guy pulled it back to hit him again.

A red rage swept down over Bolan's vision. He jabbed the ragged end of the broken stick at the guy's face, feeling the splintered end pierce his flesh, making him falter. Yanking it away, the soldier hammered the club on the man's head. He felt hard blows punishing his ribs and chest, but ignored them. He felt no pain; although he was aware of the club hitting him, it felt as though he was outside his own body, watching it happen, instead of experiencing it himself.

When he raised his own club again, he saw the ruin he had made of the man's face. Both eyes were blackened and rapidly swelling shut, his nose had been flattened and his teeth broken.

Yet he still attacked, spitting teeth and blood out as he slashed at Bolan with his club. The soldier whipped his bludgeon against this opponent's right forearm, snapping both bones. But the man brought his weapon back again, grabbing Bolan's shirt with his left hand.

Taking his adversary's left hand, Bolan forced him to let go by crushing the joint of the first metacarpal bone in his thumb. Still holding on, the Executioner stepped around the man's back and wrenched the guy's arm into a hammerlock. He brought his club down on the man's left shoulder, hearing his collarbone break under the blow. He repeated the maneuver on the man's right shoulder, rendering his arms useless.

The fight raged on until Bolan finally found an opportunity to bring his club down on the back of his adversary's neck, breaking it. The body toppled over. Panting with the effort, Bolan just stood there for a moment, staring at the corpse.

As if coming out of a thick mental fog, he stared at the club in his hand as if he'd never seen it before in his life. Opening his throbbing fingers, he let the crude weapon fall to the floor. His lungs heaved as if he had just run a marathon, and his left side ached as though it was on fire. Taking a tentative step away from the body, he felt sudden, stabbing pain as one of his broken ribs rubbed together.

"Mr. Cooper? Can you hear me?" A disembodied voice spoke from all around him. Bolan turned around, looking for the source. "I'm afraid you cannot see me right now. If you understand the words you hear, raise your right hand and give a thumbs-up sign."

His brow furrowing, Bolan slowly did as he was told, wincing at the movement.

"Very good. Some men are going to come into the room. I would like you to not do anything while they are in there. Can you do that for me?"

"Y-yes." Bolan swallowed through his suddenly very dry throat. "I'm thirsty...I—I need some water."

"Very good. We will bring you some right away. Just stay right where you are, and our men will be with you shortly. Remember, it is very important that you do not interfere with them in any way. Is that understood?"

Bolan nodded, his eyes never leaving the body in front of him. Walking over on legs that felt as stiff and unyielding as carved blocks of wood, he knelt to get a closer look at the body. Vague memories of the last few minutes flitted through his mind, disjointed images of some kind of fight—leaping from a tree at him… beating his face in…crushing his throat…snapping his neck…. He remembered it; felt both the injuries the man had given him, as well as his bruised knuckles and sore muscles.

Reaching out with sore fingers, he grabbed the body by the shoulder and pulled it over. When he saw the man's ruined face, Bolan grew angry.

He had killed before, of course, when the situation warranted or when his life was in danger. But being manipulated—forced into killing another man, even if he was doing it in self-defense—that was something else altogether.

"Easy now—you're all right—just relax and let us take a look at you." Bolan saw a quartet of silver-suited men, their faces hidden by full masks, surrounding him. Two held rifles in their hands, both pointed at him, the third walked over to him and shone a small, bright light in his eyes while the fourth man went to the body, zooming in on it with a small digital recorder.

"Can you hear me?" the man holding the light asked Bolan, who nodded.

"How many fingers am I holding up?"

Bolan registered four fingers and told him so.

"What is your name?"

"Matt…Matt Cooper."

"How do you feel?"

"Tired…really tired."

The man nodded and gave Bolan a plastic cup of water. He spoke as if he was dictating to a recorder. "Pupil dilation is normal…subject responds to visual and aural stimuli within normal parameters…"

The fourth man looked up from his examination of the corpse. "Multiple fractures of the arms, shoulders and bones of the face. Death caused by blunt trauma."

He rose and walked over to Bolan, training the camera on him the entire way. "What do you remember about the encounter with the other subject?"

Encounter? Bolan frowned. *As if I had just met the man walking casually while walking through the jungle, instead of methodically stalking him and killing him?*

He gulped water to gain a few seconds to think, unsure of what, if anything, he should tell them. "It all happened so fast—sort of a blur—one moment I saw him, the next I was standing over his body."

The blare of a warning klaxon startled everyone as a red light flashed in the room. A pleasant female voice issued orders from a loudspeaker on the wall.

"Intruder alert. Intruder alert. This is not a drill. All personnel secure all equipment and data and report to assigned stations. All personnel secure equipment and data and report to assigned stations. Repeat, this is not a drill."

The four men looked at each other just as the entire lab shook slightly. The man examining Bolan got his attention by waving his hand. "Stay here, Mr. Cooper, we'll be right back."

The four men ran to the door and exited the room, leaving Bolan alone with the body. Dizziness suddenly swept over him and the last thing he saw as he toppled to the floor was the brutalized face of the nameless man he had killed.

CHAPTER TWENTY-SIX

Jack Grimaldi studied the strange compound through his powerful night-vision binoculars. Instead of a rough campsite hacked out of the jungle, or an isolated village, he saw armed guards patrolling in front of what looked like an ordinary cliff face. But when he scanned the rock wall with his thermal vision, he got a different air temperature, not to mention the distinct outline of air several degrees colder leaking out around the edges of the wall.

Once Charlie Mott and he had received the coordinates of this location from Akira Tokaido, the Stony Man pilots had taken to the air at nightfall to conduct a thorough reconnaissance of the area. Their FLIR suite had located three leopards, a group of apes moving through the area—and several men grouped near what had looked like a heated rock wall. They had found a clearing four klicks away large enough to land and approached the place on foot. Once Grimaldi had gotten a better view of the rock wall, he realized what was off about it.

"The damn thing is hollow," he muttered.

Mott, lying on his stomach next to Grimaldi, studied the incongruous scene, as well. "You're sure the last position of the truck was right around here?"

Grimaldi didn't take his eyes off the armed guards as

he replied, "It wasn't just 'right around here.' The GPS tracker from the satellite placed it literally about fifty meters from our current position. If you look carefully, you can see the tread marks where they drove it inside. They go right up to the wall and disappear."

Mott grunted. "I think we just figured out what happened to the DRC soldiers, not to mention Bolan the Army doctor. So what's the plan now?"

Grimaldi scanned the area again, paying close attention to the trees surrounding the rock face, as well as the craggy cliff wall itself. "One, two, three cameras watching the entrance. Also, these guys are wearing headsets, so they most likely report to a security command post inside. That all makes sneaking in problematic. However, there's always the direct approach."

"Direct approach? What are you talking about?"

The Stony Man pilot lowered the binoculars. "What I'm about to suggest is a very risky plan, some might say suicidal. The right insertion plan could get one of us inside, but I've got to be honest—it relies on the element of surprise and boldness, and there's a strong chance one of us could get seriously hurt or killed while executing it."

Mott turned to regard him with a frown. "I love your optimism, but I know you too well. You must have an ace up your sleeve."

"A big one."

"Okay, what'd you have in mind?"

Grimaldi looked at him with a grin. "I thought we'd walk right up to the front entrance."

Mott stared at him. "You've got to be kidding me." He looked at the four armed men in front of the false wall. "In case you forgot, Striker's inside there and we're out here."

"Hey, I've saved his butt more than once, remember?"

"Yeah, when you were at the controls of a helicopter most of the time, remember that?"

"Exactly. I haven't told you how I was planning to knock on their door first. Come on, let's head back to the *Dragonslayer*. I'll fill you in on the way."

As they jogged back, Grimaldi contacted Stony Man. "Akira, I need construction schematics for an underground site at the following coordinates, Priority One. The location was probably something built in the 1950s through 1970s—I don't know what kind, but it's been converted to some kind of underground facility capable of holding about forty to seventy people. Send whatever you find to *Dragonslayer*'s tactical computer ASAP."

After signing off, he detailed his plan to Mott, whose expression slowly changed from incredulous to skeptical to reluctantly convinced.

"Okay, if we go that way, I doubt we'll have any problem opening the false wall. The real problem will be getting through the inner door. If the outside guards don't have a way in, we're stuck until the reinforcements come out to try to blow us away."

"I'm kind of counting on all the other guards running to the front once we breach the entrance. Either way, we use speed and surprise to break in and do what we have to do before they can mount an organized resistance. A hidden operation like this can't have too many security guards. I'd say we're looking at fifteen, maybe twenty tops, and spread out through the complex. Some will be off duty, probably sleeping at this hour, so if we'll take out the ones at the door, we might only be facing ten more inside at the most."

Mott shook his head as they crested the last hill and came upon the parked combat chopper. "Maybe so, but we're still only two people. You're assuming we can get in, find Striker and Briggs, and get out alive. It's a tall order, to say the least."

"Yeah, but if this goes down how I figure it will, we'll be inside their perimeter before the second wave can mobilize. And once the security alarm's tripped, I'm sure the big guy will seize the opportunity to create his own distraction, so we'll have two flashpoints occurring at the same time."

"Assuming he's not stuck in a cell somewhere." Mott rubbed his chin thoughtfully. "You are planning on letting mission control know about your plan, right?"

"Of course," Grimaldi said as he punched in the number to Price's direct line. She picked up immediately.

"Yes, Flyboy?"

"We've found where Striker's being held." He described the location and the security. "I have a plan to get him out, however." He also went into the same details he'd explained to Mott.

"Are you sure your assessment of the layout is accurate?" Price asked. "I don't want any friendly fire casualties."

"Neither do we," Grimaldi replied as the combat helicopter's computer beeped. "Hold on, I just got the files from Akira." He quickly scanned the structure schematics. "As I thought, they sealed off the compound from the outside environment. And there's some kind of large staging area ahead of the main airlock, so we've got some space between the two. Besides, if I'm reading this right, even if they were right on the other side, they're protected and then some."

"All right, I'm authorizing you to use whatever force you deem necessary to recover Striker and Doc One. Be careful, all right?"

"Always," the pilot replied. "We'll contact you when the operation's done."

"We'll be waiting. Good luck, Flyboy."

"We're green," Grimaldi said as he began the preflight warm-up. "Lay out an urban assault kit for both of us, just in case." He flipped a switch and the rotors overhead began turning. "Ready?"

"As I will ever be," Mott replied while loading an HK MP-7 A-1 submachine gun with a 40-round magazine.

TWENTY-FIVE minutes later the four guards at the front of the false wall looked up at the distant sound of a helicopter approaching.

"Think that prick Firke is coming back?" one of them asked.

"Don't know and don't care, as long as he doesn't fuck with me again," said the second, who'd been in the control room the night he had made his unscheduled visit. "The bastard gives me the creeps."

"It's coming closer," the first guard said as he hit his radio. "Control, this is Front Door, do we have any scheduled visitors this evening?"

"No, but the last two times we did, we barely got any notice, so it wouldn't surprise me if this is someone from HQ showing up unannounced again. Let me check with the doctor."

"Affirmative," the first guard replied, nodding at the second. "He's checking on it."

"Well, he better hurry up," a third guard said, raising his voice over the sound of the approaching aircraft. "Whoever it is, is almost here."

"Take it easy. It's not like they can land anywhere close," the first guard replied. "Probably a government hotshot heading to his mistress in the boonies."

The other three guards chuckled at that, then the first guard heard the control person in his earpiece. "Front Door, this is Control, there are no scheduled visitors for this evening, over."

"Roger, Control." The guard scanned the night sky. "Reporting an unknown aircraft in the vicinity—"

Those were the last words that guard—or any of the others—ever said. Before anyone could react, six high-explosive 66 mm Hydra 70 rockets streaked down onto their position. Two-point-one seconds later, their world was obliterated in a huge chain of explosions as the seventeen pounds of B-4 high explosive in each missile detonated, shattering the false wall and pulverizing the men standing in front of it.

The night-black helicopter adjusted its position slightly and then launched six more rockets in a staggered spread at the ground in front of the kill zone. The second Hydra 70 volley leveled the trees and foliage in a twenty-meter radius, creating a rough but usable staging point for the next phase of the operation.

Mott, his head covered in the advanced VR helmet that gave him visual and detection clarity beyond anything found in the U.S. military, scanned the large chamber beyond the demolished front door as he brought the helicopter down into the improvised landing area. "No movement sighted. Debark in ten seconds!"

"Not too low! Don't need to have the tail chew into a stump!" Grimaldi shouted back.

"Jeez, teach my grandmother to suck eggs, why don't you?" Mott replied with a grin. "We're here! Go, go, go, and good luck!"

Three meters above the jungle floor, Grimaldi jumped out of the chopper, tucking and rolling on a bare spot on the still smoking ground. With the rotor wash blowing leaves and twigs over him, he came up facing the compound entrance and charged inside, dimly lit by fading fires left over from the explosions.

He could see a rough garage had been hacked out of the mountain. One of the deuce-and-a-half trucks had been shoved over by the force of the blast, although it still looked drivable. Sweeping left and right for any gunners, he spotted the motionless forms of three people killed or knocked unconscious by the blasts. Heading for the main door on the far side of the chamber, he was halfway there when it cycled open and disgorged the first of the relief guards.

The man stared at him in a fatal moment of shock before bringing his FAMAS assault rifle into play. Grimaldi squeezed the trigger of his HK twice. The two bullets punched through the man's heart and rib cage, dropping him where he stood, but not before he squeezed the trigger of his rifle. Three bullets puffed harmlessly into the floor with a loud bark. However, as he fell, two more guards charge into the garage, rifles at the ready.

"Shit!" Grimaldi leaped toward the nearest cover, a mud-splattered Land Rover, as they opened fire. Peeking out to see if he could return fire, the pilot found that the two guards had been reinforced by two more, which covered the first pair as they began advancing into the garage, firing short bursts to keep him under cover. "Ah, *Dragonslayer,* this is Flyboy. I'm pinned down by four, repeat four, hostiles. Requesting immediate assistance, over."

"Roger that, Flyboy. Backup is on the way. I suggest hugging the ground and covering your ears."

Scooting back to the wall, Grimaldi did exactly that as what sounded like the world's largest chain saw tore through the room a few moments later. He heard loud plunks and thunks as projectiles carved through the vehicle next to him. It only lasted about five seconds, but when it was over, and Grimaldi raised his head again, the garage had been transformed.

Any vehicle in the combat helicopter's line of sight had been destroyed. The Land Rover he hid behind now sported two-dozen palm-size holes from the armor-piercing ammunition. The vehicle settled heavily on a flattened tire as coolant and oil leaked from its destroyed engine. Grimaldi warily searched for the guards, but found none living. "*Dragonslayer,* this is Flyboy…nice work. Standby for further assistance if needed."

"Roger that, Flyboy," Mott replied.

Leading with his submachine gun, Grimaldi headed for the steel access doors, which were starting to cycle closed. Slipping inside, he hugged the left wall as he approached the second set of doors leading to the rest of the compound. A calm, female voice announced that the airlock was compromised and needed repair. Glancing at the half-dozen holes in the steel door, the pilot shrugged. "Gonna need a lot more than repairing, honey," he said as he slapped the open-close control button on the side.

The moment the door cycled open, a burst of gunfire spit bullets into the airlock, forcing Grimaldi to flatten against the wall as bullets panged around him.

"Damn it!" he growled as he stuck out his MP-7 and returned fire blindly. Taking two smoke grenades off his tactical harness, he pulled the pins on both and let the bombs cook for two seconds before tossing them into the hallway, drawing another burst of fire. Pulling down his thermal goggles, he activated them as the hissing smoke began to fill the hallway.

Taking a small, thermal-vision camera from a side pocket and extending the flexible end around out the corner, Grimaldi was able to get a look at the opposition. The camera revealed six security men at the other end of the smoke, all in covering fire positions. The rest of the compound could be accessed once this obstacle was out of the way.

Popping a tear gas grenade, Grimaldi replaced his thermal goggles with a gas mask and then adjusted the goggles over them so he could see through the mask well enough. When he judged the room sufficiently wreathed in the expanding smoke and tear gas, he hit the floor and began firing. Scattered coughs came from the two far corners and the Stony Man pilot aimed there first. Continuing along the edge of the room, he aimed at the hacking, doubled-up figure in the corner and squeezed the trigger of his MP-7 twice. The form stopped coughing and slumped to the ground, wheezing once before going still. Grimaldi swung his weapon over to find the second man when he heard the sound of multiple footsteps approaching and saw three more men emerge at the far end of the hallway, each with the distinctive shape of a rifle in his hands.

Automatic fire roared at the same time. Muzzle-flashes strobed in the near-darkness and Grimaldi crawled forward to avoid ricochets off the walls. He methodically fired toward his attackers, rolling right, then repeating the process in reverse. His targets, illustrated in shades of red, gold and yellow, all crouched and fired at the entry. Occasionally a shot would come near him, but the guards didn't seem to have any idea where he was. Grimaldi, however, tagged one, then another. The only problem was that more kept coming out, two replacing his previous victims almost immediately.

"Get the fans going!" a guard shouted. "Open the main doors!" Aiming carefully, the Stony Man pilot put a pair of bullets into the man's upper chest, making him gurgle and fall backward, his hands going to his spurting throat. Grimaldi ejected his empty magazine, slapped in another one, then rolled away again, this time to the left. Holding his fire, he crawled forward. When he put his left hand down, it landed on a limp yet breathing body.

The main door began to open again, swirling smoke around the room as fresh air rushed in. Grimaldi switched his sensors to regular vision, and saw one of the guards in front of him wounded and unconscious. Grabbing the man's assault rifle, he pointed it at the reinforcements and squeezed the trigger, pressing down on the barrel to keep the gun's recoil from pushing it up. The long burst of bullets smashed into the remaining guards at the far end of the hallway, with many of the bullets punching through to star the glass windows behind them.

When the gun ran dry, Grimaldi tossed it aside and picked up his HK again. After the furious firefight, the hallway was now eerily silent. Even the alarm had stopped. The smoke and tear gas were dispersing, revealing a charnel house of dead bodies strewed along the back length of the hallway. A flicking fluorescent light popped and went dark.

The pilot got to his feet and carefully stepped down the hall, checking and confirming that each body was in fact dead as he went. No sense in getting plugged in the back because he wasn't careful enough.

At the intersection, he checked left and right, consulted the layout schematic he'd memorized, then turned left. "Heading to the security section," he transmitted to Mott as he penetrated deeper into the complex.

CHAPTER TWENTY-SEVEN

When the intruder alert sounded, everyone in the laboratory, Briggs included, looked around in momentary confusion. As soon as the two guards glanced toward the door, she snagged the hypo gun and a black ampoule, holding both behind her back. Twisting to one side, she tried to be as inconspicuous as possible as the four silver-suited men returned from the testing chamber and filed out of the observation room.

Richter pointed at the two guards. "Take her back to her cell."

The doctor grabbed the PA mike. "All personnel, secure the data and computers, then report to your assigned stations." He ran out of the room.

Briggs fumbled with the little container and the sleek, silver pistol, trying to remember how Richter had loaded it. The operation was made more difficult by doing it blind. Finally she got the little cartridge inserted correctly and felt it slide into place as one of the guards walked over. "Let's go."

She smiled at him as she stabbed the hypo gun into the back of her leg and squeezed the trigger. "Okay, just a moment."

"Come on, quit stalling. What the hell are you—? Oh, shit!"

Those were the last words he said as Briggs brought

the hypo gun around and smashed the barrel into his temple. Her eyes dilating with sudden, animalistic fury, she wrenched the submachine gun out of the man's hands as he fell.

"Virus subject in the lab! Everybody evacuate now!" The second guard pointed his weapon at Briggs and fired as she dived over a lab table, scattering papers and knocking over a computer as she hit the floor on the far side. The submachine gun's bullets chewed into the cabinet, punching through the wood and raining splinters around and on her.

The drug kicked in full-force now and Briggs saw everything around her as if it was happening in slow motion, from the frantically fleeing lab staff, one of whom caught two bullets in the chest and skidded to a lifeless heap a few yards away, to the pattern the guard's fusillade made as he destroyed the lab table and cabinet. From the angle of the exit holes, he was walking his shots up the table dead center, leaving her two ways to go.

Making sure her weapon was charged and ready, Briggs pushed off and slid across the floor to her left. Rounding the corner, she shot out from behind it, her submachine gun tracking the guard, who was a half second behind her—just enough time for three bullets from her gun to enter his chest, pulping it as they tumbled through.

Briggs scrambled to the guy, grabbed his weapon, his extra magazines and ID card, then scanned the rest of the room for other targets. Other than her, the lab was empty. Although everything in her wanted to go chase all those bastards down and kill them, instead she forced herself to go to the nearest active computer, take a small flash drive from her pocket and insert it into a USB slot. Hitting a few keys, she let the machine work while she headed for the observation room door. There was a slot at the side, and she shoved the guard's card in, waiting for what seemed like agonizing seconds before the door cycled open.

It was hot and muggy inside, but Briggs ignored the discomfort and headed for where she had last seen Cooper. She found him lying unconscious beside the tree, next to the obviously dead black man she had watched him kill. Briggs had to concentrate to control her quivering hands from closing around his throat as she pulled him into a sitting position.

"Cooper? Come on, wake up." Shaking him, then slapping, lightly at first, then harder, had no effect. She pondered how to wake him up. Then, squatting, she hoisted him in a fireman's carry on her shoulders, lifting his two-hundred-odd pounds with ease. Carrying him to the laboratory, she set him on the nearest table, sweeping away the computers and assorted lab paraphernalia with her hand. Checking her flash drive, the green light indicated it had finished working. She pulled it out and jammed it in her pocket.

Casting around for the hypo gun, she remembered where she'd left it and ran back to the first dead guard to pull it out of his fractured skull. Finding several uncrushed ampoules on the floor, she grabbed a few, stuffing them into her pockets and then inserting one into the gun. Wiping the nozzle on her sleeve to clean off the blood and bone matter, she jammed it into the motionless man's arm and pulled the trigger.

Bolan awoke with a jerk, sitting upright as if someone had administered an electric shock to his genitals.

Instinctively his balled fist lashed out at Briggs, who deflected it with the stock of her submachine gun. His gaze narrowed as he recognized her, his chest rising and falling rapidly with every breath.

"Sorry about that," Bolan said, "but I have to tell you I'm trying hard not to kill you." He looked around, his head moving in quick, nervous jerks. "What happened?" he shouted over the alarm.

Briggs found the offending speaker and fired a burst, silencing it in a shower of sparks. "I think the cavalry's here." She held out the second subgun. "It's time to go, but first we have to take care of something."

Bolan stared at her, taking in her half-crazed appearance, then grabbed the weapon from her, as if afraid she might change her mind and suddenly attack him with it. Once his hand closed on the grip, he relaxed a fraction. "What are you talking about?"

She led him to the holding cells. Bolan frowned as he realized her intent. "You're not serious."

Briggs's only reply was to point her weapon at the glass. "Turn away and cover your ears."

He did so as she shot a short burst into the top of the window, ejecting the magazine and inserting a fresh one. The glass was tough, but not bulletproof, and burst into thousands of tiny fragments, held in place by the layers of safety laminate. Briggs grabbed a nearby overturned chair and battered the safety glass, breaking it out of its frame in one big piece. She scanned the long room, keeping her weapon leveled. "I know there're at least two people in here. Come out with your hands up right now."

For a moment no one moved, then a young man and woman, both in stained lab coats, stepped out from behind the cages. "What are you going to do with them?" the woman asked, her gaze leveled at Briggs.

"I'm going to free them. Keep your hands up as you come over here and give me your ID badges. Then get out."

Puzzled frowns on their faces, the two scientists followed her orders. The male, a young man barely in his twenties, said, "Please don't hurt them," as he passed.

"I won't. Now get out of here before you both get killed."

The two scientists scrambled for the door, which Bolan kept an eye on as she approached the cages. "How do you think you're going to get these apes and gorillas out of here alive?"

"I have an idea," Briggs replied, not bothering to tell him that it was based on the flimsiest of hypotheses. "Do you still know the way out of here?"

"Yeah, right at the corridor, then left, a second right, and we're at the main airlock. Why?"

Slinging her subgun over her shoulder, Briggs took an ampoule out of her pocket and held it in her left hand while holding one of the ID cards in her right. "When I say run, you run. In fact, you might want to stand by the door and be ready to open it when I tear out of here."

Briggs walked by the row of cages, swiping the ID card through each electromagnetic key lock. At the far end of the row, she turned, dropped the card, then crushed the ampoule and smeared it across her chest.

"I hope this works." She walked slowly in front of the open cages, pausing just long enough to leave her scent in the air. When she reached the far end, she half turned to see the reaction.

Long, black fingers curled around the side of one of

the cages in the middle of the row. They were followed by a simian face, its nose sniffing the air. The gorilla turned toward Briggs and, upon seeing her, cocked its head in curiosity.

"That's it...come on..."

As if hearing her entreaty, the other gorillas and apes began emerging from their cages, as well, all sniffing the air. Briggs took a big step toward the window, then another one into the laboratory. All of the animals watched her move, their heads tracking her in perfect synchronicity.

She took another step toward the door.

The lips of the largest gorilla curled back in a silent snarl. The rest of the group tensed, leaning forward in anticipation.

Briggs took off, running as fast as she could toward the door. "Open it!"

With screeches of rage, the creatures erupted from the room into the laboratory, swarming over the tables and equipment, all of them coming straight for her. Bolan stood on the other side of the door, holding it open with one arm and waving her on with the other. When she was a yard away, he reached out his hand. Briggs grabbed it and he pulled her through the door and whipped her around so that they were both running down the hallway.

Two security guards approaching from the hallway on the other side of the door spotted them and gave chase. "Stop right there!" was all they said before being buried in a running avalanche of fur and fangs. Briggs glanced back to see the limp forms of the two guards lying on the floor as the horde of crazed apes rushed toward her.

"This way!" Still holding her arm, Bolan pulled her into another corridor on his left. Scrabbling and screeching, the troop pursued them, bowling over or cowing anyone who got in their way.

"Great trick, but how are you going to stop them from chasing you?" Bolan asked as they tore down the corridors.

"I haven't quite figured that out yet!" Only the sudden turns in the corridors had prevented the apes and gorillas from catching up so far, but once they got into a straightway, Briggs figured they were both probably as good as dead. "Any ideas?"

"We need to find a secure place where they can't get at you, a vehicle, or something protected." Bolan yanked her right, straight into a pair of scientists running the other way. The four bounced off one another, Briggs somehow managing to stay on her feet as he half dragged her down the hall.

"Hey, wait—" The man's startled query was cut off by the unstoppable tide of furious, furry simians slamming into them. There was a muffled scream, then nothing.

"The truck—where is it?" Briggs asked.

"The outer room, where we came in—I hope. Run faster, damn it!" Bolan pulled her along as they pounded down the hallway toward the airlock where they first came in. They were joined by other scientists and scattered security personnel, all of whom had only to look back once to flee the imminent danger coming at them. The small group, knitted together by pure fear, bolted to the airlock, where Bolan jammed his card into the doors.

"Come on, come on!"

The cacophony of howls and screeches grew louder and Bolan unslung his subgun and whirled. "Get down!"

"No, the door's opening!" Briggs pulled him through, along with a crowd of others that stumbled into the small airlock. "Clear it, clear it now!"

The last person shoved through and the doors slowly started to close. "Not fast enough— Hold on!" Bolan leveled his subgun and was about to blow out the other side when a security guard grabbed his weapon and pushed it up.

"No, that's bulletproof glass, you'll kill us all!"

"Jack must have knocked down the front door," Bolan said. "Is there an override on this side?"

A tall blond woman pressed her card into Bolan's hands. "Here—use my card and enter 4-5-5 on the keypad."

"The rest of you, hold that door shut!" Men and women sprang to obey just as the first wave of gorillas hit the doors, making them shudder under the impacts.

On the other side, Bolan oriented the card and inserted it into the slot, then pressed the keys. Nothing happened. He took the card out and tried again, with the same result. "It isn't working!"

"You'd better do something fast!" a security guard shouted from the far side. "They're pulling the doors open!"

A gray-haired scientist came over and looked at the dark security lock. She ran the card through, then punched the buttons again. "The keypad's broken. We're trapped in here."

Bolan examined the lock. "There has to be a manual override somewhere if the power fails."

The entire airlock shook from the determined assault

outside. "Shoot a couple of them. That'll scare the rest off!" someone shouted.

"No, don't!" Briggs held her hands out. "They just want to be free."

"Anyone who can open this door get over here and work on the override!" Bolan pushed his way through the crowd to Briggs. "It's either them or us. Stand back! Everyone cover your ears and open your mouths!"

She reluctantly moved aside and Bolan aimed his gun at the space between the slowly opening doors and pulled the trigger. The burst impacting the ceiling made the troop scatter, howling in terror as they fled.

"That worked, but probably not for long," a skinny scientist, whom Briggs recognized as the young guy monitoring the chimps and gorillas, said. "They'll be back, and probably even more pissed off."

"All the more reason to get out right now," Bolan said. "You guys got the door figured out yet?"

Two of the security guards fiddled with the lock mechanism, popping the bottom off and freeing a small handle. One began moving it back and forth as fast as possible. "This is it, but it's going to take time to lever the door open."

"Then you better pump faster." Bolan kept an eye on the gorillas at the far end of the hall. Most of the troop had retreated out of sight, but the large males had walked back into the corridor, sniffing the air. "Once they catch the scent of that stuff again, they're going to go crazy."

With a hiss, the outer doors cracked open. One of the male gorillas, a giant silverback almost as tall as Bolan, even with its hands on the ground, stalked forward, a snarl on its lips.

"They're coming!"

"Almost…there!" The airlock doors widened another inch, then another. As soon as there was enough room to squeeze through, Bolan shoved personnel out one at a time while the sec men continued widening the portal.

The apes had recovered their bravado and were only a few yards away from the door now, hooting and snarling. Bolan hustled the older, gray-haired scientist through, then the skinny kid. "Cheryl, come on!"

The loudspeakers crackled, and the female voice spoke again. "Evacuation of laboratory commencing. All personnel report to designated areas and await further instructions. This is not a drill. All personnel evacuate the compound immediately and report to designated areas."

"Now they tell us," someone muttered.

One of the gorillas smacked at the glass doors with its hand. Another one trotted up and sniffed at the seal between the two doors. "All right, we're out of here." Bolan grabbed Briggs's hand and waved the two security guards through the gap.

"Hold on."

"Cheryl, come on!"

"Just a minute. I'm not going to leave them here." She walked back to the inner doors and swiped her card through the slot, then turned and ran for the other doors. "Come on!"

Needing no urging, Bolan was already on the other side. Together they ran into the bigger room, which looked as though a massive battle had taken place. Through the ruined rock wall at the entrance, Briggs saw a sleek, black helicopter, bristling with weapons, hovering outside. Upon seeing it, the rest of the personnel ran past the row of remaining trucks and headed for an archway in the far left wall.

Bolan divided his attention between the men and women leaving the lab and the airlock with the dark, looming shapes scurrying around inside.

"Damn it, Richter's not here!" he shouted over the helicopter's roar. "Cheryl, we have to go." He pointed at the chopper. "Our ride's here!"

They both ran for the main entrance, reaching it just as the first gorilla came through the airlock door. At the same time, bright lights came on from one of the trucks on their right. Briggs looked back to see one of the two-and-one-half-ton trucks gunning straight for them, scattering the gorillas out of the way as it came.

Shoving her aside, Bolan whirled, bringing his up gun as the vehicle accelerated at him. He got off one burst that went high, starring the windshield, before he had to dive out of the way. The truck roared past, aiming straight for the helicopter, which barely got out of its way. It turned left so hard the driver's-side wheels almost left the ground, and shot off into the jungle.

"Come on," Bolan shouted, pulling Briggs to her feet and running for the helicopter, which had descended low enough for them to jump into the open side door. Briggs scrambled to the nearest open seat in back as Bolan sat in another one.

"Good to see you, Striker," the helmeted pilot said.

"Good to be here," Bolan replied. "Where's Jack?"

"I just told him I recovered you and the lieutenant, but he's still inside," Charlie said. "He says he's got a bit of a problem."

CHAPTER TWENTY-EIGHT

"Here it is! About goddamn time," Grimaldi muttered.

As embarrassing as it was to admit, once deeper inside the complex, he'd actually gotten lost in the complex of sterile hallways and identical sealed doorways. Tokaido had finally come through, however, and sent him a labeled map, based on the original blueprints.

Now, instead of plain corridors and unmarked rooms, the tiny map of the floor had labels on every room. It also kept track of where he was in the complex, and the quickest route back to the exit.

Other than that small hiccup, moving through the complex had been unusually easy. Everyone else had been running somewhere else once the intruder alert had gone off, and in the crush of personnel, Grimaldi had simply blended with the rest of the security. No one had questioned him as he'd made his way deeper into the complex, but after the third turn that took him nowhere important—although he now knew where the kitchens were—and finding less and less people as he went, the pilot had finally given up. He'd pulled out his smartphone just in time to receive the schematic floor plan of the base. Breathing a sigh of relief, he was pleased to find he was actually only a couple of turns away from the detention cells.

Examining the lock, he extruded a small metal prong

from the bottom of his cell phone and swiped it down through the electronic lock, then backed up. The phone contained a program that would analyze and open just about any key card lock program from commercial versions to encoded ones used by the military. This one was no exception, and the door popped open with a soft click.

The room was empty, however, and his investigation of the other five rooms, three on either side of the small corridor, revealed that they, too, were unoccupied. "Now where's the goddamned laboratory?"

He flipped through the blueprint with his finger, scanning for the lab section and finding it in a complex of large rooms about sixty meters away. Grimaldi quickly plotted out a back corridor path that would get him there in less than two minutes.

He set out at a fast walk, sticking to the walls and ducking out of sight whenever anyone came close. He heard the electronic female voice repeat the "intruder alert" announcement, and then he was just one corner away from the laboratory compound. He was about to round the corner when he heard two voices approach.

"I don't care where you think you have to be, Kepler said to check the lab, and that's what we're gonna do!"

"Fine, but if I catch hell for it later, I'm comin' after you."

"Whatever. Now come on."

Grimaldi raised his MP-7 and pulled out his camera again. Sticking the fiber-optic end around the corner, he saw the corridor in the small monitor. If he'd wanted to, he could have taken both guards out with no one being the wiser.

The guards tromped down the hall, then he heard

someone running, and one of them cry out, "Stop right there!" before a veritable crowd of what looked like screeching apes echoed down the hallway. Gun at the ready, Grimaldi peeked around the corner.

The two guards he had heard earlier lay unconscious on the floor as a group of the animals thundered down the hall, away from him. The Stony Man pilot frowned at the sight, but immediately headed to the lab they'd stormed out of.

The interior was a disaster zone, with overturned equipment, scattered papers and shattered glass everywhere. A large window had been completely broken out of its frame, and open, empty cages inside the next room revealed where the apes had come from.

Leading with his weapon, Grimaldi cleared the room, keeping an eye open for a working computer. Stepping over the body of a dead guard, he found one in the back of the room, next to another observation window, this one looking in on dirt, tall grass and a single tropical tree. He got out his phone and plugged it into the USB jack on the computer. Hitting the 9 button on his smartphone three times, the device began scanning, compressing and copying the entire hard drive. At the very least, he thought, I figure Akira and the folks at Stony Man will want to have a look at this.

While he waited, Grimaldi spotted the hypo gun on the table, containing an empty ampoule. Looking around, he found one of the plastic containers on the floor against a table leg, still full of a viscous black liquid. He picked it up and slipped it into his pocket.

His phone beeped twice, signaling it had completed its task. The pilot unplugged the smartphone and slipped it back into his pocket just as another announcement, this one ordering all personnel to evacuate the complex, echoed through the hallways.

That doesn't sound promising, he thought as he strode toward the door. Looking down the corridor, he was pleased to find it deserted. In the distance, he heard animal howls and a short burst of gunfire.

"Let's see... What's the best way to get the hell out of here?" he muttered. The straightest path appeared to take him in the same direction as the sounds. Pausing only to replenish his grenades from the unconscious guards, Grimaldi walked toward the exit, checking each corridor and doorway carefully before proceeding. The complex was completely deserted, with no sign of anyone. Two more turns and he was at the main intersection that would take him to the entrance airlock. But the snorts, grunts and yowls coming from the area indicated he wasn't the only one trying to get out.

Poking his camera around the corridor again, his eyes widened when he saw more than a half-dozen apes in the airlock. A couple were still inside the corridor and he made out a few others sniffing around the far side.

Just then, Mott's voice sounded in his earpiece. "Flyboy, this is *Dragonslayer*. I have visual on Striker and Doc One. Repeat, I have— Holy shit!"

"Say again, *Dragonslayer*?" Grimaldi asked as he watched the apes start leaving the other side of the airlock.

"I am retrieving Striker and Doc One at main entrance. Truck came out and nearly sideswiped me. Evac base at earliest opportunity. Over."

"I'd love to, except I've got a big, furry obstacle in my way," Grimaldi replied. "Several apes are still in airlock."

"One moment, Flyboy—" He heard Mott shouting to someone in the back and then a familiar and very welcome voice came on the radio.

"Flyboy, what are you still doing in there?" Bolan asked.

"Looking for you, what else?" Grimaldi replied. "If you'd told me you were already busting out, I would have waited for you at the door. Now I'm stuck in here."

"If you fire into the ceiling as you approach, it should spook the apes enough to get them moving out of the base. Charlie will pull up to give them some running room, then we'll come back down to grab you."

"Works for me." Grimaldi checked the load in his MP-7, then gulped and started walking toward the three apes still in the airlock. When he was five meters away, he pointed the muzzle of his subgun at the ceiling and squeezed the trigger. The burst of bullets perforated the tiles as the shots echoed down the hallway. The trio of apes in the airlock jumped as if they'd just gotten goosed and took off out the front door.

Grimaldi kept advancing, scanning left to right for more of the huge animals. Seeing a few scattered around the garage, sniffing at broken vehicles or even the torn-off limbs of the guards, he fired another burst into the ceiling. The apes howled and shrieked, but the majority of them headed for the exit, with Grimaldi herding them, for lack of a better term, along. At the exit, he watched the apes disappear into the jungle and exhaled in relief. The combat helicopter hovered about a hundred meters in the air, and he watched it come back down for him. The moment it was close enough, he slung his weapon, ran to it and threw himself on board, crawling to the copilot's seat and slipping on the headset.

"Thanks for the assist, Striker. We heading home now?"

"Not just yet," Bolan replied. Grimaldi glanced back to see him resupplying. "We're going after that truck."

"No problem." Mott took them up over the tree line, then took off after the escaping truck. The combat helicopter was among the fastest assault helicopters built, and since the truck had to navigate crude, rutted dirt roads, it was no contest. Within minutes they had caught up to the vehicle, which was slewing back and forth as it tried to go even faster on the narrow jungle lane. Even in the pitch-black darkness, the thermal suite picked out the truck as if it was broad daylight.

Mott and Grimaldi saw activity from men in the back, but couldn't quite make out what was going on. They got the answer a moment later when the olive-green canopy flew off to reveal three men clustered around a heavy machine gun. The canvas top hadn't even fallen to the ground when they opened fire on the pursuing helicopter.

"What kind of scientists are these?" Mott asked as he dodged the stream of ball projectiles. A few plunked off the undercarriage armor, making Briggs clutch her armrests tightly.

"Are we all right?"

"Oh, yeah," Grimaldi replied. "She can handle regular .50 caliber, although it's probably going to mean replacing a panel or two. Good thing they weren't using armor-piercing or high-explosive."

"Yeah," Mott said as he brought the helicopter around again. "Of course, they probably figure a Ma

Deuce would be enough to take an ordinary chopper. But the *Dragonslayer* isn't an ordinary chopper."

"Remember, guys, I want the people in the cab alive."

"Not a problem," Mott said. "One disabled .50 caliber and truck coming right up."

Highlighting where he wanted to fire the under-turreted 30 mm chain gun, Mott gave the order even as the heavy machine gun started up again. The large bullets chewed up the back of the truck, punching through the bed and demolishing the rear tires and drive train. Twenty or thirty rounds later, the Browning machine gun was nothing more than a broken hunk of useless metal on the back of the heavily damaged vehicle, its operators blown apart. The truck immediately slowed as the rear tires shredded away.

Even as battered as the vehicle was, the driver still tried to get away on the remaining tires. Grimaldi and Mott glanced at each other with a smile. "Now, for the engine," the Stony Man pilot said.

One of the remaining guards stuck his upper body out the passenger window of the cab and aimed an automatic rifle at the combat helicopter, hosing it as it moved into position. "He can do that all day. It won't do anything but scratch paint," Grimaldi commented. "Us, on the other hand…"

Leading the truck a bit, Mott put a two-second burst into the engine compartment. The hood exploded off the front of the truck as the engine disintegrated under the assault. The vehicle skidded to a stop, with the menacing helicopter coming down to hover fifteen meters off the ground, lighting up the ruined vehicle with an external spotlight.

"All persons inside the truck have ten seconds to

throw out their weapons and come out with hands up," Grimaldi announced over the loudspeaker system. "Failure to do so will force us to open fire. Do not try to run. You'll just be tired when we catch you."

Two assault rifles flew out of the passenger window and then two guards and a lab-coated man climbed out of the cab, hands in the air. Grimaldi instructed them to kneel on the ground, which they did, resigned expressions on their faces.

"Dr. Richter, I presume," Bolan said. "Let's pick them up." As he spoke, a series of loud yet muffled explosions could be heard, even over the steady beat of the helicopter's rotors.

"What the hell was that?" Mott asked, scanning the horizon for the burst of flame that typically accompanied such a blast.

"The logical conclusion is that the base was just destroyed," Bolan said with a grimace. "Come on. Let's pick up Richter."

CHAPTER TWENTY-NINE

Dressed in shapeless, light blue maintenance coveralls, Reginald Firke parked his small white van in the parking lot at the water treatment plant on Lake Märalen in Lovö, on the northwest side of Stockholm. He got out, removed a small tool kit from the backseat, clipped an identification card on his breast pocket and walked into the main building.

"Standard maintenance check and inspection on filtration unit number three," he told the receptionist in flawless Swedish, waiting patiently as she scanned his task invoice and compared it to the records in her computer system.

"You're right on time," she replied with a smile. "Just let me give you a temporary ID badge." The printer next to her spit out a laminated card, which she handed to him. "Do you know where you're going?"

He nodded. "Through those doors and to the back of the facility. The tank I'm looking for is on the left side of the building."

"That's right. It's all marked, anyway. Just let us know if you need anything."

"I will, but this should only take a few minutes," Firke replied with a smile and a nod as he walked through the doors leading to the rest of the facility.

The noise from the thousands of gallons of water flowing in from the lake outside through the various pipes and huge filtration tanks was louder than in the entryway. Firke walked down the main corridor, which ran through the middle of two rows of large tanks filled with lake water on its way to becoming tap water. True to his word, he stopped by the filtration unit—manufactured and sold by Stengrave Industries, which was also contracted to supply maintenance and repairs—scheduled for inspection and looked it over. It was in perfect working order. The last inspection had been four months ago and the tank had passed with no issues.

When he was finished with his "inspection," Firke walked to a staircase and descended to the facility's lower level. Casually glancing around, he walked over to a steel pipe one-meter in diameter that passed through the wall and outside the plant. A control panel regulated the pressure and flow of the clean water, distributing it into the network that more than 150,000 people used every day.

The plant supplied the bulk of the water to the northern and western parts of the city, including the neighborhood of Husby, which had become predominantly Muslim over the past decade, and which had already born the brunt of riots in the streets in 2013 in the wake of a protest after police had shot an elderly man they claimed had brandished a machete at them. It was, Mr. Stengrave claimed, the perfect place to begin bringing change to the city, then the country, then the world. For his part, Firke couldn't wait to do the same for his beloved city of London.

A small valve allowed samples to be drawn off to test for contamination. Setting down his tool kit, Firke took out what looked like a small canister of compressed air attached to a small hose. By threading it up through the nozzle, he would be able to introduce the virus into the clean water, bypassing the facility's numerous testing stages.

With the device ready, all he needed to do was to screw the virus sample onto the socket, which he started to do. He was so engrossed in his work that he failed to notice the shadow that fell over him, until the man it belonged to spoke.

"Firke, put the device in your hands down, then raise your hands above your head," Mack Bolan ordered.

The wiry, slender man froze upon hearing his name, then slowly looked up at the tall American who now stood in front of him. "You don't understand. They have to be stopped. They're a cancer spreading over everything we've worked to build for the past two thousand years."

"Your opinion doesn't give you or your boss the right to attempt to commit genocide," Bolan replied, the SIG-Sauer pistol in his hand not wavering an inch. "Set that thing down and raise your hands."

Firke frowned. "You got Stengrave?"

"Not yet, but I'm visiting him next," Bolan replied. "Dr. Richter, however, told us everything we needed to know about him." He moved the pistol's muzzle from Firke's chest to his head. "This is your last warning. Drop what you're holding and raise your hands."

"All right, all right, I'm unarmed. Just let me—" Firke lifted the hose as if he was going to set it down, then tossed the device at Bolan's face. The moment the canister left his hands, he dived for his tool kit.

The gunshot was swallowed by the rush of moving water, although it still echoed around the large room.

His hands inches from his bag, Firke slumped over, a red stain spreading on his back. The frangible bullets Bolan was using had fragmented upon impact, but still contained enough power to penetrate his target's clothes and tear through his chest and heart. Firke's chest heaved for breath once, twice, and then, with a wheeze, stilled for good.

Bolan stepped over and kicked the bag away. As he'd suspected, the mercenary had been going for his pistol. Next he took out a large plastic bag and carefully nudged the small ampoule next to the fallen canister into it. Only when it was sealed did he call for backup on his radio.

Dr. Bellamy, along with three Stockholm policemen, rushed up to him. Bolan handed the doctor the bag, which he immediately locked in a biohazard case. "Is the area safe?"

Bolan nodded. "There was no way I was going to let him release that into the water supply."

"I still don't know why you simply didn't take him in the parking lot," Bellamy said. "He had the virus on him. It wouldn't have risked contamination of the area."

"There was never any danger of that," Bolan said. "And I had to throw him off guard enough so that I could confirm that Stengrave is involved."

"But why? Richter told us everything we needed to know," Bellamy said.

"He did, but Stengrave and his company have done a damn good job of disassociating themselves from what was going on at that Congo facility. We needed another corroboration source."

"Well, you got it—too bad you had to shoot him," Bellamy replied. "He would have been an excellent source of information on what he saw during his time in the Congo."

"You've got Lieutenant Briggs's and my interviews on that, not to mention Richter himself—it should be more than enough," Bolan said. "By the way, how's working with him going?"

Bellamy adjusted his glasses. "Amazingly well, actually. He's been classified as a high-functioning sociopath, but he's really been quite easy to work with—" he frowned slightly "—that is, as long as you're addressing his favorite subject, scientific research on the human body. Any attempt to change the subject induces an unresponsive state. I'm bringing in the best psychologist from the U.S. to consult. We'll be studying him for years."

"And the virus?"

"The pure samples Lieutenant Briggs brought back have been a godsend in creating a vaccine for this particular strain," Bellamy said. "All of European law enforcement and hospitals are on the lookout for outbreaks matching the symptoms we've described, just in case. We're calling it variant of the rabies virus that should be quarantined immediately if found."

"Of course," Bolan said.

"The lieutenant has been working on learning everything about the virus almost nonstop since she arrived here," the doctor continued. "She's immersed in researching why it had little effect on her, and she thinks it heralds a major medical breakthrough for transmitting beneficial material to targeted genotypes. No doubt she will want a good quantity of your blood to investigate why the virus had little effect on you after the second injection."

"I'll give her what she needs. What about the others?"

"The two medical students are heading back to London with letters of recommendation from the ECDPC for their bravery, as well as official invitations to return to for a paid internship next summer. It is my hope that we will be able to hire one or both of them after graduating. The little boy has been put in foster care, but his social worker tells us she's already connected with a potential adoptive family. As for the young lady, we are getting her settled in Stockholm, and she has already expressed an interest in medicine. I'm working with her on evaluation of her intelligence and education to see how best we can help her." He cleared his throat. "After everything she's done for you and Europe, I think it's the least we can do."

"Damn right. I think your boys have this well in hand." Bolan turned to leave.

"So, you're heading back to the States, then?" Bellamy asked as he fell into step beside him. "After all, since Stengrave doesn't know he's been compromised, the Stockholm police will be moving to arrest him tomorrow."

"I know," Bolan replied. Which was why he intended to pay him a visit this night.

CHAPTER THIRTY

Twelve hours later Bolan stood in the open side entrance of the *Dragonslayer* as Jack Grimaldi maneuvered into a place high above a very Gothic, medieval-looking castle at the head of a narrow inlet of water that joined with the Gulf of Bothnia two kilometers away. The night was overcast, with hardly any wind, and the black helicopter was just another shadow hovering at 3,000 meters over the white, stone building.

"You sure you want to do this alone, Striker?" Grimaldi asked. "Just say the word and I can soften up the defenses with a couple passes first."

"Thanks, but I've got a better chance of catching him off guard if I go solo," Bolan replied. "How's that roof grid hack coming?"

"Ready when you are, Striker," Kurtzman's voice said in his ear.

"All right." Grimaldi made a few adjustments to the controls, placing the combat chopper right where he wanted it. "We're at the drop zone. You are green for insertion—now. Good luck."

"Beginning insertion on my mark. Three, two, one, mark," Bolan said as he stepped out into the cold night air. Although he was more than a mile above ground, his increasing velocity ensured that he would hit the ground about thirty seconds after he started falling.

The main hall of the castle, a large, cube-shaped structure, quickly loomed large in his night-vision goggles. Bolan maintained the classic skydiving free-fall position—arms outspread, legs bent at the knees—as he rushed toward it. After twelve seconds, he pulled the ripcord on his parachute. The square ram-air chute opened above him with a jerk, slowing his speed from more than one hundred miles an hour to just over fifteen.

Coming up on the roof of the building, Bolan pulled on his toggles both to slow down and correct his course. Unlike the start of his misadventure in Armenia, this insertion was going off without a hitch so far. Right about now, Kurtzman would be circumventing the rooftop laser-grid motion detector system by turning it off and running a dummy program that would make the security system seem still operational to any observer. All of the roof cameras had also been hacked and fed a broadcast loop that made it look as though the surface was empty, as well.

Bolan hit the graveled roof without a problem and pulled the chute around him to minimize being seen.

The castle was oddly quiet and dark around him. Even the floodlights on the lawn, normally illuminating certain architectural features, were off. However, Stony Man's intelligence said that Kristian Stengrave had arrived twenty hours ago and had not left since. Bolan intended to go through as many guards as necessary to find the man.

"I'm onsite. No guards detected," he whispered into his throat mike. "Unusual."

"Roger that, Striker," Kurtzman said. "Be advised that we are not picking up any guard activity on the grounds. Maybe target has pulled them all around him for additional security."

"Maybe. I'm going in to find out. Striker out." Stepping out of his harness and pack, Bolan stashed his parachute in the bag and stowed it around the corner from the doorway into the castle.

The access door was a stout steel model, set into a correspondingly tough metal frame. The soldier scanned it for an electronic signature that would indicate any sort of contact alarm that would go off the moment the door was opened. But he didn't pick up anything. Setting to work with his pick gun, he forced the tumblers into place and had the door open in under a minute. Standing to one side, silenced HK MP-7 at the ready, he opened the door.

Nothing. No lights burst on to blind him, no one charged out to attack him, no bullets flew up at him. The stairway was as silent as a tomb.

Still, Bolan ducked his head in to get a quick visual on the space before beginning his infiltration. The night vision turned the landing and staircase into lambent green day, highlighting the lack of opposition. He took the stairs one step at a time, every sense alert for a trap, but reached the bottom with no difficulty. "Stony Man, this is Striker," he whispered. "Have reached main level. Still no opposition. Heading to main hall."

"Roger that, Striker. Still no alarms sounded and still no guard activity detected. Maybe he somehow found out you were coming and offed himself?" Kurtzman suggested in a moment of levity.

"We could only be that lucky," Bolan replied. "Will be in touch."

"We're with you."

According to the building plans, the roof access opened to an upper maintenance hallway running the entire length of the main hall. The door at the bottom of the stairs did indeed open into a bare hallway. Bolan advanced carefully, finger on the trigger, ready for the door at the far end to burst open with each step. He reached it, and tried the knob. The door was unlocked. Before opening it, he scanned this one for any e-signature, as well, but it wasn't wired. Slowly, carefully, he turned the knob and slipped through.

The next room was small, with a closed trapdoor in the middle. Bolan knew it would lead to a walkway that ringed the main hall—exactly where he wanted to be. A scan of the hatch revealed that it was also unwired. Standing to one side, Bolan pulled it open.

This time he could hear faint noises from the other side—what sounded like a crackling fire. Bolan paused for a minute, straining to pick up anything else. Then he pulled a camera unit similar to the one Grimaldi had used in the Congo, and stuck the fiber-optic end down to get a look inside.

The hall was cavernous, about the size of a small gymnasium. It was decorated in an odd combination of medieval ornamentation—pennants and woven tapestries on the stone walls, full suits of armor lined up in two rows down the middle, mounted animal heads above all that—and smooth, angular Swedish furniture. What really caught Bolan's attention was the slumped figure sitting in front of a fireplace at least as tall as he was on the far side of the hall. The man sat perpendicular to the roaring blaze, the long, distorted shadow of his body flickering in the bright red-orange light.

"Have visual on target. Going in." Stowing the camera, Bolan slung his weapon before switching off his goggles and pushing them up on his head. Then he silently descended the ladder and stepped out onto the walkway ringing the hall.

Keeping his eyes on the figure in the chair, he took out a 60-foot length of climbing rope, tied it off at the ladder, then at the railing, and slowly, quietly, climbed over. The figure in the chair didn't stir. Bolan descended hand-over-hand to the floor, dividing his attention between the man in the chair and the huge double doors at the other end of the room. The figure didn't move. Unslinging his submachine gun, Bolan crept behind the left row of armored figures and moved in on the man at the fireplace.

Something was wrong. While Bolan knew he made little noise, the man should have heard something. He moved forward quickly. From several yards away he could make out the blank expression of a mannequin. "I must confess I am a bit surprised that someone so skilled could be fooled so easily." The toneless voice came from several small speakers mounted around the room, slightly echoing throughout the large space. Bolan looked all around, but there was still no movement anywhere in the room.

"Kristian Stengrave," Bolan said loudly. "You know I'm here about the virus."

A deep chuckle was the only reply for a few moments and then the unseen speaker fell silent. "You are here to defeat me. That is what I know."

Bolan stepped away from the mannequin and the chair, heading for the center of the room. "Yeah, I'm here to defeat you."

"Splendid!" Now the voice was positively cheerful.

"I knew it from the moment I saw you moving in the observation room. You are a true warrior, come to test my own abilities—"

"I'm here to take down a cowardly psychopath who tries to destroy what he fears most," Bolan said.

"Think what you will of my methods, they were the only way to save my country, our way of life—"

"By killing tens of thousands of innocent people?" Bolan asked. "That's genocide."

"It is righteous if performed for the correct reason!" Stengrave replied. "The saving of one's culture, one's race, so it doesn't become lost to history, washed away by a flood of refugees who just take and take, and do not give, do not add anything to their new home, their new country. It cannot—it *must* not be tolerated any longer!"

"That's not up to you to decide," Bolan said. "And it doesn't matter anymore. You've failed in your mission, Stengrave, so you might as well give yourself up. If I have to come and find you, I won't be happy about it."

"Oh, I am closer than you think. In fact, I am right here in this very room."

Bolan's brow furrowed as he looked around. There weren't many places to hide...or were there? He walked to the beginning of the double rows of armor and spotted a rack of weapons in the middle of the aisle.

"You're in one of these suits?"

"Very good. Your challenge is to identify which one. If you choose correctly, I will surrender. But if you choose incorrectly, then we will fight, and may the better man win."

"I don't play games."

"On the contrary, I would think the warrior in you would revel in it," Stengrave replied. "Too long have

I been denied the pleasure of pitting myself against a worthy foe. Now, however, it would seem that my wish has been granted."

"Well, prepare yourself for disappointment." Bolan turned to the nearest armor, an intricately engraved suit of black steel. "I'm doing this my way." He raised his MP-7 and sent a single bullet into the helmet of the suit. The 4.6 mm copper-plated, steel-cored bullet lanced through the front and back of the metal, knocking the helmet off and revealing a holed mannequin head underneath.

"What are you doing?" Stengrave asked as Bolan turned and shot the suit of armor across from him. This one, too, had a dummy inside.

"What does it look like?" Bolan asked. "I'm going to put a bullet into each of these suits until I find the one that bleeds. Then I can leave."

"You can't! That is not the tactic of an honorable warrior."

"You destroyed any semblance of honor you ever had by making undeclared war on women and children!" Bolan said as he shot two more suits of armor, going back and forth down the row. "Honor? You don't even deserve to say the word, Stengrave!"

"No!" The protest was a deafening shriek. Bolan kept at his task, taking out two more dummy suits of armor. He was turning around shoot another when he caught movement out of the corner of his eye. Whirling, he brought the submachine gun around as a full suit of armor flew at him.

Bolan triggered a burst instinctively, but the bullets didn't stop the thirty-five-kilogram metal missile. One arm fell off as it sailed through the air, but the torso and legs smashed into Bolan before he could move. Although he was braced for impact, the suit slammed into him, forcing him backward, into another steel-clad mannequin. Caught off guard, he went down, dropping his weapon in an effort to break his fall as the armor landed on top of him.

"You do not tell me what a warrior is!" Stengrave tore off his helmet and shouted as he stalked forward, barely pausing to grab two broadswords from the rack and pull them both out as he passed.

Shaken by the fall, Bolan shoved the breastplate off him. Standing, he reached for the SIG-Sauer in the holster on his leg. He drew it just as Stengrave lunged forward and swung his blade.

"No!"

Bolan was sure he had pulled the trigger, but Stengrave had managed to swat the weapon out of his hand with the flat of the sword. His hand stung, and he thought the blow might have broken at least one finger. Stengrave tossed the other broadsword at his feet. "Pick it up."

Bolan looked around for his gun, but it was out of reach.

Stengrave stepped closer and pointed the tip of his blade at Bolan. "Pick it up. I will not tell you again."

Bolan reached for the sword, which was definitely not a practice weapon as its edge looked razor-sharp. Testing its heft and balance, he found it to be excellently crafted. "An armored warrior doesn't give himself an advantage by facing an unarmored foe."

"Shut up and fight," Stengrave said as he began circling his opponent. Bolan began moving, too, trying to gain every second he could to evaluate his foe. Stengrave was tall—a few inches taller than Bolan's six-three—and in tremendous physical shape, as he didn't even seem to be bothered by the clanking, creaking armor he wore. He held the sword loosely in one hand, as easily as a child might wield a wooden sword, and Bolan wasn't about to underestimate him. He could tell by the way Stengrave moved that he knew how to use it.

Bolan tried a feint at his head, but the larger man didn't fall for it. His counterattack came immediately, a swift overhead chop at Bolan's forehead, which he barely got his sword up to block. The impact rang both blades and sent tremors up Bolan's arms, making his injured hand go completely numb.

Stengrave followed up with a swing from the shoulder that would have cleaved through Bolan's skull if it had connected. He ducked that one and retreated down the hall, trying to ward off the relentless powerful blows of the white-haired warrior. Although he was able to parry most of them, each clash of blades took more out of him. By the time he reached the end of the hall, the sword felt as though it weighed a hundred pounds in his aching hands.

Stengrave stopped before Bolan hit the back wall and regarded him with a slow shake of his head. "You are no warrior. You are a soft, weak pathetic thing, relying on your guns and technology to save you." He stepped back and spread his arms wide. "Come at me."

Bolan raising his sword, trying to figure out where he could strike the tall man that would count and thinking, He'll expect me to go for the head.

"Come at me in the next three seconds or I'll gut you where you stand," Stengrave commanded.

Bolan sucked in a breath and charged, ready for the

man to bring his sword around to try to stab him. At the last second he spun to the side and hacked down on the man's left arm with all of his strength. The heavy blade smashed on the steel vambrace with a loud clank. Bolan heard the stifled grunt of pain as he pushed past.

"Ha! You have some surprises left in you yet!" Stengrave said.

Bolan turned to face him, sword out, and saw his opponent draw his left arm in to his side and hold it there.

While his left hand dipped into the pocket on his fatigue pants, Bolan raised his sword. "Let's finish this."

"With pleasure," Stengrave said, stalking forward.

Finding what he was looking for in his pocket, Bolan withdrew his hand as he charged at the other man again, his main goal to ensure that Stengrave didn't chop him in two. He kept his sword out and up across his body, trying to protect as much of himself as he could.

Steel rang on steel. Stengrave attacked Bolan's blade first, beating it out of the way with a ferocious cross-body sweep. But as his blade was hit, Bolan let it go. Already committed to the maneuver, Stengrave overbalanced for just a moment. He began to recover, but not quickly enough.

Bolan brought his left hand around and down hard on Stengrave's face, smashing the ampoule of black, viscous liquid into his open mouth. The glass container shattered, along with several of the man's teeth. The virus fluid sprayed into his throat, with a spatter streaking across his face.

"What is—?" Stengrave stood motionless for a moment, dropping his sword and reaching up to wipe at his face with his hand. Upon seeing the black liquid, his eyes widened with panic. He grabbed for his throat with both hands, hawking loudly and spitting out tooth fragments, blood and black fluid. His eyes dilated as the overdose of artificial adrenaline was absorbed through his tongue and the roof of his mouth and poured into his bloodstream. He pawed frantically at his tongue, his movements growing more frenzied and uncontrolled. Making panicked gobbling noises, he stared at Bolan with fearful eyes as his fingers clamped onto his tongue. With a long, low moan of terror, he began jerking at it, gently at first, but harder and harder. Bolan watched dispassionately as, with a terrified shriek, Kristian Stengrave pulled out his own tongue.

Blood pouring from his mouth, arms and legs trembling uncontrollably, the industrialist swayed, then dropped his bloody tongue as he toppled backward, his heels and hands flailing against the stone floor as the stimulant roared through his arteries, overwhelming his nervous system and making his heart beat wildly, until it entered cardiac arrest. He sprayed out a mouthful of thick blood to scream once more—a long, gurgling wail of agony—then collapsed on the floor to lay there in his bloody armor, unmoving.

Bolan walked back and picked up his submachine gun and his pistol. Holstering the SIG, he held the HK in tingling fingers as he walked over to check on Stengrave, whose sightless eyes now stared at the ceiling. There was no sign of life, save for the occasional spasm from a misfiring muscle, but Bolan reached down to check for a pulse. He found none.

Straightening, he opened the main doors and trudged through the entry foyer and out the main entrance onto the deserted grounds. He breathed in the cool night air, savoring the quiet for a minute before radioing in.

"Striker to Base, mission is complete. Stengrave is dead. Come pick me up, Jack."

"Roger that, Sarge. I'm on my way," Grimaldi replied.

"And, Base?" Bolan said.

"Yes, Striker?"

"Get a message to Lieutenant Briggs. Tell her, 'it's done.' She'll know what that means."

"Copy that, Striker," Kurtzman replied. "Come on home."

"Affirmative," Bolan said, listening to *Dragonslayer* coming in for a landing as he watched the first rays of sunlight break the horizon.

* * * * *

Don Pendleton
MIND BOMB

A drug that creates homicidal maniacs must be stopped…

Following a series of suicide bombings along the
US–Mexico border, the relatives of a dead female bomber
attack Able Team. Clearly these bombings are far more
than random killings. Searching for an answer, Stony Man
discovers someone is controlling these people's minds
with a drug that gives them the urge to kill and then
renders them catatonic or dead. While Able Team follows
leads in the US, Phoenix Force heads to investigate similar
bombings in the Middle East. With numerous civilians
already infected, they must eliminate the source before the
body count of unwilling sacrifices mounts.

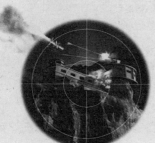

STONY MAN

*Available February 2015
wherever books and ebooks are sold.*
